Heaven Bearers

The Great Rest of 1834 and the Mud Flood

Janine Helene

FANTASY - ROMANCE

Copyright © 2019 Janine Helene Heggenstaller

All rights reserved

The characters and events portrayed in this book are fictitious. Any similarity to real persons, living or dead, is coincidental and not intended by the author.

No part of this book may be reproduced, or stored in a retrieval system, or transmitted in any form or by any means, electronic, mechanical, photocopying, recording, or otherwise, without express written permission of the publisher.

ISBN-13: 9798650848783
ISBN-10: 1477123456

Cover design by: Art Painter
Library of Congress Control Number: 2018675309
Printed in the United States of America

To everyone who loves history, question everything.
Not everything is what is purports to be

FOREWORD

Having a curious mind is a wonderful thing. You can see the world differently to others, at least with regards to certain aspects. I followed the path followed by most, went to University, got my degree and went to work at a respectable firm. In the meantime, YouTube started to boom in popularity. YouTube is a both a blessing and a curse. You can find anything and everything on it, but it can also lead you down some very weird paths.

My family is from Europe and I visit every couple of years. I remember walking around the town square, of a big city, and I was admiring the magnificent buildings all around me. I noticed some had very big doors, while others had windows that were semi submerged into the ground. I found it odd at the time, but I am no expert in anything relating to construction, so I didn't give it much more thought. I continued to enjoy the different buildings, their details, the workmanship and their size. *Especially their size.* I noticed that the buildings were almost the same all over Europe, sure some had different building styles, but a lot seemed to be built by the same *type of people*. Right across Europe, from France to Russia and there were even similar buildings in Australia and in Africa. What struck me most was that buildings all over the world had sunken windows, massive doors and I found the details on the ceilings or on the roofs over the top. It was beautiful, but was it necessary? I thought about what it costs to build the average three building house in a medium-sized city, I couldn't even begin to wonder what it must cost to build these buildings? Especially in cities in America. People arrived as immigrants and built up a life there, working hard and not having much. Who paid for some of these magnificent buildings and why spend so much on them in the first place?

During high school, I attended an exchange programme with a German school in Reutlingen, and we were taken to the Cologne Cathedral. Wow, this building was massive, I couldn't believe that people, with less technology than what we have currently, were able to build something so big and intricate. There is perfect symmetry everywhere, every stone or brick was cut with precision and I wondered how these more "primitive people" managed to lift these heavy blocks, of the different types of material, up so high? Was this even possible? Standing down below and looking up, my logic told me it wasn't. They didn't have cranes; the material would just be too heavy. I had many questions that were left unanswered, it bothered me, but not enough to sit down and spend hours researching it. I also found it interesting that we couldn't replicate those buildings, or rather we didn't want to. We, as a modern society preferred to build less appealing, glass buildings, sometimes with very weird architecture and we classed them as "modern". Truth is they are completely out of place and don't belong in some of these city squares. These modern building, no matter how big or expensive they are, could never compare to the beauty and workmanship of the older buildings. Not even a little bit. At least, in my opinion and those of friends and family.

Years passed by and I still wondered about these anomalies here and there, but I put no effort into my curiosity. And then one day, I stumbled upon a video on YouTube, it was about interesting rock formations. I watched it briefly and another video caught my eye, it was "recommended" and so I gave it a try. It was long and one of three parts. It was all about odd photos from the 1800's and the narrator had an interesting accent that really caught my attention. He displayed photos from many of the different cities in Europe, showing these immaculate buildings. But what was strikingly odd, was that there were hardly any people around in all of the photos. There would be a person here and there, but city squares were empty and seemed deserted. I scrolled down to the comment section and noticed there were many people talking about something that happened, rather about something that *they think happened* and that no one talks about. **They call it the mud flood.**

I have heard about Noah and the flood, but never of a mud flood. It piqued my interest and I watched all three of the videos in a single sitting. There were pictures depicting what looked like mud being cleared away from buildings and there were some odd piles of sand or mud, but the pictures were old and I couldn't quite make out anything specific. It would all be assumption on my part and so I kept digging. I noticed there were other old photographs of buildings that were "dug out". Yes, I couldn't believe my eyes, but there were buildings that extended many metres into the ground and they had been "modified", entrance doors were added to them or windows were turned into doors and so on, even though the original entrances were way below, in the ground. Fascinating I thought. But perhaps this was all just a coincidence and this happened to *one building and only in one city.*

It was not coincidence and there were many buildings that extended into the ground. A simple *Google* search of the "mud flood" revealed buildings all across the world, that extended into the ground and it finally made sense why some windows were semi submerged. The architects would, surely, not have built like that without a good reason, and what reason did they have? I couldn't think of one, neither could I find one. But the mud flood, that made sense. There were plenty examples and although, I can't know for sure if something such as a mud flood happened, it was evident that the buildings were a lot bigger, higher rather, than what the average personal realised or could see from the ground level. I implore you to google it some time, then you can understand what I mean. A simple search term such as "mud flood" will yield many results. Photos of renovations of the Capital building in the USA will appear, a row of buildings in France and even some in Russia, among many others. Take a look at Salt Lake City, what about the Parliament building in Budapest? Take a few minutes out of your day and really look at them. Whether there is some truth to the mud flood or not, the photos definitely are very interesting to look at.

I was pretty convinced by the mud flood theory, I had to admit. I even warmed up to the idea of a so-called societal reset of some kind. The theory goes that whole cities of people disappeared or died and new people were introduced. They didn't know what the different buildings were used for, so they gave them a purpose. Sounds crazy, I know. I found information on some of the weirdest things. Look at any old map and you will notice a place called "Tartaria" situated near Russia. The same name is on all the old maps, which means this place *did exist* at some point in the past. I, however, had never heard about it, nor was I taught anything about it in school. Weird right? No, it gets weirder. There were orphanage type homes, called foundling homes and they were filled with unwanted children. There were many photos and in them, were these creepy men in suits, always. Possibly another coincidence, I am not sure. But and these children were then shipped all over the world, especially to the Americas and this became their new home. There were photos of many people, with no children and vice versa. Then there were the "Electric Parks" in America, that were some kind of Amusement Park, which strangely enough had babies in incubators as an attraction. People paid a couple of cents to view these babies and it seemed to be a very exciting attraction, with the way this was advertised. Very weird, I thought. I don't think I'd want to pay to see that at all. But that is just me, I guess. Weirder still, in the photos of the "Electric Parks" there were never children, at least none that I could see. Where are all the children? In the Foundling Homes perhaps?

Star Forts (bastion forts) were another topic I found interesting. They are in almost every country, all over the world and they are always built near the water. Their function was explained as a type of fort, where canons were stationed, and they were used to fight off any approaching enemy. Does make sense, but also it doesn't. There are thousands of them, they all have a similar shape, but they are not all built the same. The sizes and styles differ, but they all seem to be based on the same concept. Then the kicker, the Statue of Liberty, currently found on Liberty Island in the New York Harbour, take a look at the shape of it. Never noticed it? Neither did it. But it is a star fort. My mind was blown. Most of all I wondered why? What was it used for, really used for, and why put a statue on it? There are even whole towns built on star forts in the Netherlands and Belgium, among other places. It isn't noticeable from the ground, but a bird's eye view is a magical thing.

I found the topic of the mud flood and the missing "Tartaria" fascinating and with my active imagination, I decided to turn it into a fictional story. And although this story, including the characters, are *completely* fictional there are some truths, rather gaps in our history and the official narrative, which does leave some unanswered questions.

Does the mud flood topic interest you?

Write me an email: Janine.helene7@gmail.com or visit my blog Janine.helene.wordpress.com.

Follow me instagram @authorjaninehelene

Please leave a review and tell me what you think.

"THE IMAGINATION IS THE GOLDEN PATHWAY TO EVERY-WHERE." – Terrence Mckenna

PROLOGUE

The city streets are bustling with people. Women, dressed in the finest silk and lace, roam the streets, while children giggle and play in the fountains in the city square. The great *Empire of Tartaria*, home to the Tartarians, a people of high moral standards, honesty and kindness. There is no jealousy here, no want and no need. Everyone is equal, man women and child. There are no classes of people and no one is rich or poor.

A group of children are kicking a small rubber ball around the streets, while others are eating the finest quality ice creaming and watching their friends play. There is laughter everywhere, the sun is shining bright and the air smells like a field full of blooming flowers. The sky suddenly turns a dark grey and big, bushy and heavy clouds roll in. Sleet starts falling from the sky and the sun disappears.

The children drop their ice cream and start walking around, desperately looking for their mothers, who in turn, are left standing frozen on the spot, staring up at the Canopy above them.

A young man, of only nineteen years of age, holds out his long and slender arm and with his palm faced upwards, he lets a single snowflake land gently onto it. He glances at it carefully and wonders what it is. He continues to stare at it in awe and watches it quickly melt away after making contact with his warm skin.

'What is that?' He mutters and looks over at the elderly lady standing next to him. Her face is completely expressionless and pale. Her eyes are big and bright blue and her hands are trembling. She shakes her head, while she watches the sleet fall around them and land on the pavement. The sleet turns to snow and the air becomes cold, thick and heavy.
The sky begins to crack with anger and people start to scream and take cover under tables, chairs and even behind the fountains in the city square. There has not been a war, or any kind of battle in Tartaria, in over one thousand years and the Tartarians don't even remember what conflict is.

A young, blonde girl, wearing a bright yellow summer dress stands at the edge of the park and tears are rolling down her soft cheeks. She is clutching onto her little sister in fear and her eyes are darting back and forth, she is looking for someone. She starts to scream and then cries frantically for her mother, but no one comes to her aid. Another loud crack lights up the sky and the windows shatter and the glass tumbles down to the floor. A crack forms in the firmament surrounding and protecting the Earth, just above the Canopy and seven black figures fly inside. They start to hiss as the fly around and the snow becomes heavier and covers everything in a thick and white layer of utter cold.

The trumpet of King Finn sounds in the distance and the one-billion-strong army of Tartarian warriors, put on their armour, ready for the battle that could end all life and the Empire as they know it.

A man dressed in white and gold armour stands on a podium and addresses the people who fill the city square. He is almost four metres tall and he stands with authority and strength in front of his people. They are terrified, the women are crying and have their arms clutched around their children and horror is painted across their faces. The sky is still dark and the snow hasn't stopped falling. For the first time ever, the Tartarian people experience cold.

'Tartaria, the Great Empire of Tartaria! Fear not my people, my family and friends. The Great Army is ready for any and all incursions by enemies from within and beyond. This Empire will celebrate its seven thousandth year of creation next month and we shall not fall to anyone, not now and not in another thousand years.' He pauses and swallows hard. 'Go out and continue with your day and put your trust in me, your King. I serve you and only you. Everything is under control.' He says with passion and grace and musters up a warm smile, while his eyes briefly dart towards his General, who is standing slightly to the right of him.

His face is stern and the King is gravely worried.

There is no applause this time, people are unsure and don't know how to respond. The atmosphere is an empty one, people look to their friend and neighbour for reassurance, but there is none that can be given or shared.

Meanwhile, back at the Office of Great Men, King Finn stares at his reflection in the large and oval shaped, gold-coloured mirror, which is encrusted with pearls and moon rocks. It was a gift that he was given on his Union Day with Queen Ariella and his eyes fill up with tears.

'War is coming and I am powerless to stop it.' He says and can see his wife, the mother is his two daughters, stand near the marble arch with concern all over her beautiful face. Her eyes are a pale blue and her cheeks too have lost their colour.

'What do we do?' She asks and her concerned expression changes to one of worry.

'Flee to the Mansion in Montreal today! You will be safe there and I will come for you. Take the children and go at once!' He replies and watches her turn around and call for the girls to start packing a bag for a little trip they are going on. He waves them off, with sadness in his heart and looks up at the Canopy.

The creatures are still hovering up in the night sky and

haven't come down to the ground in over seven days.

'What are they doing?' King Finn asks his most trusted General, as he watches them circle the sky.

General Jokkiel and his men have been watching them day and night, trying to anticipate their every move. They have not yet learned what that is or, more importantly what they are, yet.

'We don't know my King, but they have been doing the exact same thing for days now. It seems they are waiting for the right time to strike.' He answers without taking is eyes away from them.

'Hold down the fort, I will go meet mother nature and see what she makes of these strange creatures. Perhaps she will know how they entered our realm, what they want and how to stop them? Together, we can figure out how to best approach them and ask them kindly to leave.' His eyes flash a bright blue suddenly. 'They are not welcome here!' He pats him on the arm and picks up the platinum staff, which is hanging on the wall above the Energy port. It has blue encrusted diamonds and some inscriptions on it. The stones light up individually, the moment he touches it.

'This staff contains all of my ancestors going back fourteen generations, each ruling five hundred years. Each one of these diamond stones represents an ancestor and their power which they gifted to the Empire upon their death,' he says to the General who is staring out into the distance. His heart is heavy and it is left wanting.

'War is in the air my King; you need to hurry!'

King Finn walks out into the garden, places his mighty hand on the stone structure and wholeheartedly mutters four simple, but powerful words. 'I today, tomorrow never.'
Within a matter of seconds, he is standing in the Canopy and looking around for *her*. It is quiet, too quiet and there is a quick and bright, yellow flash, that semi blinds him for a brief moment.

'Ahh!' He mutters and turns his face away quickly. He can

smell something and realises it is the smell of burning flesh in the air. His body fills with fear and he looks down at his abdomen. There is a big tear in his armour and his flesh is exposed.

'Reveal yourself creature!' He orders sternly, anger fills his voice and his eyes scan the space ahead of him. There is snickering in the distance that echoes all around him and then suddenly fades.

'Expose yourself you coward!' He shouts and clutches the staff as hard as he can.

His eyes dart back and forth, he is not sure what to expect, but he can smell it and he covers his nose and mouth with his arm to block out the awful stench.

'I can smell you creature, now I ask again, expose yourself.' He sits his staff down hard onto the branch that he is standing on and the leaves all around him rattle from the force of this motion.

The snickering gets louder and he turns to his left side to face the creature, but the sound disappears again. The stench that fills the room gets much stronger and he knows it is close. The hair on the back of his neck stands up and it pricks his skin. He places his hand on his neck and gives it a soft rub, while he slowly turns around, his right hand still firmly placed around the staff. The diamond stones light up one by one and he sees a wretched creature standing in front of him grinning with its sharp teeth exposed. It is twice his size, with pathetic small eyes and long, but broken claws.

'Who are you and what do you want?' He asks and his voice carries his authority proudly.

The creature's grin suddenly turns into a gentle smile and it hides the two rows of teeth and forked tongue in its mouth.

'I come in peace.' It replies and bows its head before the King.

These creatures, the *Heaven Bearers*, did not come in peace. They came for blood and death. They took the Old World and turned it upside down. Everything that was once good and pure, was no more. The screams of the mothers fighting to protect their children lasted for days. Their goal was the children and they took the women for themselves. What did they want and why did they want it? Tartarian women are beautiful, the most beautiful beings to have ever graced the Universe and they wanted power! The children were to be captured, re-educated, taught a new history, a new language and introduced to a new religion. The New World Order! This was the goal and they were willing to do any-and-everything necessary, in order to achieve this.

The New World Order, a world run by elite creatures, who will hide in the shadows and have complete control over the earth and her resources. The ultimate goal is to create a new race called the Humans. They will become the daily workers, slaves, who will work themselves to death in order to procure riches for their masters.

But then something unplanned happened, something outrageous that killed off the majority of the population before the creatures even had the chance to succeed with their initial goal. The *mud flood.*

The screams of the terrified Tartarians were loud and deafening, but they were starting to fade. The will to fight these creatures was dwindling. The soil began to rise and it quickly turned to dust, while the Canopy above opened and unleashed a constant flow of water that lasted for almost two weeks. The wind blew from all directions and a wall of mud, wood and rock formed and it consumed the whole Earth. It covered every garden, it destroyed houses and buildings and all fields filled with their ripe harvests. Animals perished and so did the Tartarian people. No one could escape the mud that did not stop flowing for one week, three days and two nights.

Until one day the rain stopped and so did the mud. Those who found higher ground and managed to survive in the mountains, with what little food they could carry and find, tried in desperation to shovel the dirt away from their homes, but it was too thick and too deep. Without food and clean water and no means to replant the fields, three quarters of all Tartarians starved to death.

Most don't remember that day. Those, who survived it only ever heard about it. But there was one little girl that sat all alone on the outskirts of the city, crying for her mother. The mud had formed all around her, but had not touched her. She had no food or water, but was not hungry or thirsty. Her tears eventually dried up and she waited two weeks and one nights for someone to find her.

'There you are sweet thing.' A young, thirty-year-old Tartarian lady, dressed in black, with golden blonde hair and dark blue eyes, gently picks her up and wraps her up in sweet smelling blanket. The soft tassels tickle her nose and she starts to cry out again. 'You are safe now dear Bonnie. Dry up those tears, I am taking you home.'

CHAPTER ONE

'Bonnie! Bonnie, come down here at once!' Ms Estes is calling her and she doesn't like having to wait.

She quickly slips on her nude coloured stockings, puts on her black shoes and hurries down to the foyer, clutching the railing of the stairs, as she glides down the stairs as quickly as she can.

'You are late Bonnie; you will miss the train if you keep this up!' She eyes her sternly and gestures for her to enter the dining room and join the rest of the girls for breakfast.

'Listen up everyone.' She glares at the dozen girls in the corner of the dining room. Her face is stern and her voice is cold with a touch of sadness in it. She swallows hard and clutches her hands that she is holding out in front of her. 'We have just fifteen minutes and then we need to leave.' She looks over at Mary, who is sneaking into the room and scoffs at her. 'Chop chop you silly girl!'

It is 1851 and the next group of girls have just reached majority age and it is time for them to be introduced into society and *given* to their new husbands.

The girls are unwanted and unloved foundlings, abandoned by their parents shortly after birth, who now have the opportunity to become productive members of society. They don't know who their parents were or where they come from. They grew up together, along with the matrons, such as Ms Estes, and it is their job to take care of the girls and teach them how to be ladies and more importantly, mothers.

'I wonder what kind of husband I am going to get.' She blushes bright red. 'I am so very nervous!' Claudia suddenly looks down at her porridge and plays with her spoon. 'I think it very silly that we don't at least get to choose,' she says with a heavy heart.

Bonnie isn't paying any attention to her. She eats her porridge slowly in small bites, completely oblivious to the fact that it is oat porridge, which is her least favourite and it is slightly burnt. She takes the spoon and mechanically inserts it into her mouth and swallows the lumpy porridge, without noticing just how tasteless it is today. Her mind is on other things. She thinks about her new life and she is terrified at the thought.

'I am going to Canada and I wonder if I will ever see you again,' she snaps and breaks her own thought pattern. Bonnie wants to start to cry and her eyes fill up with tears, but crying is forbidden here and she quickly wipes them away before anyone notices.

Stacy places her hand on hers and gives it a soft rub. 'We will visit each together all the time and our husbands will become friends and everything will work out just like we spoke about all those many late nights when we couldn't sleep.' Her smile is infectious and mellows the mood immediately.

Stacy is strong and brave; she will be fine and make a good wife and mother. Bonnie and Mary, on the other hand, they are shy and timid by nature. Personalities are not encouraged here at the St Catherine's Foundling Home for girls. The objective is to educate the unwanted or left behind and have them find appropriate husbands. Nothing more.

The girls come and go every year and only a handful ever return to share happy stories of their new lives. It does happen, but it is rare.

A disaster struck seventeen years ago, they call it a *mud flood,* and it covered the entire Earth in a matter of days.

Earth? Bonnie doesn't really know what the Earth is, she just knows it is a big place, with many cities and people spread all over, millions of people. In Canada, the place where she is going, it is cold and very far from where Stacy and Mary are going. Stacy is going to a place called New York and Mary will settle in Salt Lake City. They say they will see each other all the time and remain good friends, but deep down inside, Bonnie knows that this is very unlikely.

'It is time girls!' Ms Estes is yelling and ushering the girls outside and into the horse drawn wagon. It is cold and there is sleet falling down around them. Bonnie clutches onto her coat and buries her face into her thick, black scarf. It smells like nothing and she imagines it smelling like her mother, or rather, what she imagines her mother would have smelt like. She looks back at Ms Estes and wonders if she will ever see her again. The carriage starts to move and Ms Estes walks back inside, she doesn't even wave them off and it saddens Bonnie deeply.

They arrive at the ocean after a few hours on the road. The waves are loud and there are things floating in the water. They look like long and oddly shaped buildings, scattered all over the place. Ships? These are the things we learnt about, she thinks. People are climbing into them and they all have the same, sad and lost look, on their pale and unsure faces. It will take them two months to get to a place called the *Americas* and from there, the girls will be dispersed to their new homes and more importantly, to their new husbands.

'Bonnie, come over here and stay by me. You stay close and don't listen to anyone else. You two will stay with me until we get there, do you understand?' Stacy grabs them both by their frozen hands and toddles off towards to the big, wooden ship that is docked at the harbour.

Stacy looks out for them, she has always acted at their

protector and in a way, their mother. She keeps them by her side all the way to the Americas, takes care of them when they got sea sick and made sure they had enough to drink and eat.

The days pass by slowly and the air is stale and foul smelling inside the cabins. Five girls are squashed into a small room, with only two beds between them and they are forced to take turns sleeping on the floor. There isn't nearly enough food and the water is dirty and tastes re-used at times.

They finally arrive in New York and it is just as cold here, as it was in Ireland. Bonnie stands near the deck and takes a peek outside and her weary eyes fixate on this huge metallic looking structure, standing in the middle of the water. It is of a lady. She is painted gold and she is wearing some sort of band around her head, with spikes coming out of it. In her one hand, she is holding a flame and in the other, is a metal staff.

Bonnie stares at this lady and is mesmerised by her, wondering who she is?

'Bonnie, come back inside, it is freezing and you will catch a cold.' Bonnie duly follows Stacy back inside and takes a seat on the floor next to Mary.

'Now listen to me girls, in a few minutes we will part ways.' She looks them each in eye individually. 'You will be on your own and you need to go to where you were told to go, okay?' She looks at Mary and can see she isn't listening properly; she is too nervous.

'If you are unsure, you must just ask someone to help you. They will know where you need to go.' She takes an excited breath and fixes her hair.

'Always remember to put on a pretty smile and say thank you.' She says as her eyes glow with excitement for her new life.

The girls stay seated for a while and when they hear the horn honk, they slowly get up and stand in line waiting for the ship to dock. Each girl has a standard, small and compact, wooden suitcase clutched in their sweaty and nervous hands. Inside is an extra outfit and a piece of soap. This is all they own and their entire identity.

It will be the job of your husband to provide for you. This is what Ms Estes would always say to them and they never questioned anything she said or did. Bonnie always wondered how the men chose the girls. She asked Ms Estes this question once, about three years ago and she got ten lashes as an answer.

'You don't ask questions to certain things Bonnie, you do as you are told. It's a terrifying world out there and the less you know, the better!' She would always bark at her and shake her head in anger and frustration, then stomp off loudly.

A horn honks in the distance and it means they can leave the ship. Stacy grabs Mary by the hand and in turn, Mary grabs Bonnie, and they start to march off the ship and onto the dock. Stacy is confident and Bonnie can see a hint of adventure in her, even though the rest of the girls are terrified and Bonnie wonders if she knows something that perhaps the rest of them don't?

They reach a counter with a man in a black top hat and Bonnie is last in line. She patiently waits her turn and notices that he is wearing a dark grey suit. It doesn't fit him properly and he has a big, thick and black moustache.

'Pass Miss?' He says routinely, without looking up at her.

Bonnie just freezes and stares at the man and doesn't respond to his request.

'I can't let you in without a pass.' He says, visibly irritated. He has a weird accent and a certain calmness about him that reminds her of home.

'Oh, I am so sorry, here it is.' She hands him her pass and notices her hand is shaking.

She blushes and he hands her the pass back with a red stamp on the middle page.

'Good luck to you miss.' He smiles and calls out for the next person to step up to the counter.

She returns a nervous, yet sincere smile and quickly picks up her suitcase and follows the crowd in front of her. She looks around for Stacy and Mary, but she can't see them anywhere, they must be gone already? That was quick and she wonders why they didn't wait for her?

There are many people in New York and she has never before seen so many people in one place. Her eyes suddenly wander to her surroundings and she realises she is in a massive structure; she would guess it is twenty meters high and wide. It is so very long.

'What is this place?' She mutters while her mouth hangs open in awe of what her eyes are permitted to witness.

'Out of the way!'

A nervous looking girl bumps into her and scurries on ahead. She is wearing a bright red coat and Bonnie wonders where she got it? She has never seen such nice colours before and the thought of wearing something, other than black, suddenly excites her. At the Foundling Home the girls were only permitted to wear dark clothes, black and navy blue. Ms Estes said it made them more equal this way and Bonnie never thought more about it.

'A real lady doesn't draw attention to herself,' she would say to the girls during their etiquette lessons, that Bonnie was always so fond of.

In that moment Bonnie tears up and she realises that she will miss her. She was mean, the meanest of all the care takers, but she is all she had and all she knew.

Bonnie turned eighteen years of age, just two days ago and was told that she was fortunate to be going to Canada. Apparently, it is very nice up there and the men are handsome, at least that is what Ms Kent used to always tell her.

Bonnie has only ever seen a few men in her entire life and most were old. She can't even imagine what a young man her age must look like. She starts to smile at the thought and carries on walking briskly.

She hears a man calling for Montreal and her head instinctively turns in that direction.

'That is where I need to go,' she calls out and pushes

through the crowd to reach him.

'I need to go to Montreal, Canada. Please and thank you.' She hands him her ticket and he lets her climb onto the train. This train is much bigger than the one she took back home and the seats have a pretty, blue and grey fabric covering them.

She walks inside and finds an empty seat and sits down gently, completely unsure of herself. She stares out of the window and watches the people scurry around outside, like the ants did in the garden at the Foundling Home. She always found the ants to be very fascinating. There were days, when she would sneak outside and just watch them climb the wall, with whatever they found firmly in their mouths. They never seemed to tire or lose their way and she admired that about them.

'Do you mind if I sit here?'

Her thoughts are interrupted and Bonnie looks up to put a face to the squeaky voice that startled her.

'No!' She quickly moves over and leans into the window to try and make space, even though there is plenty already.

'Thanks, my name is Dora.' The young girl says as she sits down.

She is elegant and has porcelain skin, that is almost white. 'I'm from a small town near Manchester, do you know where that is?' She asks and puts some more red lipstick on. She is confident and it reminds her of Stacey.

Bonnie looks at her and shakes her head, 'No. I don't I'm sorry.' She looks down at her hands in embarrassment.

'Don't look so nervous girl, I'm sure the men are just as nervous to meet you and I!'

'Why? Why would they be nervous to meet us?' She asks confused.

'Well, they don't know what kind of girl they will be stuck with. Then again, I heard from a girl, basically a friend of a friend, that some of the men don't approve of the girls they are assigned and they outright refuse to marry them.' She pulls a face or horror and giggles to herself. 'That won't happen to me or you, luckily. In fact, that's why I chose to sit next to you.' She pats her on the leg and gives her a wink.

'What do you mean?'

'What do I mean?' She crinkles her nose and pouts her lips briefly like she is confused by Bonnie's question. 'Well,' she leans in closer to her. 'You are pretty, have you seen some of the other girls? They really don't have very pretty faces. Men like pretty girls, it is just the way it is.' She leans back in her seat and wiggles to get comfortable.

Bonnie clears her throat and rubs her hands together, but she doesn't make eye contact with Dora or anyone else.

'What...what happens to the girls that get rejected by the men?' She finally asks and swallows hard.

Dora looks over at her and takes her right hand in hers. 'No idea sweety, but you won't have to worry about that. Now close your eyes and gets some rest, it is a long trip from what I hear.'

Bonnie does as she says and she falls asleep, an hour into the trip.

She dreams that she is standing in front of a small stone house with big, square and wooden windows. There are orange curtains swaying in the wind and the air is crisp. Inside it, is a man dressed in a suit and he calls out to her, to join him inside. She walks into the kitchen happily and he tells her to sit down, he has important news to tell her.

'I found your parents, they are alive! And you have a sister, her name is...' He pauses briefly. 'She is lovely.'

She stands up and gives him a loving hug. 'Thank you, thank you for finding them. When can I go see them?'

He looks at her confused. 'See them? Why would you want to see them Bonnie?' He asks and tilts his head in confusion.

'Well, I, they are my family?!' She stands there confused and watches his expression change to one of anger.

Another man appears at the door and he is holding some chains that clang against each other and he has a stern look on his face.

'Young girls aren't allowed to ask questions.' He scoffs at her and reaches out to grab her.

'No!' She mutters. 'Please I am sorry!'

She feels him grab her by the shoulder and shake her hard.

'Wake up Sweety, it is all just a dream. We are almost there.' Says *that* squeaky voice, which is familiar to her now.

Bonnie opens her eyes slowly and looks around, trying to orientate herself. She looks over at Dora and she is sitting on the edge of her seat with anticipation. She all of a sudden, notices her light reddish-blonde hair. It is illuminated by the way the sun is shining through the window of the train and it bothers her just how different she looks. She is pretty, even Bonnie could say so and her husband will like her.

Will my husband like me she wonders?

The train finally stops and she climbs out looking around her and watches all the people hurry to their destinations. It is cold and it is snowing, but the snow seems heavier and thicker here, than back home. There is chatter and giggling and it makes her look towards the left of where she is standing and she notices a massive building and it completely takes her breath away. She has never seen something this big before and she wonders who could have built it? It is made of a red looking stone or brick, it has a green roof with many point edges and she notices these odd, long metal poles and interesting looking ornaments all over the roof of this building.

As she gets closer, she sees a small golden sign that has "Château Frontenac" written on it and she wonders what that means and walks inside. She pauses at the door and traces the detail of the stone statue that is right in front of her with her eyes and can't help but feel it doesn't belong there, but rather somewhere outside. In the town square perhaps, she thinks?
The man is holding a metal pole of some kind and it has fourteen little nobs on it. She wonders who he is and what the pole is for? He is tall and looks like a warrior. She can't help but feel that he looks like her somehow and it gives her goose bumps on her

arms underneath her warm coat. She shakes them off quickly and walks past the statue, admiring everything around her.

The rest of this building is even more breath-taking than the foyer was. There are big, white and grey marble pillars at every corner, red carpets and golden ornaments and finishing's, on every single window and door. There is another big statute of a man in the middle of the room, but he looks less important than the first one. He is smaller and he exudes an arrogance that makes him seem left wanting and lacking of any real talent and prominence. The material used is also of a less superior quality and so is the workmanship. This man is definitely of no real significance, yet he is placed in the centre of the room and it bothers her.

The clock chimes suddenly and it breaks her thought. She walks up to the front desk and smiles at the lady with the white-blond coloured hair and blue eyes.

'Hello, I'm...my name is Bonnie. I am here to see Malcom Harrington please.' Her hands are sweating in her gloves and she wipes them over her coat, reminding herself that this is the moment she has been trained for, since the day she arrived as a foundling.

'Please head over to the sun-room dining hall and ask for Walter, he will take you to him.' She points to where Bonnie must walk and Bonnie trots off.

She stops at the door to the dining hall, quickly fixes her hair, gives each cheek a little pinch for some colour and enters the room.

The room is bright and cheerful. People are sitting at round tables, with white table clothes, enjoying a cup of coffee and a slice of cake. There are bright orange roses in the corner by the window and she wonders where they came from?

'Can I help you miss?' A polite voice asks her and she turns to look at him.

'Yes, good day, my name is Bonnie. Mr Harrington, as in Malcom Harrington, is expecting me.' She smiles awkwardly at the man and she can feel her heart pounding hard in her chest.

'This way madam.'

He walks briskly ahead and stops at a table at the far end of the room. There is a man seated with his back towards her. He is reading a book and sipping on a small cup of coffee. The aroma is strong and it fills her nose as she walks up to him.

Walter leans in and whispers something to the man and hurries back to the entrance to help the next customer. The man gets up and faces her with a warm smile. He pauses and gives her a surprised look, then stretches out his hand to greet her.

'It is nice to finally meet you Bonnie.' He says and his eyes glisten a soft blue.

She takes his hand in hers, they are big and warm and she is suddenly much calmer.

'Please take a seat. Can I order you something, are you hungry?' He asks politely.

Bonnie nods, she is very hungry. He orders her a slice of apple pie and a cup of coffee. He watches her eat and doesn't say a single word. He just watches her.

She eats her pie and feels much better. Malcom seems nice and kind. He is young and handsome, has blonde hair and blue eyes. His smile is comforting, his hands are soft and gentle and he has a sparkle in his eye that is infectious.

He suddenly gets up and shakes the hand of another man and his demeanour changes to a submissive one.

'I'm sorry I am late, is this the girl?' The man says and his tone is curt.

He nods and looks at her. 'Bonnie, please meet Malcom Harrington.'

Bonnie is confused, but she gets up from her chair and gives him her hand. He doesn't shake it; he merely holds it gently in his own and frowns.

'I expected...you are not what I expected.' He says rudely and quickly looks at his pocket watch, then then back at her. 'You will just have to do, come on we are late.' He snaps at her and it makes her flinch.

He marches off and she grabs her gloves from the table and follows him as quickly and ladylike as she can. She never even got to ask the other man who he was and wonders if she will see him again?

Malcom helps her into the carriage and they sit in an awkward and bitter silence for about twenty minutes. He doesn't glance at her or even acknowledge her presence, but rather feels uncomfortable around her. The carriage stops and he climbs out and mumbles something at her and walks inside the building. She stands in front of the carriage and has a good look at her surroundings. Nothing is familiar, but it is beautiful here and it is cold, there is snow everywhere. She hears children laughing down the street and a few stray leaves blow over her feet. She watches them carry on down the street and notices the atmosphere is eerie. A man gestures for her to go inside and she duly does as he asks.

'Welcome Mrs Harrington.' A lady not older than forty appears out of nowhere and is helping her take off her coat and scarf. She hangs them up by the door and smiles, while looking her up and down. She has a soft face, blonde hair, light blue eyes and a small scar on her left cheek that is a slight pink colour.

'Is this my new home?' She asks and her voice is meek and unsure.

'Yes, it is. My name is Jane and I run your household. If there is anything you need, you come and ask me.' Her smile is warm and genuine and Bonnie feels calm around her.

They both suddenly flinch to the sound of glass breaking. Bonnie locks eyes with Jane and can hear Malcom shouting at someone and she tenses up like a ball of yarn.

'Coffee or tea?' She asks and takes Bonnie by the shoulders and leads her towards the drawing room.

'You will get used to it dear, now look happy and smile,' she says and hands her a cup of warm camomile tea.

Malcom enters the room and sits down opposite her. Jane hands him a cup of coffee and he takes a healthy sip of coffee and swallows it loudly. He watches her and opens his mouth as if to say something, only to close it again and say nothing instead.

'You are too young for me and not what I want.' He clenches his jaw and balls his hand into a fist. 'I will speak to Ms Estes in the morning and have her send me someone else.' He says and takes another sip of his coffee. His eyes are fierce and mean and Bonnie can't bear to look at them.

She shakes her to acknowledge that she understands what he just said and her eyes tear up in shame, while he gets up, finishes his last sip of coffee and walks out of the room.

She waits until she can no longer hear his footsteps and she starts to cry, all alone and in a strange place.

CHAPTER TWO

She can't sleep that night and lies in her bed staring at the ceiling. She left the dark blue curtains wide open and the moonlight is shining inside softly, making the room just bright enough for her to stare at the artwork on the ceiling. Why would someone paint such a magical piece on the ceiling for no one to appreciate, she wonders? It seems weird to her and she lets her mind wander to Malcom. She replays the look of complete and utter disappointment, that he had on his face when he met her, and she wonders where she will be going to next? She remembers Dora, the girl on the train, telling her she is pretty and that her husband will like her.

'Why doesn't he like me, what did I do wrong?' She cries out and she can feel the tears run down her cheeks.
Who will want her now? She has heard the stories, women who don't get placed with a husband need to work, some end up at the factories or in the colonies. Perhaps she can run someone's household, like Jane? But I don't know anything about running a household, she reminds herself.

She turns over and a single tear runs down her cheek and onto her pillow. She has cried enough tears for tonight and decides to try and fall asleep in the big, warm bed. She misses her mother. She doesn't know what happened to her, but she remembers the face of a lady with crystal blue eyes and gentle hands. She was blonde, with long wavy hair and a bright and loving smile. When she spoke, her words sounded like that of an angel, but she didn't recognise what she said, it wasn't English as she knows it.

'One day I will know what happened,' she whispers out loud, hoping that wherever her mother is, she will hear her and finally doses off, with a clear and exhausted mind.

She wakes up to Jane placing a tray of coffee next to her bed. She opens her eyes slowly and feels groggy and exhausted.

'Good morning Mrs Harrington, did you sleep well?' She asks with a cheerful voice.

She turns to open the curtains and pauses for a minute when she realises that they are already open. She watches the snow fall and places her hand onto the glass pane on the window, as if she is remembering something from her past.

'It is still snowing, but it should clear up soon.' She mutters, but it sounds to Bonnie as if she is talking to herself and not to her.

Bonnie sits up in her bed and she feels sore and tired. Most of all she feels sad and hopeless.

'What is going to happen to me now?' She asks and she pulls the blanket up to her chin.

Jane pours some tea in a small light pink tea cup and hands it to her.

'Nothing at all, you will be joined in union by this evening and you will become his wife.'

'His wife?' She takes a sip of tea and keeps her eyes on the tea cup.

'Mr Harrington, he has changed his mind and he will marry you. Today in fact.' Her voice is chipper and full of life. She places her hand on Bonnies cheek and brushes it softly with her finger. 'He is a harsh man, but you will understand him, eventually. Now finish your tea, we need to get ready.'

Jane runs a bath for her and puts something scented into the water. She can smell it all the way by the bed and wonders what that is. It is sweet and earthy, with a hint of warmth and something that is familiar to her, but she doesn't know what it is.

'What is that smell?' She asks with curiosity filling her eyes.

Jane smiles and hands her a little bottle with a golden cap. There is a small metal chain dangling from the bottle and the letter "A" is engraved on the front of it.

'It's a gift from Mr Harrington, use it sparingly and only on special occasions,' she admonishes her and Bonnie nods in agreement.

She takes the bottle from Bonnie and places it back inside the little, white cupboard by the sink, in the bathroom. There is a single white face cloth next to it with a red "A" stitched onto it and she knows these things belonged to someone else at some point.

'Now come on and get in, we need to give you a nice wash.' Bonnie has never had her long blonde hair washed with anything other than soap. But this bathroom is full of products and she watches Jane and what she uses for her hair and skin and it makes her feel special for the very first time in her life.

'I feel quite pampered,' she chuckles and Jane shares her smile.

'You are the future Mrs Harrington, it is a big deal, you are basically royalty.' She pauses. 'Not quite royalty like the Queen, but you understand. He is filthy rich, there is nothing you can't have.'

'Except you forget that he doesn't want me, not really. I wouldn't be surprised if Ms Estes is on her way here to fetch me.' She replies and traces her fingers through the foam. She can see her pale body underneath the water and she thinks about him placing his hands on her, this evening, and she can feel her skin crawl.

'You have beautiful hair.' Jane ignores her previous statement and gently combs her hair; she is deep in thought herself.

She finishes up with her hair, hands her a silk gown and instructs her to wait in the dining room for breakfast.

Bonnie chooses to eat a bowl of fruit and can't believe all the different colours that are staring back at her, in her white bowl with golden edges.

'I have only ever eaten apples,' she says as she takes a bite of the little, blackish-blue round balls that are balancing on her spoon. She asks Jane what they are and she explains them one by one. 'Blueberries are these small blackish-blue balls, these red things are strawberries, this a peach and over there are bananas. She points to an oddly shaped, yellow fruit and Bonnie can't help but smile after setting eyes on it for the very first time.

Bonnie notices someone standing in the corner of the room and realises it is Malcom. She swallows hard and immediately stands up with a stern look on her face and forces a smile to appear on her face, but her lips struggle to part at the sight of him. His face is mean, his demeanour is unkind and she can feel the tension that radiates from his body. His eyes are cold and unhappy. She guesses he must be in his thirties; he has an aged face and green eyes that are intimidating to look at.

'If you don't know what fruit is, what on earth do the foundlings eat?' He scoffs while he pours himself a cup of coffee.

His voice is surprisingly calm and he gives her a sarcastic grin while he puts a single blueberry into his mouth.

'Porridge,' she replies and feels silly.

'Well there is no such thing as porridge here, we are not peasants.' His voice is suddenly cruel and unkind.

He gives Jane a look and she quickly pours him another cup of coffee.

'Have her ready by six pm, that is when the proceedings will start.'

'Yes, Mr Harrington.' She smiles and leaves the room.

Bonnie finishes her breakfast and enjoys the explosion of flavours in her mouth. She thinks about Mary and Stacey and wonders where they are? Are they happy and are their husband's kind and friendly, she wonders?

She puts on a long and elegant white silk dress, with long lace sleeves and gold decorative buttons down the back.

'This is beautiful.' She runs her hands down the fabric and looks at herself in the mirror.

'Now listen to me Bonnie, when the celebration of your union is done, you will need to go back to his bedroom with him, do you understand?'

Bonnie looks confused, she has no idea what she is talking about.

'He will take off your dress and tell you to lie on the bed. He will then climb on top of you, make love to you.' Jane starts to feel embarrassed by the topic and her cheeks turn a soft pink.

Bonnies eyes go a deep blue and she looks down at her feet.

'You understand now?' She asks and plays with a curl that is out of place and pins it back where it belongs.

Bonnie blushes at the thought and turns her head away in embarrassment. Her body suddenly feels weird and the thought excites her, but she doesn't understand why.

'This is how I will give him a baby?' She replies coyly.

'Yes...'

Jane doesn't make eye contact with her and tenses up while she looks for the diamond tiara that she needs to place in her hair. There is something she isn't saying and Bonnie can't help but wonder what it is?

'You look stunning dear, look at you in that dress, he will be very pleased.'

Bonnie smiles and touches her arm. 'Jane...what aren't you telling me?' Her confidence surprises Jane and she wonders if she should say something. She decides it is best if she doesn't and leaves the room for a few moments while she gathers her thoughts. Telling Bonnie that this is his third marriage is only going to make her more nervous, she convinces herself. She walks back inside the room with a more composed smile and demeanour.

'I have nothing to tell you. Besides this is your big day, you need to focus on that.' She smoothes over her hair one last time, to makes sure no strand is out of place.

'We need to leave in ten minutes, I will come fetch you if you would like a moment to yourself?' She asks and gives her a motherly look.

Bonnie nods that she would like to be alone and turns her back towards the mirror and stares at her reflection. She walks to the side of the room and sits at the big window and just watches the snowflakes fall, one by one, and thinks about Stacy. She decides she will ask him about it someday, if he is as important as Jane says, he will know where she is. Perhaps she could write her? The though excites her and she feels giddy inside.

'Bonnie, it is time.' Jane is standing at the door and stretches out her hand and gently guides her down the stairs and to the carriage.

'Good luck, I will see you later.' She fixes her hair one last time; her hands are suddenly nervous and she runs back into the house. She doesn't wave her off, she doesn't want to wave her off.

Bonnie suddenly feels very nervous as well and clutches her silk dress tightly. She looks straight ahead and thinks about Stacy and how brave and bold she was. Her mind wonders to the day she stole a piece of cake from Ms Estes and gave it to her for her fifteenth birthday. It was the best surprise she ever got and to this day no one knows who took the piece of cake. It has become the local mystery at the Foundling Home. She giggles softly under her breath and covers her mouth with her hand like a naughty foundling girl.

The carriage stops abruptly and her heart starts pounding hard in her chest. She sits forward to see where they are and she can see a big, cold and oddly shaped building in front of her. She wonders where she is and climbs out with the help of the carriage driver. She walks up to the door and notices the abnormal size of it. It is as tall as three of her, perhaps even four. Why do they need such big doors she wonders? She stretches out her hand to knock on the door and it opens before her hand even touches the cold, smooth steel.

'Mrs Harrington, welcome, please do come in.'

A man dressed in a black pair of pants and jacket, with a small white patch on his neck, stands in front of her with brown eyes and a big grin.

'Mr Harrington is waiting for you, but first let me ask you. How long are you a believer?'

Bonnie doesn't answer him and he notices the confused look on her face. 'That is alright, we can discuss that later.'

He takes her by the arm. 'Ready?' He asks her enthusiastically.

Bonnie nods and she starts to walk down the long aisle with him. She only needs to walk about fifty metres and keeps her eyes straight ahead of her, making an effort not to let them wander too much and distract her from the reason why she is here. There are no people waiting at the end of the aisle and she doesn't see Malcom. Her heart starts to race and she wonders where he could be? Perhaps he changed his mind and wants someone else after all?

A man appears from nowhere and walks into the middle of the room and stops by a podium of some kind and smiles, albeit sternly. It is Malcom and relief enters her entire body. They reach him and the man in black says something to him and shakes his hand and quickly gets into position. He grabs a thick book, opens it and gestures for Malcom to take Bonnie by the hand.

'Let us pray.'

Bonnie listens to him giving thanks and praise, but doesn't know who this God or Lord fellow is. Malcom slips a ring onto her finger, it is thin and dainty, gold in colour and gives her a very faint smile. The man in black asks her to say a few words, which she does and next thing Malcom is kissing her. She freezes and can feel the cold in his touch and it makes her want to pull away from him. The kiss is short and meaningless and, in that moment, she realises that this is not what she wants at all and it makes her feel sick. She puts on a brave smile for the rest of the evening and he takes her down the street to a place that is full of people.

She doesn't know any of the them, but there is a wonderful celebration planned after their union in that odd building. She thinks back to walking down the aisle and remembers there was a deep-red carpet, that almost caught her shoe and made her trip, the same kind of red that was in that fancy building at the train station and she is curious if all these buildings have red carpets? Malcom's mansion has red carpets too, is there is reason for this? She knows the red carpets aren't important, but she can't help but think about them. She also noticed this big, metal thing right on top and in the corner on her way out. It was shiny and had all these different-length pipes coming out of it. What did it do? Her mind is racing and she has many questions about her new reality.

She wonders if she can ask Malcom about these things, will he want to answer her questions?

'So Bonnie, how long?' A voice causes her to snap back to reality and she quickly puts on a smile.

'How long, I'm sorry I don't understand what you mean?' She replies politely and shrugs her shoulders.

The young man laughs out at her. 'How long are you believer?'

This is the second time that evening she was asked this question and she has no idea what this means. She decides to answer him anyway.

'Since tonight actually.' She smiles and takes a sip of a drink, they call wine. It is tasty and makes her cheeks feel warm. She takes another quick sip and looks at her new husband.

Malcom doesn't pay her any attention, yet he looks happy to have these people around him. They must all be *his* friends and she wonders if she will also have these many friends one day?

They arrive home and he walks with her up the stairs and into his bedroom. He opens the door for her and she walks inside and takes off her tiara and shoes. His bedroom is twice the side of hers, with a big, four post bed and a soft cream coloured carpet on the floor. The bed is dark brown and has champagne coloured fabric hanging from the sides of it. There is a very detailed pattern on the wood and she wants to touch it. She can suddenly feel his breath on the back of her neck, while he opens the back of her dress and she can feel her palms getting sweaty. Goose bumps form all over her body as he slips her dress off of her shoulders and she wants to run away, as far away from him as she can. The thought of him touching her, she just can't bear it. She thinks about Stacy and feels him runs his fingers in her hair and down her back. His fingertips are warm and gentle and this surprises her.

'Go and lie on the bed,' he orders her.

She doesn't like his tone, it isn't happy or have any ounce of excitement in it, but she does as she is told and just stares at the ceiling, waiting for him to do what he needs to do with her. He climbs on top of her, kisses her on the lips briefly, then proceeds to kiss her neck and inserts himself. She cries out and continues to stare at the ceiling, while she lies there as still as she can.

He is rough and forceful and he smells like ash and fire and some wine. A couple of minutes later, it is all over and he is next to her, facing away from her and they both go to sleep.

She wakes up to a strange sound and looks around the room. Hear heart is racing and she is scared. Malcom is still asleep next to her and she looks towards the window, wondering what that was to wake her so suddenly? She hears the noise again and her heart pounds even harder in her chest. She gently pulls back the thick navy-blue curtains, the same ones that she has in her room, in order to see what it is.

Nothing, there is nothing there. She hears the noise again and this time cries out softly with fright.

'It's an owl.' He says suddenly.

His voice startles her and she looks over at him with big, bold eyes. He is sitting up on the bed staring at her. The moonlight illuminates her body perfectly in that moment and his heart skips a single beat. He walks up to her and takes hold of the curtain. He stares out of the window; his eyes are looking for something.

'You see that tree right at the back, in the corner by the wall?' He asks her.

'Yes.'

He casually places his other hand on the small of her back and gently strokes her soft skin.

'Now move your eyes slightly upwards, do you see the bird?'

'Yes, I can!' She smiles at him, but her expression changes to confusion. 'That's an owl? Why is it awake at this hour?' She asks and crinkles her nose at being awake so late at night.

'They are nocturnal,' he replies softly, but the expression on her face tells him she doesn't know what he means.

'They don't sleep at night, but rather they hunt rodents, mice and rats.' He pauses briefly at her beauty. 'They are supposed to be bad luck, like a bad omen,' he goes on to say and wonders why he felt he had to mention that to her.

He can feel her tense up and he strokes her back with more force and gently tugs on her long, soft hair.

'But I don't believe in such things. Now come back to bed.' She climbs back into bed and turns away from him, her mind is stuck on the scary sounding bird and what bad luck she may encounter, other than being married to Malcom. He places his hand on her hip and she can feel him up against her and she immediately closes her eyes tight. She knows what he wants from her.

CHAPTER THREE

'Lala ladida lala...' she wakes up smiling. She knows this tune and hums along while she lies there sprawled out on the big bed. Her mother used to sing a song to her with that tune. She didn't even know that she knew it, until now.

'That song, I know it,' she says as she sits up holding the sheets tightly to cover her naked body.

'Good morning Mrs Harrington, breakfast is ready downstairs.' She pulls open the curtains with a strong tug and puts a gold coloured tie back around each of them. 'You will be eating alone this morning; Mr Harrington is at the office already.'

Bonnie looks over at the chunky gold clock above the fireplace and yawns.

'I didn't realise it was already nine am. Was Mr Harrington upset that I was still sleeping?' She asks and feels guilty.

Jane grabs her champagne coloured gown and hands it to her with a gentle smile, but doesn't answer her question. 'You need to head into town after breakfast and buy some clothes, Mr Harrington's orders. I could accompany you, if you would like?'

'Yes, yes please. I have never had to buy clothes before, we were given what we needed at the Foundling Home and that was it.' She puts on her gown and starts to blush. 'I didn't even realise you got clothes in different colours until I left the Home.'

This is a different world, she thinks to herself as she walks down the majestic staircase, letting her hand trace the railings and looks up at the details and fine engravings along the ceiling. She chooses to eat the fruit again and takes her time. I'm *Mrs Harrington* now, I don't need to feel ashamed for doing things at my own pace, she tells herself and pours herself another cup of coffee.

She takes a bath and puts on the black dress she arrived in. She then grabs her black coat hanging next to the others and plays with the hole where the middle button should be for a moment. She looks in the mirror and realises just how different, how sad and tragic she looks dressed as she is and slides on her black leather gloves. *I looked a like a real lady in my white gown.*

'I am very grateful to be getting new clothes,' she mutters all nervously and stares at Jane in the reflection of the mirror, she has been waiting for her. She turns to face the door and stares at it. 'The life he can give me will make it all worth it.' This time she is talking to herself and walks out the door.

She has never seen so many dresses and colours. There are over a hundred different types of fabrics and patterns, some are for parties, others are for trips to the beach. The beach?

'And to think just seventeen years ago, this place looked so different.'

Her eyes move in the direction of that voice and she sees an elderly lady, maybe fifty years of age, telling her daughter about an incident that happened over a decade ago. She takes a step closer and pretends to be looking at a pair of shoes and pricks up her ears.

'I have heard this story a hundred times mother. The mud flood was terrible, I get it, but look around, there is almost no sign of it!' The young girl is visibly irritated, crosses her arms and lets out a big groan.

The girl looks nothing like her mother. She has olive brown skin and dark, thick, straight black hair. Her eyes are a dark brown and she has very feminine features, but she isn't pretty. Not like most girls in the store. Her mother, on the other hand, looks like her and Jane. She has blonde hair, with a few grey strands in it and bright, heavy set, blue eyes.

Her smile is kind and welcoming as she goes through the different dresses on the rack and Bonnie decides to be brave and bold.

'Excuse me, I couldn't help but overhear you talking to your daughter and I was just wondering, were you talking about the mud flood?'

The elderly lady turns around and grins at the sight of her.

'Aren't you a pretty thing. I'm Mrs Wentworth,' she says as she stretches out her hand for Bonnie to touch softly. Bonnie notices that she is wearing a very big, bright yellow stone on her fourth finger and on her left hand. Her expression and posture tells her she is someone important and it makes her feel less bold suddenly.

She gently touches her hand the way Malcom touched hers and greets her back. 'It is a pleasure to meet you, Mrs Wentworth. I am Mrs Harrington.' She replies with a simple smile.

The lady's eyes widen and the grin on her face turns into a big toothy smile. 'Mrs Harrington?' Her eyes scan her entire body and face and it is evident that she knows who Malcom is. Jane was right he must be very important.

'This is my daughter Elizabeth.' She leans over and snaps at her. 'Come shake her hand stupid girl!'

Elizabeth reluctantly shakes her hand and sits back down on the black leather couch and pulls a face. The girl must not enjoy shopping or her mother, or both, she thinks to herself?

'So, about that mud flood. What happened?' She asks gently and politely.

Mrs Wentworth ignores her and checks the gold watch on her thick wrist. 'Coffee and cake?' She isn't really asking and starts leaving the store.

Bonnie agrees and asks Jane to finish up the shopping for her, she doesn't want to miss this opportunity.

Mrs Wentworth takes her to a small corner café, which is located just a few metres away from the store they were in. There is an assortment of cakes visible at the window and Bonnie can't help but stop and stare at the sight of it all. There is so much colour here, people are happy and they smile, *really smile*. She has never experienced smiling at the Foundling Home. Mrs Estes was her care taker, but she never seemed happy, no-one there did.

They reach the café entrance and a young man dressed in a dark red suit, with golden buttons, opens the door and welcomes them inside.

'Thank you, Johnny. Table for two please.' She places her hand seductively on his chest and he smiles.

They take their seats and Mrs Wentworth quickly scans through the menu. 'Do you mind if I order?' She asks her, but doesn't look up at her.

'Not at all, please order...I honestly don't know what I would order anyway.' The truth is there is too much selection and Bonnie feels out of her depth. There is so much I need to learn; she thinks and stares at the menu.

She orders them a creamy coffee and a slice of Black Forest cake.

'This is one of the many things that we got right...' She shakes her head suddenly and doesn't finish her sentence. She takes another big bite of her cake and chews in silence. 'It doesn't matter,' she eventually says and takes a sip of her coffee.

'So, the story about the mud flood?' Bonnie prompts her gently, trying to change the subject back to what she wants to talk about.

'Right, so seventeen years ago the world went through a drastic change. I don't know all the details, but there was a cataclysm, they call them "Heaven Bearers".' She takes a big gulp of her coffee.

'There was the Old World, it is basically everything you

see and the structures all around you, they span the whole Earth you know? You see there was just one ruler or so-called Empire back then, known as Tartaria and they ruled the entire Earth. They all spoke one language and were one people. It is even said that they didn't believe in any higher power.' She scoffs and looks around the room as if she wants another slice of cake.

'Anyway, so the Tartarians were a fair-looking people, especially the women. Blonde, petite, like you and me dear. The Heaven Bearers, well they are of a different kind, if you know what I mean?' Her voice changes slightly and she fidgets with her fingers.

'Truth is we aren't supposed to talk about this stuff, it is no longer history or of any importance.'

Bonnie doesn't know what she means, but doesn't want her to stop talking.

'So, these Heaven Bearers came and then what happened? How did the mud flood happen?'

'Well they took over the entire earth, a war ensued between the Tartarians and it somehow resulted in a mud flood that covered everything in twenty metres of mud, or something like that. The buildings still stood, but the Tartarians starved to death. You see they were alive and needed to eat, whereas the heaven bearers, well...I guess they didn't.'

Bonnie can see she wants to change the subject suddenly and tries one more time to keep the conversation going.

'Did all the Tartarians die?' She asks and makes direct eye contact with her.

'No dear, not all, you see...' she hears someone call her name and stops mid-sentence.

'Malcom, my dear!' She gets up and gives him a motherly embrace and sloppy kiss on the cheek and then proceeds to wipe off her lipstick with her napkin.

'You didn't tell me you had such a charming wife.' She gives Bonnie a sweet smile and sits back down. Bonnie realises she needs to greet him as well and reluctantly gives him a soft peck on the cheek. He smells like perfume and she notices the woman standing next to him. She is about his age, with curly dark hair and green eyes like him. She doesn't make any eye contact with Bonnie and heads towards an empty table and sits down facing her.

'Well, you two ladies enjoy the rest of your morning.' He excuses himself and takes his seat next to the woman.

Bonnie sips her coffee and stares out of the window. Ms Estes told her once that these rich men can have other women, in fact it is quite common. She didn't understand what she meant at the time, but she does now. She is upset and feels hollow suddenly, but reminds herself that this is the new world and this is how things are done now.

She finishes her cake while listening to Mrs Wentworth talk about the World Fair and how her husband is financing the project. The rest was just her waffling about nothing in particular. They get up and her eyes drift towards this woman sitting next to Malcom and they briefly lock eyes. Bonnie freezes and then quickly looks away. She could have sworn for a minute her eyes changed colour, to a luminous purple and then back to green. Bonnie feels cold and scared and exits the café as quickly as she can, trying to get rid of that awful feeling she felt when she locked eyes with that women.

'Jane?'

Bonnie enters the big house, that they call a mansion and walks around looking for Jane. She can't see her and gets distracted by all the effort that the builders put into every inch of it. There are details everywhere, in places that she wouldn't even notice or appreciate them, yet they are there and it bothers her. Even the door and windows have some details or finishing of some kind and she wonders how long it took to build this place? She starts walking through the mansion and is about to enter the library, when Jane interrupts her.

'Mrs Harrington, I apologise, I was busy in the kitchen and didn't hear you.'

Bonnie smiles and takes off her old coat.

'Actually, you don't need this one anymore. How about I donate it to the Foundling Home nearby? She takes the coat from her and hangs it over her arm.

'There is a Foundling Home here?' She tilts her head and gives Jane a confused look. 'Why didn't he just marry one of those girls? Why did I have to travel so far for him?' She shakes her head and is visibly irritated and upset.

Jane touches her hand softly and helps her take off her gloves. 'I don't know dear.'

Bonnie decides to ignore the thought, she is more curious about the mansion and the mud flood.

'How long did it take to build this mansion? Do you perhaps know?' She suddenly asks.

'No, I don't. That is something you will need to ask Malcom about sometime, but I don't think he will know either. Your tea will be ready shortly.' She acts like she doesn't know anything, but Bonnie can see that she is lying and Jane notices this in her eyes.

'Ask him about the Freemasons some time, when he is in a good mood. It will help you understand.'

'Freemasons? I have never heard that term before.' She pauses and crinkles her nose. 'Thank you, Jane.' She says and goes to the kitchen to drink some water and wonders about the library and what she will find inside it? She walks back towards it and opens the door. The room is big and full of books. They start at the floor level and go all the way up to the ceiling. The room is huge and she realises there must be thousands of books in it. An out-of-place glass case, in the right-hand corner of the room, catches her eye and she wants to see what it is or if it contains an object. There is something very big inside and it has her very curious. She walks towards it and realises it is just a book. But the size of it? It must be almost a metre in height! She has never seen such a big book. How could anyone even lift and hold such a big book, she wonders?

'The Freemasons perhaps?' She mutters under her breath and knows she needs to ask Malcom about them as soon as possible.

She gets bored and is too scared to touch any of the books and goes to the sun room to have her tea. Stacy is still on her mind and she wonders how she is doing and what her husband is like? Her mind quickly drifts toward the thought of her mother, Malcom and *that* woman. She has so many questions that she wants to ask, but isn't sure if Malcom would even know some of them. *Would he even tell me?* She decides then and there that she will ask him tonight, at dinner and finishes her rose flavoured tea.

Malcom arrives home just after six pm, he walks straight into the dining room and sits down clumsily. He seems grumpy, like he had a bad day and taps his finger on the table. Bonnie quickly changes her mind about asking about the Freemasons or anything else tonight, she will wait for the right moment. Perhaps he will feel better tomorrow?

He eats his food, while she sips her wine slowly and she can feel the agitation in the air. The wine makes being around him a lot more bearable and she pours herself another glass, much to his dismay.

'How was your day?' She asks politely.

He doesn't even look up from his plate.

'Fine,' he mutters under his breath and keeps eating.

They eat the rest of their meal in silence and Bonnie wonders if he will ever be friendly towards her? Malcom is a man of very few words, he is old fashioned and has a very bad temper. She watches him carefully as she sits there, at the twelve-seater dining room table with the ball and claw feet. Her eyes trace over him and for the first time she takes a good look at *her* husband. He has dark, coffee brown hair and she likes the way it covers his ears just a little, but not completely. He has thick eyebrows and a slight stubble from the day before – he is very manly and she catches herself smiling stupidly at the sight of him. He is tall and strong, but slim built, with a very hard jawline and intense green eyes. He is perfectly proportional, he is perfect. He reminds her of Jerry, the butcher that would drop off the meat at the Foundling home, he was always grump too. Malcom's hands are clenched around his fork and knife and he seems to be enjoying his meal, but he doesn't smile or reveal what he is thinking about and feeling. He suddenly looks up and locks eyes with her.

She chokes on the piece of chicken in her mouth and she can't pull her eyes away from him. She starts to cough; her eyes water and she starts to panic. She can't breathe! He gets up from his chair and walks over to her, puts his arms around her and with his hands firmly locked together around her chest he gives her a hard thud. The chicken loosens from her throat and she can feel the air enter her lungs again.

She needs to catch her breath and feels so stupid. He says nothing to her, but waits a moment to make sure she is okay and then walks out of the room.

She sits back down and wonders what just happened? She wipes her mouth with her napkin and walks after him.

'Malcom, wait!' She calls out to him.

He ignores her, walks into his study and slams the door shut in her face. She hears a loud clicking sound and realises he just locked the door. What is wrong with him?

She goes back to the library with a different kind of motivation than she had earlier and wonders what she might find if she takes a proper look? Perhaps something about Tartaria, the mud flood and even the Freemasons? She goes over the books, one by one, and goes over the conversation she had with Mrs Wentworth in her head. *Heaven Bearers*, what on earth are they? She made it sound like they aren't like her – is Malcom a Heaven Bearer perhaps? Nothing about him seems ordinary.

There are a lot of interesting books, but most are in a weird language that she doesn't recognise. She attempts to read the cover of a thick book, with a dark green cover and bold golden letters on the front page, but she can't. She wonders what language this is, Tartarian perhaps?

She walks back to the glass case and stares directly at the big, golden book inside of it and it hits her! This must be something important, why else would he keep it in glass case that is locked? The answers to all her questions must be inside it and the thought excites her. She squints carefully at the cover and she thinks she can make out a word that looks similar to "Tartaria".

'What did Mrs Wentworth say, the empire spanned the entire Earth and they had one language, one people and...?' She says out loud to herself in thought and closes her eyes trying hard to remember exactly what she said.

'No religion?' He is suddenly standing right behind her and her body tenses up immediately.

'I didn't even hear you come in? How did you walk so quietly?' She responds and her heart starts to pound in her chest.

She turns around to face him and he slowly takes a step forward and brushes the hair from her face. He lets his hands slip down over her breasts and watches her every expression.

'You like this book?' He asks her genuinely.

She turns around and takes another look at it, not realising what he wants from her.

'I do yes, I wonder what is inside?'

He pushes her up against the glass case and she knows what he wants. His hands are warm and less impatient than the night before and she feels how his fingers gently lift up her dress and move hastily over her body.

CHAPTER FOUR

He takes his hands off of her and begins to zip up his pants and then proceeds to leave the library.

'What is in that book?' She asks him in a firm and confident voice.

He ignores her and keeps walking.

'Malcom, what is in that book? I want to see it,' she says again firmly, but he can hear the slight fear in her voice and it excites him.

He stops, turns around and walks back towards her.

'What do you hope to find Bonnie? Something about your mother, your family? You girls all want the same thing!' He snaps at her.

'*You girls*?' She feels a rush of cold air brush over her entire body and her expression gets cold.

'What other girls? You were married before?' Her voice is only a whisper and her hands are shaking.

He clenches his jaw and looks her up and down as if to remind himself that she is worth keeping.

'Twice. I have been married twice before.' He raises his hand to his face and rubs his thumb over his lips. 'Not that is any of your business!' He scoffs suddenly and his facial features become hard and unkind. She reminds him of something or perhaps *someone...*

She turns pale white and faces away from him to catch her breath. What? Where are his other wives? He puts his hand on her shoulder and she cringes and wants nothing more than to smack his hand away from her. His touch is no longer warm, like it was a few minutes ago and she feels angry.

'What happened to them? Your wives? Please tell me the truth.' Her breathing is fast and heavy and she is angry. She can feel panic in her breathing and she tries to slow it down.

'Come to bed Bonnie, it is late.' He replies and he pulls her gently by the arm, but she resists him completely.

'No.'

His eyes turn *that* intense green colour and she knows he is getting angry, very angry. He leans into her as if he wants to kiss her, but he stops himself and walks away instead.

Eventually, she follows him upstairs and climbs into bed and covers her head with the blanket. He is taking a bath and she waits for him to finish, wondering what he knows and if he will ever tell her?

She hears the door open and she pulls the blanket from her head.

'Will you tell me now, please?'

He climbs into bed and turns away from her like he usually does.

'The first one left me and I don't know where she went. The second one couldn't give me children, I had no use for her,' he finally answers her and goes to sleep.

Bonnie swallows hard, his answer isn't what she expected at all and she feels sick to her stomach.

Malcom and Bonnie have been married for two months already and once a week they routinely go to that odd stone building, where they had their union. They call it a church and the man in the black suit, who is a priest, holds an hour reading and during that time he reads from that book with the black cover and symbol on the front cover. The Priest is saying a prayer and she leans in to Malcom and asks him what that symbol means.

'It is called a cross and we – you are encouraged to wear it around your neck to signify your allegiance to the *New World*. Now keep quiet and bow your head.' He says with a hint of sarcasm in his voice.

She listens to the priest tell them a story about a man that loved his fellow *Humans* very much, but they murdered him. Humans, what are they, she wonders?

The story is very sad and she wonders why people would do that do one another? She thinks back to what Malcom said *that* night, about having had two wives and her wanting to know about her mother. Did he know something about her mother? Her gut tells her that he does and she wants to know what he knows.

Her thoughts are interrupted by people standing up and she realises the reading is finished and she is relieved. She finds them terribly tedious and boring.

She greets Mr and Mrs Wentworth and Elizabeth politely, on her way out and Malcom and her walk back home. It is spring and the weather is very mild, even Malcom seems to enjoy it and she notices that he is semi calm today, *almost happy*. She enjoys having the sun shine on her face and she stops for a moment to admire some wild flowers that have sprung up by the side of the road. They are white and very dainty; she picks one and smells it.

'It smells like nothing?' She says surprised and then runs to catch up to Malcom.

They keep walking until they reach the house and he opens the door for her and just before she heads into the kitchen to make some tea, he pulls her in close and kisses her. He is rough and he holds her way too tight. She tries to pull away, but he won't let go of her. His grip loosens and his roughness changes to passion. He picks her up and carries her to the bedroom.

He is impatient, but he takes his time. He puts her down

on the bed and takes off her dress slowly and kisses her entire body while she just lies there breathing hard and loudly. He kisses her lips, really tastes them, he then proceeds to push himself up against her, but he is gentle. He suddenly stops and climbs off of her, takes off his clothes in hurry and proceeds to take off her stockings one by one while he kisses her right leg all the way up to her thigh. She lies there still and for the first time he doesn't repulse her, completely. He climbs on top of her again and kisses her breasts eagerly and she moans out. This surprises him and he guides himself into her slowly and calmly while he adjusts his thrusting to what *she wants.*

She moans out in satisfaction and they both lie there in silence, neither of them knows what to say. Eventually he breaks the silence and completely ruins the moment.

'You need to get pregnant soon, understand?' He says in an arrogant tone.

She lies there and nods, feeling suddenly very uncomfortable and exposed and quickly covers herself with the bed sheets, while he gets dressed and heads downstairs.

She wonders what got into him, why was he so gentle and kind, only to revert back to his normal cold and grumpy self? She thinks about what he said and wonders how long she has until he gets rid of her too?

She puts on some clothes, grabs an apple and leaves the house. She wants to walk around and look at all the buildings, perhaps she will find some of the answers to the questions she has herself? She has already seen a few from her neighbourhood and the church, but she wonders what other odd buildings are around? She thinks about that big metal thing inside the church, they call it an organ and it makes a weird sound, but she can't help but think that, the organ had a different purpose and so did the church? It is too big and cold to be a "place of worship" as the priest says. The church seems repurposed, almost like they didn't know what it was for and gave it a made-up purpose.

'*No religion.*' That is what Malcom said when she was curious about that big, gold coloured book in the glass case. Is that why people ask her that weird question, of how long has she been a believer for? Did no one believe in anything in the Old World? If there was no religion, then why is there one now? Her mind is racing and she accidentally bumps into a man and falls to the ground. She half catches herself, but scrapes her knee on the pavement and cries out.

'Ouch!'

'I am so sorry Miss, here let me help you up.' He helps her up and notices the ring on her ring finger and immediately knows who she is. Malcom has, in the meantime, given her another ring to wear, with a big blueish-purple diamond. It is a very rare stone and he wanted her to have it. She didn't dare say no, although it felt too big for her finger.

'Mrs Harrington, I beg your pardon, here let me walk you home.' He tries to lead her away, but she pulls away from him and rubs her hand gently over her grazed knee.

'No, I am quite alright, thank you.' She is annoyed that he knows who she is and carries on walking down the street.

'Mrs Harrington, please wait. I am very sorry; can we not mention this to your husband?'

His request surprises her and she stops to look at him. He is young, maybe twenty-four years old, with blonde hair and the same sparkling blue eyes that she has. He has full lips and a kind smile and extremely rough hands.

'Who are you? I don't know you. But you seem to know me!?' Her expression is cold and stern.

'Everyone knows who you are.' He gives her a shy grin and looks down at the ground.

'My name is Henry; I work as an engineer down at Oldbrooks. That is actually where I am heading, we need to remove some mud and fix the damage –'

'Mud?' She interrupts him and takes a step closer to him.

'What kind of mud...I mean, from where is this mud?' She asks and he can see he has her full attention.

He looks around him to make sure no one is listening to

their conversation and leans in close to her. 'From the *Old World* Mrs Harrington.'

Her eyes go big and the blue in them sparkles with exhilaration.

'I'd like to accompany you. Please lead the way.' She gestures with her hand.

He puts up his hands in protest! 'I'm afraid you can't, it isn't appropriate – I am sorry Mrs.'

She cuts him off. 'Fine, then I shall tell my husband that you pushed me to the ground and didn't even help me up.' She is posturing and hoping Henry won't call her bluff.

'Not a word to anyone, you hear me?' His voice is firm and his face is stern, she knows he is not joking.

They start walking and he explains what he is doing in the area and with the mud flood-effected building.

'We have repaired most of the damage, you know, but these building are massive, some go twenty-thirty metres down into the ground. We built new roads, so you wouldn't notice, but what you see is not the whole building.' His eyes light up and she realises he has a passion for discovering these buildings and it makes her heart swell with excitement.
She is in awe with what he tells her and she realises she could listen to him talk about this topic for hours. The whole day even.

'We have even found some skeletons, of the Old World people, they were big, much bigger than us.'

'Big enough to pick up a book that is about one metre in height?' She interrupts and asks him sarcastically, but he knows she is serious. She has a fire in her eyes and he knows he has sparked an interest in her. She is beautiful, her skin radiates youth and innocence and he has to force himself to look away from her.

He eventually stops walking and looks at her and gets drawn into her dark blue eyes, so much so that he can't look away this time.

'Some, yes, others are about double my height or slightly bigger.' She hears a banging noise in the distance and it distracts them both. He carries on walking on ahead and starts to talk as if he is speaking to himself.

'It makes sense you know, why else are the doors so big? From a construction point of view, it makes no sense to build such big doors. But, if you are two or three metres tall, it would make perfect sense.'

He shows her the building he is currently working on and he starts telling her all about the work he does, when she notices a man in a black suit and a top hat down the end of the narrow street. He disappears just as quickly as he appeared and she wonders if she is being followed?

She brushes off the thought and continues to listen to Henry and what he has to say.

He takes her to the side of the building and bends down and knocks his fist on the glass pane of a window.

'You see this window? Look at how low it is. Why would someone want to put a window halfway into the ground?' He shakes his head in confusion and disbelief.

He is right, she takes a good look and notices that the entire row of windows are half-buried into the ground.

'You see, no one would build like this, it is not practical, why put in a window in at all?' He is doing that thing again where he is talking to himself. 'I have been to all the big cities in Canada, even in New York, it is the same all over. The buildings are buried and we are brought in to make it look as if, this is what was intended by the original builders. That is why some of the important men are called Freemasons. They found the buildings; you know got them for free and claimed to have built them. Get it?' He suddenly shakes his head at what he is saying and then realises, perhaps he has said too much.

'Look, I...' she places her hand on his arm. 'I won't say a word.' She starts to smile and puts her hand over her mouth to cover just how happy she is, now that she is finally learning about the New World and what happened all those years ago.

'What about the church? My husband made a comment that there was no religion in the Old World?'

Henry nods and stares past her into the distance. She knows what he thinks he saw, the man in the top hat.

'I should go.' She turns around to leave, but stops and faces him again. 'How can I find you again?'

'I work for Old-Brooks in town, just ask for me there.'

'Jane, can you please run me a bath?' She calls as she enters the mansion, but sees that she is busy preparing a roast for this evening.

'That is a big roast, are we expecting company?' She asks her jokingly and takes a whiff of the lovely smell that fill the kitchen.

Jane looks over at her surprised. 'Yes Mrs Harrington. Your mother-in-law, father-in-law and brother-in-law are coming for dinner. They should be here in about two hours.'

Bonnie shakes her head in confusion. 'Really? Malcom didn't mention anything to me earlier?'

She runs her own bath, puts on a nice light blue dress, fixes her hair so that her neck is exposed, just how Malcom likes it. She finishes up, by putting on her shoes and walks downstairs towards the study and knocks loudly on the door.

'Come in.' His voice is deep and he looks like he is deep in thought.

'You didn't mention your family is coming for dinner. In fact, I didn't even know you had a family. Why haven't you mentioned them before?'

He can hear she is upset and doesn't understand why.

'They weren't even at our union!' She snaps at him and her voice quivers.

'They don't live in the area,' he replies coldly and puts down the document he is holding in his hand. He doesn't know what else to say to her and starts to play with a metal object on is desk.

'I like your dress; it looks nice on you,' he replies and gives her a grin. His mind is elsewhere and he is trying to change the subject. This makes her mad, but she knows there is no point in arguing with him. He will just close up and she wants him to be in a good mood for when her in-laws arrive. She gives him a fake smile and leaves the room.

She walks outside and takes a walk in the garden. She picks some flowers and breathes in the clean and fresh air. Everything is perfect here; Malcom insists on it and she does appreciate the effort put in to maintain the estate. She walks a bit further towards the stream and dips her toes into the water and thinks about Henry and all that he told her earlier in the day. She can't wait to see him again and ask him some more questions.

'First thing tomorrow when Malcom is back at the office, I will tell Jane I am going shopping and I will find him at Old-Brooks, no one will know any different,' she mutters as she plays with a leaf that she picked from a nearby tree. She is excited, she enjoyed their conversation today. She looks back at the mansion and can see him standing at the window in his study watching her. She picks up her hand and gives him a wave and laughs out loud. She is being cheeky and it's not like her at all, but she doesn't care.

It is six pm and she waits patiently in the entertainment room with a glass of wine in her hand, she is nervous. She takes another sip and swallows it slowly.

'Slow down on the wine, I will not have you drunk tonight,' he barks harshly at her.

She puts her glass down and hears voices coming from the foyer. She stands up, fixes her dress and checks that her hair is in place and puts on a big and welcoming smile. Malcom watches her and can't help but grin. He is starting to enjoy her and her quirkiness. She is different to the other two, they were cold to the touch and could never quite get used to him. He reminds himself that she doesn't know who, what he is, and when she does that will all change.

His mother walks in first, followed by his brother and his wife, then his father. They all look just like him, dark hair, slender figures, good looking and have this perfect bone structure, except for the brother's wife. She is blonde, with dark blue eyes and luscious pink lips. They also have the same intense green eyes, except for Waal, his father. His eyes are more grey-green in colour and they don't suit him at all. She feels completely out of depth around them and isn't sure how to react or what to say. She feels Malcom place his arm around her and guide her towards them and she starts to tremble.

'Bonnie, this is Leesa, my dear mother.'

They shake hands and Bonnie can see her inspecting her face, her stomach, but the dress isn't very revealing. Waal gives her a soft kiss on her cheek and has a much warmer aura around him, while Harlow, his brother, greets her from where he is standing and carries on talking to his wife. She looks very much like Bonnie, she is petite and pretty, very pretty.

She leans over towards Malcom and quickly whispers into his ear. 'I see you and your brother both seem to like the same type women.' She gives him an awkward, yet cheeky smile and he leans back in towards her and laughs.

'Indeed. After all, that is my second wife,' he replies and kisses her on the cheek.

She feels that cold air rush over her body again and goes to sit down at the table and places her fidgety hands onto her lap. The atmosphere is weird, they talk about business and no one even really acknowledges Bonnie at all. They neither ask her any questions nor include her into the conversation and she notices how Harlow's wife is ignored too. It suddenly hits her and she knocks over her glass of water by accident. She quickly mops it up and turns her head away from Malcom and his scolding look. She excuses herself briefly and goes outside for some fresh air. She can hear him walk up behind her this time, but he doesn't touch her, he just stands there.

'Come back inside now,' he orders her and she reluctantly follows him back to the table.

The rest of the night is a bit of a blur, she ended up drinking too much wine and really wasn't interested in anything her in-laws had to say.

Eventually they leave and head back to their hotel and Malcom comes to fetch her. She is still sitting at the table with her head placed on her arms, leaning on her placemat and she is mumbling to herself. Malcom picks her up gently and carries her to bed and just as he sets her down onto the bed, she reaches out her and grabs him by the arm.

'What are you people? You are not like us; we are different to you! Why do you even want us? What do you want from me?'

He takes her hand off of his arm and tells her to go to sleep.

'We can talk about it tomorrow,' he promises and proceeds to take off her shoes and cover her with a blanket.

CHAPTER FIVE

She wakes up and her mouth is dry, so she gets up to drink some water. Malcom is still sleeping and she walks over to the golden clock to see what the time is. It is four am and it is raining outside. She finishes the glass of water, it is cold and refreshing and climbs back into bed. Malcom has his back turned towards her, like he always does, and she notices a faint scar that runs down his back, near his spine. She gently traces it with her fingers, not wanting to wake him and she goes back to sleep.

When she wakes up again, he is gone and she is all alone in the bed. She drinks the glass of water that he left for her on the bedside table, but it tastes bitter. She spits it back into the glass and gets dressed for breakfast.

All the in-laws are there already, seated in the dining room and are still talking about the World's Fair that will open within the next six months. She remembers Mrs Wentworth talking about that too, at the store a while back.

'Good morning everyone.'

She politely sits down and she can feel their gaze on her. She smiles and sips her coffee and then puts some fruit in her bowl. Malcom is expressionless and Harlow's wife just stares at the wall in front of her. *Weird family*, she thinks.

'Where is this World's Fair?' She asks and tries to involve herself in their conversation.

'Chicago!' Malcom snaps at her and catches himself.

He is mad and she thinks she must have said something he would have deemed *inappropriate* last night at dinner.

She pretends she didn't notice and eats her fruit, piece by piece, with the biggest smile on her face. She is happy and she doesn't know why, but she won't let any of them ruin her day.

The conversation about the World's Fair continues and she just listens quietly to what they have to say.

'People from all over the world are coming. I spoke to cousin Geoff and he will be there with his wife. It is quite the talk of the town.' Harlow says as he finishes his coffee and gets interrupted by Waal.

'I'm not sure it is a good idea that we put so much on display, we don't want *them* to start to ask questions.' He pauses and looks out of the window. 'There are enough anomalies as is.'

Leesa clenches her jaw exactly the way Malcom clenches his and places her hand onto his.

Bonnie pretends like she isn't listening and remembers that she still wants to go and see Henry later today.

'I heard the name "Old-brooks" the other day, while I was in town. Is that the name of a dress store?' She sips her coffee and acts ignorant.

'It's an engineering firm dear.' Harlow looks at her and grins. 'Let the men handle the business-related things, you can stick to shopping.' He laughs and looks over at Malcom, who shares his laughter.

Waal stays quiet at the other end of the table and she makes eye contact with him. He knows she is acting and she starts to fidget with her spoon.

'If you are interested in such things, head on down to 3rd street, you can't miss it,' he replies and watches her reaction.

She pretends that she just made a mistake and really thought it was a dress shop and doesn't ask any more questions.

She doesn't understand why he just told her where to go and, in that moment, she thinks about the man in the top hat. Bonnie feels a soft touch on her hand and turns to see it is Harlow's wife wanting her attention. Her actions completely interrupt her thoughts and she stops fidgeting with her spoon and puts it down.

'I was hoping you would show me your new wardrobe that you bought, I'm sure you have some wonderful things now? If you don't mind?'

Bonnie is surprised by her request and happily agrees to show her anything she would like to see.

They walk upstairs and she opens the door to her mud-coloured walnut wardrobe. It is big and has large, silver handles. Harlow's wife suddenly grabs her by the arm and pushes her into the cupboard shelves.

'Ouch, slow down, you are hurting me!' Bonnie cries out. 'Do you realise I don't even know your name; no-one has introduced us yet.'

'My name is Valeria. Now listen carefully, stop asking all these questions. Or do you want to disappear like Annabeth?'

She looks at the door to make sure no-one is there, with her grip still tight on Bonnies arm.

'Annabeth?' Bonnie coughs out. Her statement has caught her off guard and she needs to catch herself.

'Malcom's first wife?' She watches her facial expression carefully and then continues. 'Do you know that she just disappeared one day, never to be heard from again? Malcom loved her; it was very hard on him. Apparently, as in, that is the official story.'

Bonnie doesn't know what to say and she wants to get away from Valeria. 'Please let go of me,' she orders firmly and smacks her hand away from her.

'Why are you even telling me this? Are you insinuating that Malcom murders the wives that ask too many questions?

Because if you are, I will take my chances, thank you.' She replies sarcastically and brushes the hair from her face.
She closes her cupboard door and goes to find Henry at Old-brooks. She can't stand being around these people, *his family*.

She has no idea where she is going, she just walks briskly down the street and looks for someone with a friendly smile to stop along the way and to ask directions from. People are in a good mood and are only too happy to help her. She has been walking around for over an hour and finally finds the building, hidden at the end of a small, one-way street. She opens the door and hears a little bell ring.

'Can I help you Miss?' A man appears from the back holding a hammer and his hair is covered in fine dust and white plaster, or concrete, she isn't quite sure.
She puts her hands behind her and slips off her wedding ring. She remembers that Henry identified her by that ring and she doesn't want anyone to know that she was here.

'Hello, I am looking for Henry, I don't know his last name unfortunately,' she says with a friendly smile and blushes slightly.

'I am sorry miss but he isn't here, he is out on the job.'

'I see – '

She pulls a disappointed face and thanks him for his time. Out on the job? Where? The old Mansion not far from the creek, where they were yesterday surely?

She slips her ring back on and rushes off that way, getting lost twice, but she eventually finds her way. She can see him; he is with two other men and they are busy taking measurements at the back of the building. He looks up and sees her. She waves and starts walking towards him.

'Hello Henry, I need to have a have a word, if you don't mind?'

'Of course.' Henry plays along and walks away with her.

'What are you doing here?' His face is concerned. 'People should not see us together, you understand why, don't' you?'

She shrugs her shoulders. 'No, not really, honestly I don't care. She pauses. 'I have more questions and you said I must look for you at Old-brooks. I went there and you weren't there.'

He laughs and rubs his hands in his hair.

'Rich women and wanting their way,' he teases.

'I wasn't always rich you know; I was a foundling. Grew up all the way in Ireland in one of those not-so-great Foundling Homes.' She crinkles her nose and her eyes momentarily turn sad.

He can see that she misses someone or something by the expression on her face.

'You never got to know you parents?' He replies.

She shakes her head and her cheeks start to fill with colour. She suddenly drops down to the floor and scurries over to hide behind a wall.

'What is Malcom doing here? Did you tell him I was coming here?' She scoffs angrily at him.

Henry laughs again. 'No...he owns Old-brooks. He owns most of the city actually.'

'Of course, he does,' she rolls her eyes. 'He can't see me. Look, I have more questions, when can I see you again?'

'If you know what is good for you, never. I need to go and you must go home now,' he orders and hurries back to the other men and Malcom.

Bonnie quietly sneaks back home and hopes Malcom did not see her. She joins Leesa and Valeria for tea in the rose garden and tells them about how busy the city was today. She makes up some story about all the irritating peasant-like people and how hard it was not to be disturbed by them.

'Well it is month end darling; people have just been paid.' Leesa is sarcastic and takes advantage of her ignorance and naivety. She continues to waffle on about something, but Bonnie ignores her.

Her gaze wonders to the flowers in the garden and she thinks about the Foundling home, how different it was growing up there and that she could never have imagined that she would be living in a place like this. She makes direct eye contact with Valeria and decides to press her a little.

'So which Foundling home did you grow up in?'

Both Valeria and Leesa are surprised by her question and Valeria looks at Leesa for approval, before she answers the question. Leesa gives her a nod of approval and she turns towards Bonnie.

'The one in London,' she replies curtly and sips on her tea.

Bonnie isn't ready to stop pressing her and reaches for a blueberry muffin and takes a small bite from it.

'How many of these foundling places are there, I mean, I thought mine was the only one?'

She chews the piece of muffin in her mouth and smiles like a silly little girl who can't understand basic instructions.

Leesa decides to take over and answers the question for her. 'There are many unwanted children Bonnie, be grateful you were taken in and given such a wonderful life.' Her eyes are full of poison and Bonnie wants to slap that cup of tea out of her hand.

Bonnie admits defeat and finishes her muffin in silence. She excuses herself and goes upstairs, lies on her bed and vents her frustration into a pillow. *I really want to talk to Henry!*

There is a knock on the door and she looks up at who it is. It is Jane and she asks if she can enter the room.

'Yes, of course Jane, do come in.'

She sits down next to her on the bed, with a motherly expression on her face. 'You have a curious mind dear, but that is a dangerous thing these days. You understand what I am saying?'

'You mean I will disappear suddenly?' She snaps and regrets being so childish.

She brushes her hair back gently and pauses. 'Lets us just be more careful, shall we. And stay away from Henry, he is a charmer and will only get you into trouble.'

'You know Henry?' She is surprised and suddenly happy and upbeat.

'He is my nephew. Now listen to me, stay away from him.

If Malcom finds out...let us just say you don't want to test his patience more than you already have, okay?'

'Okay.' She agrees and lies back down on the bed and thinks about all the children who have no parents and places her hand on her belly, wondering if she will one day have a child of her own. Her face cringes at the thought of having Malcom's baby. He has been kinder to her lately, but she still doesn't like him. He is a terrible husband and she can't see him being a better father.

She thinks about whether she would want a boy or girl and what name she would choose?

Malcom walks into the room a while later and sees that she is fast asleep on the bed and for a tiny moment, he watches her with a smile on her face.

He thinks about Annabeth and the fact that they *were happy for a little while*. Then he told her the truth. He thought he was doing the right thing and told her about the Heaven Bearers and who he really is. He explained what really happened seventeen years ago and why he married her. She sat on the chair in his study and listened to every word he had to say and was visibly shaken. He understood it was a lot to take in, but he never expected that she would run off the very next day, while he was at work and that he would never see her again. He wonders if she is alive and where she went? What he would say if he ever saw her again? Would he want to see her again? He shakes his head and reminds himself that he has Bonnie now. He looks at her again and the smile disappears from his face and he leaves the room.

Four more months pass by in flash. She wakes up before the sun is up or the birds are chirping and she is dog sick lying on the bathroom floor, in agony and clutching onto a towel. She washes her face with some cold water and she can feel her throat burning from all the puking. She drinks some water, but pukes it up within a few seconds.

'Here take this.' Malcom is standing next to her with a white linen cloth in his hand and he hands it to her. He is happy and smiling and she wants to scream at him for finding joy in her misery.

'You like seeing me sick? Or why are you so happy?' She asks and places the cloth over mouth trying not to puke again. Bonnie has learnt to be bolder and more straightforward with Malcom and to not fear him like she used to. He has never laid a hand on her and she doubts he ever will.

'I am very happy you are sick darling.' He gives her a kiss on the forehead. 'It means you are finally going to give me a baby, I almost gave up on you there,' he jokes and hands her a glass of water.

'Here, try take another sip.'

His words make her sick again and she turns her head away from him and starts to puke some more.

He has been a nightmare the last three months. He is always grumpy and snappy with her. He is rough with her when he makes love to her and he avoids her whenever he can. Except when he wants sex, he always wants sex. She doesn't understand what she did wrong, nor will she ever truly know or understand him. Malcom is not like her; she can see that clearly now. She wants to ask him about it, but knows that would be pushing her liberties too far. But now that she is pregnant, surely, she can get away with it, she wonders?

She decides to wait and see how he is at supper and then she will consider asking him.

Jane serves them their dinner, they are having beef roast, with cornbread and a mixed salad. An odd combination she thinks. She waits for Jane to leave the room and she lets him eat half of his plate, while she just pokes at her food and barely touches it.

'What are you?' She asks and makes direct eye contact with him, but he ignores her completely.

'Malcom I–'

'I heard you the first time.' He snaps at her suddenly. 'I just choose to ignore you.' He takes another mouthful of his food and then looks up and gives her a fake smile and carries on eating.

She drops her knife and fork loudly onto her plate like a child and sits back into her chair with her arms crossed.

'I'm carrying your child; I have the right to know!' She snaps back at him.

Malcom looks up and, in that moment, she realises she pushed him too far. With one swift movement he throws his plate against the wall and it shatters everywhere. She flinches, but keeps her eye contact with him. Inside, she is terrified and trembling, but she tells herself he won't hurt her, not while she is carrying the baby that he so longs for.

His eyes are striking and intense and she can't help but feel mesmerised by them. She leans forward and places both her hands flat onto the table and after a minute gets up and walks towards him. She walks up to where he is sitting and leans her buttocks on the edge of the table, keeping her eyes firmly locked onto his.

'Just tell me Malcom, I have no-where to go, nor do I plan on going anywhere at all. I would just like to know who, what you really are? It is obvious that we are not the same.' Her voice is calm, but her heartbeat tells him she is not really.

He swallows hard and breaks his eye contact with her. He remembers Annabeth and her reaction and balls his hand into a fist. She places her hand gently onto his and he releases his tight grip and relaxes almost completely. She proceeds to sit on his lap, places her hands firmly around the back of his head, forcing him to look at her and asks him again. 'What are you Malcom?'

She changes her demeanour to one of understanding and she can feel his body get less tense. He reaches for her face and rubs his hand over her cheek and kisses her.

'You are just so beautiful; your kind is always so beautiful.'

She doesn't say a word and hopes he will continue. He can see her eyes are burning with intrigue and it encourages him to continue.

'They call us Phoenicians. We are half Tartarian and half Heaven Bearers. You are a Tartarian, in fact anyone with blonde hair and blue eyes is a Tartarian.' His eyes are watching her carefully and he is very curious as to how she will react to what he just told her.

'I am a Tartarian?' She replies all surprised and the realisation isn't quite sinking in. She gets a cold shiver and immediately tries to stand up. He grabs her and keeps her as she was, seated on his lap.

'No running off now Bonnie, you wanted to know. You need to hear the complete story. Now listen carefully! Our child will be a Human and that is the goal, this is why I married you. Your sole purpose is to create more Humans. They will become our slaves. They will work and think they are free, but their sole purpose it to create wealth for us, and most importantly for the Heaven Bearers.' He tells her this without an ounce of empathy or any emotion at all.

'What!?' She moves her body away from him. 'You want our child to become a slave? No!' She shouts and her throats closes up with pain. She gets up in utter shock and takes a big step away from him. He pulls an angry face and she wonders what he will smash next.

'Our baby will be no-one's slave!' Her voice is shaking and she is upset. 'I will not let my child be a slave, do you hear me Malcom?!' She threatens him and he recognises *that* look on her face. It is the same face she gets when she wants to puke, that same look Annabeth had on her face.

He plays with his place mat and thinks for a moment. 'There are different classes of Humans Bonnie, our child will be classified accordingly.'

She doesn't even bother to ask what he means by that. She feels winded and she suddenly can't breathe. She keeps her composure and excuses herself and walks outside and looks up at the night sky. The moon is bright and it illuminates the entire yard. Tears roll down her face and she doesn't wipe them away. She looks down at her shadow and sees another one approaching her and her body tenses up at the thought of him touching her.

'Please don't touch me.' Her voice is weak and full of emotion.

'Cry if you need to, scream, I don't care. Come tomorrow you will have accepted the reality of what your purpose is and the purpose of that baby. You Tartarians are so fickle.' He laughs and his tone is sickening. She feels the tears pour down her cheeks and she sits down on the grass and lets it all out.

'What happened to my mother, my parents?' She turns her head and looks him in the eye. She now knows the answer to the question she has been asking herself for all these years.

'They are dead, but you already know that.' He squints his eyes at her and tries to ascertain what she is thinking.

'Did the Heaven Bearers kill them?'

'Probably, they killed anyone who didn't want to conform to the New World Order. Your parents were likely dissidents, rebels who refused to join the New World Order and follow the new rules and laws. Most of the adults were a threat and needed to go. We kept the children.' He sees the pain in her eyes and although he can't understand her pain, he can feel her sorrow radiate towards him.

'This is enough for tonight.'

He turns around and briskly walks back inside the mansion. He grabs a bottle of whiskey, notices Jane cleaning up the mess in the dining room and he wants to apologise, but reminds himself that he doesn't owe her, *them*, any sympathy.

CHAPTER SIX

She couldn't sleep at all, she just sat in the lounge with a million thoughts going through her mind and she felt like her head was going to explode. For all these years she has been holding onto the thought that her mother was out there somewhere, that she had a good reason for not wanting her. She would have never guessed that she was dead. Bonnie always wished that she would track her down one day and get to meet her, hear her story and have some kind of relationship with her. Jane walks into the room and begins to open the curtains and is startled by her lying on the couch with swollen and bloodshot eyes.

'Oh sweetheart.' She sits down next to her and rubs her back gently. 'I am sorry you had to find out this way, but it will all be okay. Just give it some time.'

Bonnie sits up and wipes her tears away. Her eyes are sensitive to the touch, she has never cried this much before and she feels completely silly.

'You are like me? You are a Tartarian?' Bonnie touches her blond hair lightly with her fingers.

'Yes, but some, like me, we can't bear children. At least

not with them?' She smiles and Bonnie is sure she saw a hint of pride in her smile.

'Them?' she asks.

'Not all Tartarians can get pregnant and have children with either the Heaven Bearers or the Phoenicians. The lucky ones, like you, can.' She is still smiling, but it is different to the one she just had on her face.

'Lucky!?' Bonnie cries out. 'I don't feel very lucky right now!' She throws the pillow off the couch and it knocks a candle stick holder over. It makes a loud bang as it hit the floor and it makes them both flinch.

'What does that mean for me?' She starts to cry again and blows her nose gently.

'It means that you will bear as many as my children as possible.' His voice is filled with hatred and anger. 'In exchange you will be taken care of by me and be given a very luxurious lifestyle.' His voice shatters the atmosphere in the room and brings with it, arrogance and no empathy whatsoever.

'If I couldn't have any, what would you do to me then?' She shouts at him in anger

'I wouldn't do anything to you! You would be given a job and you would be expected to work and live as a Human, just like the rest of them!'

He looks at his watch, it is almost six am and he snaps at Jane to make him some coffee.

He gestures for Bonnie to come to him, but she ignores him flat and turns away from him. He disgusts her and he knows it.

'Bonnie, listen to me and listen carefully.' He walks up to her and sits behind her, runs his fingers through her hair and inhales calmly. 'You have a job, just like me and everyone else. You do as you are told or you will join your mother. Bearing my child doesn't give you endless privileges.'

He grabs her gently by the shoulder and turns her so that she faces him. He wipes the last of her tears away and is surprised at how upset she really is. He has never experienced so much pain and sorrow. Phoenicians have no emotions, yet he can feel a sharp pain inside of him that he has never felt before and he can't explain it.

He kisses her softly and she doesn't kiss him back. He kisses her harder and forces her to kiss him back. He needs to taste her and feel her emotions as they radiate from her. His want for her consumes him and he lets himself get carried away. He is suddenly interrupted by a knock on the door.

'Mr Harrington, it is time.' He pulls away from her abruptly and she watches his facial expression turn cold and hard. He gets up and walks out of the room leaving her humiliated and alone.

Jane tries make her feel better as best she can. She helps her take a bath and insists she eat something, but Bonnie is exhausted and goes to the bedroom to lie down. She sleeps the whole day and awakens when Malcom climbs into bed that evening. She opens her eyes and she can feel just how swollen her eyes are now and notices it is pitch dark. She doesn't move a muscle and pretends she is fast asleep. He moves in closer to her and gives her a tender kiss on her shoulder, one that is so tender she isn't sure if she is actually dreaming it. He smells like a warm summer breeze and she wonders where he has been all day.

She turns onto her back and places her hand onto her stomach. She thinks about the baby and she is strangely aroused knowing it was Malcom who got her pregnant.

She shakes her head and tries to push the thought away. *I hate him,* she tells herself and I will never love him!

She can't shake the thought and realises she wants him suddenly. She lifts her night dress off, over her shoulders and turns him onto his back and hastily climbs on top of him.

He grabs her by the wrist, he is surprised by her actions.

'Bonnie, what has gotten into you?' He gasps at her and can feel how eager she is.

She leans down and starts kissing him and he lets go of her arm. Her mouth and hands are full of passion, so much so, that he feels momentarily overwhelmed by it. He flips her over and lays her down on to her back gently and slows down the pace.

He kisses her neck softly and her hands trace up his back and she pulls him in close and he knows he needs to have her immediately!

She lies there for a few minutes waiting for him to fall sleep and notices his breathing is soft and shallow. She sits up in the bed and looks over at him.

'Malcom?' She whispers. He doesn't move, he is finally asleep and she goes downstairs and looks for something to eat. She is starving and she can smell something delicious in the kitchen. She opens the fridge and finds some left-over chicken pie and cuts herself a generous slice. She eats the piece of pie greedily, but isn't satisfied and looks for something sweet to eat. She scrounges around the kitchen, opens a few cupboard doors, but can't find anything. No cake? She pulls a face and scratches her head wondering what else she can eat.

She eventually finds a small tin of chocolate chip cookies and eats a handful of those. She feels much better and decides she needs to go for a walk and get some fresh air. She grabs her coat and a pair of shoes and walks down the street. It is quiet, everyone is fast asleep and it is strange not to hear the children giggle and play outside.

She suddenly flinches with fright at the sound of a terrifying screech and she remembers her first night here and waking up to that exact sound. Malcom said it was from a bird and that it means something bad will happen. She looks around for the owl, but can't see it. Her eyes examine the rooftops and trees and the hair on the back of her neck starts to stand up and she hurries on down the street. She walks all the way to the building where Henry took her that day, when she met him, and has a look around in the dark. She can't see much and there is no lighting anywhere.

She enters the building and finds a few old rags that the work crew left behind and lays them out so she can sit down on them, rather than getting her new light-brown coat dirty. The floor is cold and she huddles herself into a ball and thinks about her mother. She closes her eyes and sees her smile, those striking blue eyes and she hums along to the song Jane was singing the other day.

'Ladidi dada lala...'

She wakes up to deep whispering and opens her eyes. 'Henry?' She blinks her eyes twice.

He is standing in front of her with a big and confused grin on his face. He starts to giggle softly.

'Good morning Mrs Harrington.' He moves down and sits next to her. 'Are you okay?' He has genuine concern on his face.

'Yes, I am fine, I just... I couldn't sleep so I went for an early morning stroll, but got tired. It is nothing at all.' Bonnie is embarrassed and he notices this.

He helps her onto her feet and she hurries back home. The other two men that are standing there greet her gently and watch her as she walks out of the building and away down the street.

Malcom will be so mad; she tells herself and her heart starts to race with fear and worry.

She gets to her street and starts to pick up her pace back home. She rushes up the stairs and pulls open the big entrance door and it bangs loudly against the wall.

'Jane?' She catches her breath and hangs up her coat. She takes off her shoes and throws them into the corner without any care. She is still wearing her night dress and it hits her just how badly she messed up.

'Jane are you there?'

There is no answer and the mansion is dead quiet. Her hands start to shake and she walks upstairs to check the bedroom. Malcom is not there and the bed is already made. She looks at the time, it is eight am and she figures he must be at the office. He knows she has nowhere to go and he doesn't really care about her, everything is fine, she tells herself.

Maybe he is in his study? She knocks on the door, but

there is no answer. She turns the handle, but it is locked. She knocks again.

'Malcom, are you in there?'

Still, there is no answer at all and she leans up against the door confused. *No one is home? Weird, the house is never empty...*

She makes herself some coffee and eats some more chicken pie and goes to sit in the library. She pulls out a leather book and runs her fingers over the front page. She puts it back and takes another one out and is suddenly interested by the look if this one. The book is heavy and has a gold cover, with red writing and it makes her think about that grand hotel, where she met Malcom. All these enormous and majestic buildings have a lot of red and gold in them, it must have been the colours of Tartaria she thinks and attempts to read the cover of the page, but she can't.

She snaps it shut out of frustration and throws it onto the floor. She pouts and then picks it up and puts it back where she found it.

Foundlings aren't taught to read properly, only the mere basics, so that they can fulfil their duties. She knows the language isn't English and wonders what language they spoke? Do Phoenicians and Heaven Bearers speak the same language and can they understand each other? She takes the same book back out from the shelf and opens it again. She flips through the pages and this time she notices a picture of a family. They are all blonde with blue eyes and the photo looks like it was taken here inside the mansion. A handsome man, with a stunning wife and their three children. She looks pregnant and she wonders who they are?

She is startled by the sound of footsteps and notices Malcom standing in the doorway. There is a man behind him, with a top hat, but she doesn't recognise him. Malcom turns to the man and says something, but she can't make out what he is saying and decides she doesn't care. He closes the door and locks it behind him and she freezes with fear.

'Who is this family?' She holds up the book and shows

him the picture.

Her question surprises him and he rips the book from her hand and throws it onto the floor!

'Where were you?!' He shouts and grabs her by the shoulders and gives her a shake. He is angry and his eyes rush over her to make sure she is alright and not harmed in any way.

'Who is the family?' She asks again and stands her ground. He doesn't like to be challenged, yet he doesn't do anything about her disobeying him and not answering his question.

'They are...they were an important Tartarian family. They are dead. They wouldn't conform to the New World Order. I don't know much about them to be honest.' He finally answers her.

'Did you kill them? What were their names?' She responds and her tone is bitchy.

He shakes his head. 'No, I did not kill them.' Her question bothers him and his smile becomes tense and agitated. 'Her name was Ariella, Queen Ariella, she was a kind and gentle woman.' He clenches his jaw tighter, but keeps talking.

'Her husband was King Finn, he was an intrepid warrior with mystical powers, but they proved worthless to the Heaven Bearers.' He gets that sick and twisted look on his face and it makes her wonder if he was there to witness them die.

'If you didn't kill them, who did? I can see by the look on your face you are well aware.' She replies and glares at him.

'I was just a boy when they died, but my father, Azrael, he killed them.'

'Azrael?' She says out loud. 'I have heard that name before as a little girl. They call him the *angel of death,* at least that is what I heard—'

Malcom's eyes flicker a shade of purple and he turns away from her. His real father is the angel of death? He did say he was half Heaven Bearer. This means it is impossible for Waal and Leesa to be his real parents, she realises suddenly.

'Who is your real mother then, if it isn't Leesa? Is she even alive?'

'No, I don't talk about her. I won't, not with you and not with anyone. Now, I have told you enough for today.'

She walks up to him and gives him a meaningful hug. 'Thank you for telling me.' Her actions surprise him, just as much as they surprise her.

He gets *that* look in his eyes and she knows that there was a particular reason why he locked the door behind him, he wanted privacy with her.

He rips off her night dress and drops it to the floor, leaving her naked and exposed. He is ravenous and he doesn't bother to hide it. He picks her up and sets her down on the table in the middle of the room and kisses her passionately and quickly moves to her breasts. Her nipples are hard and the taste of them is driving him wild. He kisses her up to her neck, spins her around and inserts himself hard so that she cries out softly. He doesn't hurt her, but he wants to hear her loudly. He wants her to like it, to like him inside of her so her thrusts slowly and deep and goes according to her breathing and her pace.

She notices a change in him, he is more attentive to her and her needs and this surprises her. He has been so harsh the last while and she is grateful for this change in his character.

She wonders if her wanting him so badly and unexpectedly last night has something to do with the change in him? Perhaps the fact that she came back and didn't leave him like Annabeth did has something to do with how he is around her suddenly? She isn't sure, but she is happy to have him this way. He is suddenly more attractive and he doesn't repulse her like he did before.

'I will be good to you, if you just let me Bonnie. And do me a favour, stay away from Henry.' He kisses her on the forehead and leaves the room.

The man with the top hat is working for Malcom? She isn't surprised. She picks up her night dress and realises he basically tore it half. She puts it back on and sneaks back upstairs to take a bath and to put on some proper clothes.

She doesn't know what to do for the rest of the day and decides to explore the mansion. There is still so much to see, she has only been in a few rooms of the house and there are many rooms. *Freemasons*, she thinks and remembers what she was told about them. They found these buildings and pretended to build them. This would mean that Malcom was a Freemason too surely? She walks outside, up to the side of the road and takes a good look at the entire mansion. The door to the mansion it big, bigger than what she or Malcom would ever need it to be, practically speaking. The windows are big too, but she can clearly see that none are half buried. She looks at the roof and sees all of these metal rods and weirdly shaped metal structures on it. She doesn't know what they are or even how to explain them. She walks around towards the back of the house and inspects every inch of it. She finally reaches the back and stops in her tracks. She sees a window half buried into the ground and bends down to look inside. She can't see anything and wonders how she can get inside there?

She looks around her and finds a small rock and uses it to smash the window. It takes her a few hard hits and eventually the window breaks and the glass shatters and lands on the inside, on the tiled floor. She takes the same stone and knocks the big and sharp pieces, that remain, away from the frame so that she can stick her head inside.

She pulls her head out of the window and sits down hard. 'Wow, there is actually an entire room down there!' She stands up and looks round her. There is no one here and she is so curious as to what awaits her down there. Should I go inside?

CHAPTER SEVEN

There is an entire level down there, rooms with doors and she can see a staircase in the distance, which means there is at least another level besides this one. Her heart starts pounding with excitement and she wonders what she will find. She takes the rock and cleans out the glass neatly from the window frame until there is no more glass. She sticks her feet in through the window first and climbs inside slowly, so as to not to cut herself accidentally.

The room is dark and stuffy, but some light manages to reach inside now that the window is missing. There is an old chair in the corner of the room and it is the only piece of furniture in the entire room. It is big, for someone twice her size and there is a folded piece of paper on the floor. She picks it up and opens it to read what is inside. There is a single sentence:

Vi er ute av tiden

It is in that same language that the books in the library are written in and she is slightly irritated that she can't understand it. *The old Tartarian language?*

She folds up the piece of paper and puts it into her pocket. Jane should know what the sentence means, Bonnie is sure that she knows more than she is letting on. She walks out of the room and into a little passage way. There is on old painting on the wall and a broken mirror. The door is different, older than the ones above on the ground level and she can't help but notice this. She wonders if Malcom had them replaced? It is very likely that he did.

She looks up at the ceiling and can see a faint depiction of something or a pattern of some sort, but it is too dark and she can't make out exactly what it is. It is probably the same patterns that are on the upstairs ceiling, she assumes and she continues to explore the rest of the rooms.

She puts her left foot onto the staircase and pulls it away. She is scared to go down there; she doesn't know what she will find.

'I need light,' she mutters out loud and quickly runs back to the window and carefully begins to climb out. She places her hands out in front of her and notices a pair of shiny black leather boots. She reverses back inside the window and a hand reaches in to grab hold of her. She screams and runs towards the staircase and doesn't look behind her to see if he is following her.

She can hear him grunt and she decides to go down the stairs and find a corner to hide in. She has no idea where she is going and she can barely see anything. It is very dark down here and none of the sunlight from outside is able to reach this level at all. She stretches her hands out in front of her and uses them to guide her and she puts one foot in front of the other, walking very slowly and carefully. If she can't see, then neither can he and she doesn't need to rush, she reminds herself and she can feel her breathing slow down. She bumps into something hard with her foot and has to stop herself from crying out. She carries on walking and can feel her heart pounding so hard in her chest, she worries that the man will hear it. She can feel a table of sorts or perhaps a cupboard and feels underneath it, it is hollow and she climbs inside.

She wants to cough and sneeze from the dusty and cold air, but pinches her nose shut with her finger tips. The air is very thick and heavy suddenly and she can't breathe in enough of it. She puts her knees up and puts her face against them counting to a thousand in her head, until she can no longer hear him looking for her.

Who is this man? This is the second time that she has seen him, but this time he seemed violent. When she sees Malcom later, she will tell him about this incident and how he scared her.

She starts to yawn and lays her head against the side of the wooden piece of furniture she is hiding in and closes her eyes, for what only feels like a couple of minutes.

She suddenly hears voices and opens her eyes wide. It takes her a moment to remember where she is and she wonders who else is coming after her? She closes her eyes tight hoping they will go away so that she can sneak back out. She hears more glass breaking and a loud and angry voice. It makes the hair on her arms stand up and she crawls out from under the table and crawls along the floor trying to find her way back. She is lost and the voices disappear. Did I just imagine those voices? Am I going crazy, she wonders?

She starts to cough as she breathes in the dusty air and then opens her eyes even wider and tries to orientate herself, to see something, anything. But it is pitch black and she can't see a single thing. She carries on crawling along the floor and she touches something cold and metal. It feels like a metal pole of some kind. She runs her fingers along it and she can feel fourteen bumps on the one side of it. They feel hard, but they are not metal and she carries it with her thinking that she will use it as a weapon, if she needs to.

The sun starts to set and she is still down there. She hasn't noticed the time; she keeps wandering around trying to find her way back and she is quite confused as to how she got this lost.

She hears the sound of wood creaking not far from where

she is crawling and she holds the metal pole she has in her hands as tight as she possibly can.

What was that? She listens carefully and pushes herself up against the wall. Her hands are starting to sweat and she takes a deep breath ready to defend herself.

'Bonnie?' She hears a soft voice, a voice she recognises. 'Bonnie? Are you in here?'

Henry? Is that Henry?

She lets him get a little closer, until she can hear it is him. She sees a light and decides to call out to him.

'Henry, I am over here!' She whispers loudly and lowers the metal pole.

The light turns towards her and he starts to walk in her direction. He finally spots her and gives her a toothy smile.

'First you fall asleep at the Asher building, much to the amusement of my men, particularly Harris. Your husband, however, wasn't very impressed, as we could both have guessed. And the building is off limits to the public by the way, public health standards and all that.' He gives her a cheeky wink and she knows he is teasing her.

'And now I have Mr Harrington thinking I have you locked away somewhere. He is a scary man, I'm not sure if you have ever noticed that?'

She stands there all shy, her face and hair are covered in dirt and spider webs.

'I admit, it wasn't my finest moment, but I was curious about what was down here.' Her voice is apologetic and she gives him an ashamed smile.

'What were you hoping to find down here?' He asks and shines the lantern around the room. 'There really isn't much here. There wouldn't be, they would have taken anything of value out, a long time ago I would suspect.'

She shakes her head and puts her arms up in defeat. 'I don't know, I was just looking to see if my home was also mud flood affected, then I saw the window and realised there are levels underneath the mansion. I just wanted to do a bit of exploring, it is my home after all.' She rolls her eyes and walks closer to Henry, not wanting to be too far away from the light he provides.

Henry takes the oil lantern he is carrying and moves it around to the corner of the room; something has caught his eye.

'Wow, look at that.' He says.

Her eyes follow his and she realises there is a large organ in the room. There is a fire place, like they have upstairs, but it looks slightly different and has no place for any air or smoke to enter or exit. There is a family portrait above the fireplace and it doesn't look too old and faded.

'Henry, please move closer to the painting, I'd like to have a better look at it.'

The blood rushes from her face. 'It's them!' She steps away and trips over something and lands hard on her buttocks. 'Ouch!' She cries out and starts to giggle.

'Are you ok?' Henry reaches for her. 'Do you know these people?' He asks her and frowns softly. He helps her up and she dusts over her dress to get rid of the dirty on it.

'I'm fine,' she laughs awkwardly and then shakes her head. 'No, I don't know them! But Malcom knows who they are, they were a King and Queen of some sorts, this was their house!'

'You mean King Finn and Queen Ariella?'

She turns to him surprised that he knows who they are.

'Yes, I have heard of them.' He gives her another cheeky smile. 'Rumour has it, your beloved Malcom is her son you know? That is why he is so special. I figure his daddy must be...' He doesn't finish the sentence.

'Azrael?' She answers and says what he is either too scared to say or not sure if he should mention it or not. He doesn't confirm or deny the name. He just walks back up to the family portrait and takes a good look at it.

'Don't tell anyone you found this, please Bonnie. There is not much left of them or anything really. They have taken over it all and given things a fake purpose and name. They even lay claim to the design and buildings that our people built for you and I!' His voice turns to anger and he is clutching the edge of the fireplace.

'I won't. I don't know why things happened the way they did, but we have to live with them now, it might not be forever, but it is reality for right now.' She places her hand on his arm and tries to lighten the mood.

'I'm sure there is a lot down here, we need to explore this place some more...'
Henry interrupts her rudely. 'And what do you hope to find? Your mother? Bonnie, she is dead, you know that.'

Her facial expression changes suddenly and she is hurt by his insensitive comment. 'I know she is dead!' She snaps at him. 'This world doesn't belong to them! It never has and it still doesn't. We can take it back. They want to create a species of slaves; did you know that?' She did a complete 180 degrees just like that and her voice if full of anger and she is shaking. 'They are going to take my child and make him into a slave!' Her eyes fill with tears and he understands why she is suddenly so upset.

'You are pregnant?' He is surprised and saddened at the same time by this revelation.

'You are the first in quite a while around here, turns out it isn't so easy for the Phoenicians to get our kind pregnant. It was much easier for the Heaven Bearers, but you see they tricked the Phoenician woman.'

'What do you mean they tricked them? How?' She asks, Malcom hadn't mention this, no one has said a word about it.

'They can shape shift or at least take over the form of another being, so they pretended to be their husbands, it is genius if you ask me.'

She watches his eyes trace the family portrait again and he touches Ariella's face softly. 'She really was beautiful, wasn't she?'

They stand there in silence and she takes hold of his left hand while they take in the once magnificent Tartarian King and Queen and time stands completely still.

Eventually he leans over and tells her they need to head back and she knows he is right. Her stomach starts to grumble and she realises that she is really hungry and thirsty.

'Promise me we will come back here Henry? It doesn't have to be tomorrow or the night after, but soon?'

He is reluctant to agree, but eventually does.

'It will have to be soon. I have a feeling your husband is going to make sure no one can come down here ever again, he will most likely close up the window nice and tight.'

She nods that she understands and they navigate their way back to the ground level.

She is still holding his hand as he walks her back to the house like a real gentleman and just before she reaches the door, she stops him. She takes out the note she had put into her pocket and shows it to him. 'Can you read this?'

He looks at it for a minute. 'My Tartarian isn't the best, but if I had to guess I would say it says "we are out of time".' He takes the note from her and puts it in his pocket. 'Your husband is watching, now go to him.'

She keeps her head down and walks inside the house.

She greets Malcom and Jane and asks her to get a bath ready for her, while she heads upstairs.

'Please leave us.' Malcom enters the bathroom and Jane hurries out. Malcom has been furious all day. Bonnie and her disappearing acts are driving him crazy and he has been needing to vent his anger a lot more, than he usually needs to.

He puts down a white cotton towel and sits on it so that he is at eye level with her. 'I have noticed me getting angry doesn't stop you from being reckless. Perhaps I need to keep you locked up inside or have someone escort you at all times?' He says calmly, but his voice is serious.

He looks over at her and his eyes are soft and a happy-green colour. She expected him to be a lot angrier and demand an explanation from her! She is glad that he isn't behaving like that, not yet, she cautions herself.

'You mean your top hat man? I figured he already reports my every movement?' She replies sarcastically and gives him a cheeky and happy smile back.

'No, he doesn't work for me.' He pauses and processes what she just told him. 'Did you get a good look at him?' He dips his finger into the water. It is nice and warm and he considers joining her. He stands up and starts to remove his clothes.

She watches him slip off his shirt and can't help but stare at how manly he is. She carries on watching him take off his clothes and doesn't hide her smile.

'He looked like the man that was with you earlier when you found me in the library, but it wasn't the exact same man. He gave me a heart attack you know, that is why I hid. He just grabbed for me and I panicked and got so lost. I was very glad that Henry eventually found me.'

'Move forward.' He orders her and he climbs into the bath and sits behind her, then gently pulls her back close to him.

'You made me very angry today Bonnie.' He speaks softly and calmly and rubs his hand over her breasts and down to her stomach, where it stays. 'I can feel it you know, the baby.' He takes his fingers and tickles her stomach and his touch is much warmer than the water.

'I'm sure you can,' she says all sarcastically and rolls her eyes.

'I can hear it, feel it –' He kisses her gently on the side of her head and she realises he is being serious.

'I have very sensitive senses Bonnie. They allow me to sense many things, including reading minds. It doesn't matter if it is the mind of a Phoenician, Tartarian or even a Human, it is all based on how their bodies reacts and smell. I will know if you are lying, because I can hear your heart beat, smell the sweat that starts to form on your forehead and hands. The body as many giveaways. I can tell how much you despise me and I know you are not happy to be the mother of my child.' He stops talking and sighs. 'I can't blame you completely, but I do expect you not to harm this baby, do you understand?'

Her heart has a sudden change in rhythm. 'I would never harm my child! Please don't say something like that to me ever again!' She isn't angry and her voice is completely calm, but not entirely happy. This surprises him and he isn't sure how to respond to her. She runs her fingers over his hand and thinks about what he just told her.

'What am I thinking about right now?' She decides to test him and see what he comes up with.

'I know you found something down there, something about my mother. What did that note say?'

Her body tenses in horror. How can he know that? She decides to lie and test him further.

'The note was in some language and I can only read the basics, foundlings aren't toughed how to read you know.'

'Hmmm...And what did you find?'

'Nothing, it was dark. Oh, I did find a metal pole with some bobbles on it. But I left it down there, it was just a stupid metal pole.'

'And what else?' He asks gently and he kisses the side of her head again.

She can feel his breathing get slightly heavier and she knows that she must tell him about the painting.

'A family portrait of the same people from that book. And an organ, like in the church. I don't think its real purpose is meant to make sounds, just by the way.' She immediately regrets mentioning the organ and rolls her eyes again. 'Please, don't close it up just yet. I would very much like to go back down there again, I find it all so very interesting.' She turns her head so she can see his face and expression and she batters her eye lids at him softly.

'You are asking me for permission?' His hand moves back up her breasts and he massages them gently.

'Yes, I am. Thing is don't want to lie to you, but I will if you don't give me some freedom. I have a curious mind Malcom and I want to learn things, completely understand them.'

'Tell me what the note said and I will think about it.' He

replies and she can hear he is being serious.

'It said "we are out of time". At least that is what Henry said. I really can't read that language; I can't read very well at all.' She splashes the water with her hand and is ashamed by her admission and she can feel her cheeks getting warm.

'Would you like to learn how to read?' He asks her and stops playing with her breast.

She sits up and turns to look at him, to see the expression on his face. 'Are you being serious?'

Malcom nods his head and gives her a sweet and gentle grin. 'I wouldn't ask you as a joke, that would be cruel.'

'And would you allow me to learn that language as well?' She tries to test her luck, since he is in such a good mood.

He laughs and touches her face. 'No, not that. That is forbidden, it is law Bonnie. But I will have someone teach you to read English, if you would like?'

'Why? I mean why are you being so nice to me all of a sudden? You don't even have emotions or care. I have a purpose remember and that is all I am worth?'

Her question surprises him and he needs a minute to ponder what to say to her in response.

'I am not sure Bonnie,' he answers honestly and closes his eyes and just lies there. He is thinking and she has never seen him like this before.

'I want you to tell me more about the Old World and in exchange I won't see Henry anymore.' She is testing him again and hopes he will take the bait.

'That is not up to you Bonnie, you know that.'

She lies back down against him and can feel how hard he is as he presses up against her.

'I know.' Her voice is full of disappointment.

She lies there, while he traces his fingers and hands all over her body and she can't help but think that she is a traitor to the Tartarian people, *her people*. Not only is she sleeping with the enemy, but she is carrying his child.

'Turn around,' he says softly and he pulls her onto him

and watches her every expression. He finds her form and emotions mind-blowing. She is *different* to the others.

CHAPTER EIGHT

The wind is howling outside and the raindrops are big and heavy. They smash up against the glass on the dining room window and she watches how the wind blows them all over the place. There are light brown and yellow leaves stuck against the window and she can't help but want to scratch them off with her finger. She sits in her chair and scratches gently at the table and imagines it is the window.

There is a loud bang and she jumps in her seat. A branch hits the window and it snaps her out of her day dreaming and brings her back to reality.

Malcom puts his fork down for a brief moment and looks towards the window and then takes a sip of his coffee and they continue to sit in silence and eat their breakfast. She is four months pregnant and he wants to keep her housebound to *protect* the baby. They argued the night before and he slept in the guest bedroom, it was the first time he was so angry with her, that he couldn't bear the thought of being near her. She started crying and he couldn't handle her and so he left. It was the right thing to do, before he said or did something he would regret. She is feisty now that she is pregnant and her emotions are all over the place, more than he would have expected them to be. He reminds himself that it is a good thing she is pregnant, but deep down inside he can't wait for the entire pregnancy to be over with, so that she can return to her normal self.

'I am not an ornament and you can't keep me locked up here Malcom!' She slams her hand onto the table and starts to cry. She takes her napkin and wipes away her tears out of frustration. 'Why am I always crying?' She blurts out between the tears and puts her face into her hands.

Malcom has no idea what to say or do, so he chooses to say nothing and lets her cry. Eventually, he can't take it anymore and decides to say something that should cheer her up.

'You are pregnant with twins! If only you knew how rare that is, you wouldn't be crying, but rather you would be celebrating! This will be a first since we took over.' He takes a sip of his coffee and she can see that he is very happy, proud even.

'Twins? What does that mean?' She asks while she blows her nose.

'It means I hear two heart beats, so that would mean there are two babies inside of you,' he says sarcastically and immediately regrets it.

She starts crying again and he snaps at her to stop! 'Bonnie, you need to stop crying, I just can't handle it anymore, please.' Both of his hands are balled into a fist and his eyes are agitated.

'How is it that you feel nothing, but you are always angry? I thought Phoenicians have no emotions?' She snaps back at him unexpectedly.

Her comment angers him even more and he loses all self-control. The rain stops falling for a moment and the wind disappears and his eyes flash a slight purple. As they return to their normal green colour, he grabs the table and flips it up against the wall. Everything happens in slow motion and she watches the coffee spill out of his cup and splash up against the white wall. Plates break into tiny pieces and she swallows hard.

She looks over at the window and focuses hard on the

leaves stuck to the window, the yellow one falls off and the rain starts falling again.

'I would like to see Henry today; I would like him to tell me some stories about the Old World and the mud flood. I am bored and he can't even come here, because you won't allow it.' She says under her breath, but loud enough for him to hear her.

'Well, how can I say no to such a reasonable request?' He barks at her and catches his breath. His voice is suddenly filled with pure sarcasm and his expression softens just slightly.

'Please Malcom. I am not sneaking off to go and see him and after all, you are his boss, he has to do what you say. I ought to have some perks being married to you.'

Malcom is standing a couple of meters away from her and he wants to hurt her and he knows he shouldn't. He sits back down on his chair and neatly places his hands on his lap. He looks like a school boy, but his expression doesn't match his posture.

'I need to think about it. Being my wife...' he pauses. 'Your perks are being *my wife*, that is all.'

'Fine,' she mutters and looks away from him. She hates what he just told her, but she knows that he is right, she has one purpose and, in a few months' time, that purpose will be fulfilled. He will then decide if she is worth keeping or not.

He suddenly starts talking softly, his tone is sincere and it interrupts her thoughts and she looks back at him.

'Phoenicians have a problem with anger, we can't always control it. One day I might just...hurt you Bonnie. You won't always be pregnant and I won't always have a use for you. Do you understand what I am saying?' He doesn't wait for her to reply or even nod that she understands him. He immediately stands up and begins to leave the room.

'Lock the door and stay inside this room for a while,' he orders her and slams the door shut.

She lets out a deep breath and rubs her hands together to stop them from trembling. She really believed that he was going to hurt her, throw her against the wall perhaps?

Her face changes its expression and she wants to cry again, but the tears won't come.

He doesn't understand her, he doesn't even try. She doesn't want them to take her children away from her and make slaves out of them, how could he be okay with that!? All he can feel is anger and nothing else. He doesn't want to care.

'It's not that hard,' she mutters to herself and looks over at the mess of food and broken crockery all over the floor. She picks up a chair and throws it against the wall and it shatters into pieces. She grabs the next chair and the next, until all twelve chairs are in hundreds of pieces on the floor. She is shaking and she can't believe what she has just done.

She hates him and knows she needs to get away from him, she needs to save her babies. But how, where will she go? There is nowhere to go and she knows this. I need to see Henry and soon, she tells herself and sees Jane standing at the entrance to the room, pale as a white bed sheet and she has a look of horror on her face.

Bonnie ignores her and brushes past her, just barely touching her. She puts on her coat and shoes and then stops with her hand on the door handle.

'I could get him into trouble,' she mutters under her breath. She opens the door and then slams it shut again.

'That is right, don't do that to him Bonnie,' Jane says from inside the dining room and starts to clean up the mess. Bonnie walks back towards the dining room and peeps her head around the door.

'I need to do something Jane, they are going to make slaves out of my babies.' She starts to cry and Jane completely ignores her. She can't bear to see her cry and she is powerless to stop them.

Bonnie stands in the door frame and watches her for a while and eventually helps Jane clean up the mess. She decides to stay home and obey Malcom this time, perhaps he will be pleased and eventually allow her to see Henry, she tells herself?

She grabs a black umbrella, it is Malcom's, but she doesn't care and takes an oil lantern from the shelf and lights it.

'He never said I couldn't go down to the underground,' she says to her reflection in the mirror by the door and smiles.

He had someone board up the window with sheets of wood, but hasn't replaced the glass yet and she wonders if he plans to? She climbs inside and takes a good look around now that she can see properly. She remembers the staircase and wonders just how far down it goes? Each room has exquisite details on the ceilings, the window frames and doors, just like the rest of the house, but every room down here is painted a different colour and that surprises her. She keeps thinking back to the grand hotel she met Malcom in, and wonders what it was used for seventeen years ago? What did they use it for in the Old World, was it perhaps someone's home? It is much bigger than the Mansion she lives in, maybe it really was a hotel? But there aren't even enough Phoenicians and Tartarians around to justify needing such a big hotel, at least not currently. Perhaps they will use to house the Humans?

She isn't sure and continues to explore the rooms. She finds that metal pole she held the other night and notices it is full of engravings, in that same language that she doesn't understand. There are fourteen bright blue stones placed in perfect symmetry on the one side and she brushes over them with her thumb.

I will take it with and ask Jane about it, maybe Malcom, or maybe she won't ask anyone about it, she tells herself and places it in the corner, for her to take with her later.

She can feel her frustration growing from not knowing certain things and she wonders suddenly if her mother, her parents where important, like King Finn and Queen Arielle? There must be something in those books, if only she could read them!

Malcom was kind enough and arranged that, twice a week, a local teacher comes by the mansion and teaches her how to read. But the English lessons aren't much help considering almost all of the books in the library are in that Tartarian language.

The English language is new, it was created by the Heaven Bearers in order ensure that, should any Human or Tartarian accidently stumble upon the objects from the Old World, they wouldn't understand them.

'Reprogramming and the destruction of history at its best!' She scoffs and wants to throw the lantern onto the ground. This makes her extremely mad and she realises everything she knows and was taught in the Foundling home is a lie. History as she knows it, how most Tartarians know it, is all a big lie!

She continues to search through the house, but most of the furniture is gone, only a few pieces of furniture remained. It is evident that the Tartarians of the Old World were bigger than she is and she doesn't understand why they were bigger?
She finds a bedroom, is looks like a child's room and she can't help but look under the old, broken bed to see if something was stashed there. She gets the impression that the family left in a hurry and took their most important possessions with them.

She finds nothing of importance anywhere, it was only that note that she gave to Henry, the family portrait and that metal pole. The bottom half of the mansion is empty. She is quite disappointed, she really thought she would find something down here.

She takes the family portrait off of the wall and takes it with to put it in the library, where it belongs.

'Something so beautiful and important should be preserved,' she says to herself as she walks back to where she entered the house.

She reaches the room with the broken window and as she is close enough to the window to climb out of it, she recognises those black shoes standing on the bottom of the window frame and she drops what she is carrying. This time she isn't quick enough and he grabs hold of her and throws her against the wall. In his right hand he is holding a rock, it looks like the same rock she used to break open the window with and he hits her over the head with it. There is pain that spreads all over her body and she can feel her body go limp and hit the hard, cold tiled floor. Her eyes close and she can see *that* smile. She is finally with her mother and she lets out a tiny sigh.

Malcom is at the office; he is in charge of the entire city of Montreal and his responsibilities include making sure that all the buildings have been re-purposed and are in full use. Things need to run smoothly and everything must have a predetermined function. He has hired engineers, Henry being one of them, who need to draw up the plans, fake construction photos and thus create a false narrative and a new history of how the city was built. This new narrative needs to be air tight, dates must be included, architects must be invented and there can be no contradictions. It is quite the task, but they have finished most of it. This is what will be taught in the education homes that were set up five years ago. All human children will be required to attend them from the age of three, on a semi-permanent basis and from the age of five, it will be permanent and compulsory.

They will not be taught about the Heaven Bearers, as officially they do not exist. They merely sit behind the curtain, in the shadows, and rule over all living beings on Earth. They decide on the laws and they tell the newly created tribunals to enforce them. No questions may be asked, there is no such thing as a democracy, but it must appear as if the notion of freedom for all and equality exists.

The Tartarian's are permitted to have children, but any children born from a Tartarian couple will be removed from their care at the age of one year, or sooner, depending on the circumstances and sent to the Foundling Homes, to be reprogrammed and educated. This is law. The Tartarians have a strong will and some are born with memories that they inherit from their parents. It is essential that these memories be erased soon after birth.

The Heaven Bearers are a sadistic species. They are greedy and their only purpose and goal is to make money, to gain power and control and become the ultimate rulers. They find pleasure in nothing else. This is what they did before they came to Earth, this is what they have done for the almost eight hundred years. They find a new host, take over and kill all who disagree with their leadership, strip their new home of all its resources and then move on to find their next host. Their method is unsustainable and their greed, their need to make more and more money, is what destroys them each and *every time.*

They do not want to live in equilibrium with mother nature and she will eventually let herself die and with her death, the Heaven Bearers will start to die too. This is what happened to Plerth. Mother nature took her last breath and the entire planet imploded into itself. Evil, however, is hard to destroy and seven of the ten Heaven Bearers managed to escape, alive. They wandered directionless for sixteen years in open space until one day, an opening in the firmament appeared over the flat Earth and they discovered their next host. They deceived the Tartarian people and more importantly mother nature, and conquered them easily. Tartarians are smart and have invented many things, things that the Heaven Bearers can never replicate. They however, don't make very good slaves. They aren't particularly strong, physically speaking, and they have very strong will. Many did not follow the orders of the Heaven Bearers and they were killed as a consequence of that.

The Heaven Bearers quickly realised they will need to create a new race of slaves that can mine the Earth and all of its minerals, in order to create a frequency strong enough that will open the firmament. Once they have achieved this, they will be in complete control and they may come and go as they please.

The biggest challenge thus far was the repurposing of the building, that is now the church and the creation of a religion. Tartaria had no religion, no one attended church once a week, nor did they read from a book and pray. This did not mean that there wasn't a higher power, he was just not worshipped. Azrael wanted a sure way to create a measure of control over the Humans and together with the other Heaven Bearers, namely, Baird, Enid, Kismet, Niamh, Samira and Ard, they found the ultimate control through religion. They managed to escape the carnage of Plerth, just barely and split up the newly discovered Earth in to seven pieces, which they call continents.

Azrael rules over North America, Baird over South America, Enid over Australia, Kismet over Africa, Niamh over Europe, Samira over Asia and Ard over Antarctica and the unclaimed islands.

The Tartarians were a very humble and trusting people who lived in perfect harmony with mother nature and the Tree of Life, who together, were the beating heart and lifeline of Earth. They had one race, one language, and one culture. The Tartarian empire spanned the entire Earth and had only one King and Queen who did not rule over the people, but made sure that the empire was always in perfect harmony with mother nature. When mother nature was sick, the Tartarians would nurse her back to health and she rewarded them with good harvests and the purest of water.

They did not take without giving back and there was complete equilibrium. There was no pain and suffering, poverty did not exist, neither did money. Everything was free and people merely followed their passions. There was no such thing as a job, not like what the Heaven Bearers have created for the Humans. The Tartarians have very high mental capacities and found a way to create free energy, from nature and they built mega structures to harness this power and divert it to the different homes, via ornaments and metal structures on top of buildings, known as antiquitech.

Three massive power station were built in the northern part of Africa and they are so big they can be seen for miles above the Earth's surface. They have pointy tops and produce no waste and make no sound. There is water all around them and they channel this free energy through the water to all the different cities around the Earth. The energy is centralised and converted into usable power via the buildings, that are now used as churches, and distributed to all the homes via frequency that is created by the organs found inside of them. The energy flows to each home, connects with the antiquitech on the roof of the particular home and powers up everything, including the fireplace.

The Heaven Bearers couldn't understand how this Tartarian technology worked, so they destroyed most of it after they had arrived and started to work on plans to create their own.

Malcom comes home just after the sun sets and he is sorry, at least he thinks he is. He is starting to feel emotions and he doesn't understand why. It makes him feel weak and being a Phoenician, he has to try very hard to brush these thoughts and feelings away. He calls for Bonnie while he takes off his coat, but there is no answer.

'Bonnie!' He calls again and his voice is harsh.

'I haven't seen her all day, Mr Harrington! Jane appears from the kitchen with a red and white table cloth in her hands and she has a look of worry on her face. 'She went for a walk outside in the garden and she just didn't come back.' I asked her stay away from Henry, but I'm not sure... '

'She isn't with Henry, I was with him most of the day,' he snaps and interrupts her.

'Then perhaps...' She pauses and has a revelation. 'I think she went down to the underneath part of the mansion then.'

Malcom walks around to the back of the mansion and the window is boarded up tight and nailed in, exactly as he instructed Henry to do. He can smell she was here earlier in the day and he allows his senses to go into overdrive. He closes his eyes and focuses hard. He can smell fear and blood, he can smell her blood.

'Jane, go back inside and get supper ready.' His voice is calm and relaxed.

He pulls away the wooden board, with ease and the nails used to hold it into place are no match for him. He climbs inside and sees her lying in the corner of the room. Her blonde hair and head are bloody, but the blood isn't fresh and this pleases him. He looks around the room and notices the portrait lying on the floor and the metal pole, with the blue stones, leaning up against the wall and a shock of electricity rushes over him. He knows what this metal pole is and it is definitely not any ordinary metal pole. He takes the metal pole, picks her up and carries her into the house. I will come back for the portrait he tells himself.

'Jane, fetch me some warm water and a cloth, now!' He shouts as he enters the mansion.

There is a sudden urgency in his voice, but it is gentle and she drops what she is doing and rushes over to help him.

She cries out at the sight of Bonnie. Her lips are a light shade of blue and her neck has bruising on it.

'She is fine Jane, I can hear her heart beat, in fact I can hear all three heartbeats, they are faint, but they are there.'

'What can I do?' She asks and places her hand on his shoulder.

'Fetch me a blanket, she is ice cold and we need to warm her up. Start a fire in the sitting room when you are finished.'

Jane rushes off to do as he asks and when she comes back, he dips the linen cloth into the warm water and he cleans the blood off of Bonnies face and hair as best as he can. As he slowly removes the blood from the side of her head, he notices the wound is already healing itself and he stops breathing for a split second. He blinks hard and takes another good look at what he is seeing.

Tartarians don't have the ability to heal themselves, he thinks to himself. No, it cannot be! He takes a closer look and the wound looks a few days old already and his left hand starts to tremble, slightly.

He finishes cleaning her up and then carries her to the sitting room and sits with her in front of the fireplace using the fire and his body heat to warm her up. He wonders what happened to her and more importantly wonders why she is healing herself at such a fast pace? He can smell a scent, a man on her, but he doesn't know this person and knows that he is definitely not from around here.

CHAPTER NINE

She feels warm and can feel the bright, yellow sunlight on her face. She is sitting in a field with thousands of purple and white flowers and she picks one, just to make sure they are real.

'Daphne! Come over here Sweetheart.'

She looks around, but there is no one else there and she picks another purple flower.

'Daphne, I said come over here! The voice is sweet and flows away gently in the wind.

Bonnie looks around her again and sees a woman, with bright blue eyes and a big smile signally for her to come and join her. It is her; it is her mother! She is young and beautiful, her golden, wavy hair blowing in the wind and the white dress she is wearing accentuates her petite structure.

Bonnie takes a deep breath and runs, with wobbly and clumsy legs, as fast as she can with her arms stretched out in front of her.

'There you are Sweetheart. She picks her up and kisses her all over her face and she realises she is small, only a baby. This is a memory of when she was a baby and her heart sinks in her chest. She is suddenly standing there, as a *grown-up Bonnie*, and she watches her mother swing her younger self around in her arms. The flowers in the field stretches for miles and her gaze move towards a man, playing with another little girl. She is older than her, maybe three or four years old.

'Cassidy, come and join us!' She calls out and she comes running towards her. The man follows with a smile on his face and she knows him too. It is them; it is *her family*. She reaches out her hand to touch them, but she can't get close enough. She opens her mouth to call out to them, but she makes no sound.

'You can't edit or recreate dreams Bonnie. Just enjoy them as they are,' says a soft and young voice and she realises it is her, talking to herself. She can hear another voice suddenly, but it isn't hers, it is from a man. She looks over at her father, but he is laughing and spinning Cassidy around. The voice is not his.

'Bonnie, darling, wake up!' The voice is familiar and it gets louder and louder. Her face feels very warm suddenly and she opens her eyes. He is staring back at her with *those* intense green eyes, there is a sparkle in them and for the first time she can feel her heart melt away, by the mere sight of him.

'I'm in love with you,' she blurts out and locks eyes with him.

He feels her face and is confused by what she has just said.

'It is me, Malcom. You were dreaming, but now, this is real life Bonnie.'

She sits up and smiles at him. 'I know, silly.' She grabs hold of him and gives him an intimate kiss.

'I got to see them for a while, my family. I have…had a sister, named Cassidy. She was older than me and she was beautiful too. We were all so very happy.' She looks around the room and her expression changes with a suddenly realisation that hits her.

'Why?' She asks and kisses him again and then pulls away.

'Why what?' He asks, genuinely confused by her behaviour.

'Why did the Heaven Bearers decide to conquer and destroy us? Everything was so beautiful back then, people were happy. They chose to cause chaos and destroy everything that was pure and good. I just can't understand why?'

He sighs and brushes a single strand of hair away from her face.

'Can we talk it about it another day, I would prefer it if you would just rest.'

'No, we can't!' She shakes her head and gives him a sweet smile. 'I have just this one question for now and I expect a thorough answer Mr Harrington.' She kisses him again and he doesn't understand what is wrong with her. She normally cringes at the mere touch of him, she never enjoys him, not really. *He can feel and sense it.* Yet now she is suddenly all over him.

'What has gotten into you?' He asks her in between kisses.

'What do you mean?' She pulls away and starts to giggle like a little girl.

He checks her head again and it is healing nicely.

'Bonnie, I need you to look at me and answer me truthfully. Can you heal?'

'Of course, I can heal. We all can!' She is confused by his question.

'A week ago, when you angered me and I punched the wall...you saw me bleed badly, didn't you?'

She nods and recalls that evening well. He had so much rage in him and it terrified her. But he had more rage in him when he flipped the dining room against the wall this morning and she cringes at the very thought of having to relive it.

'Yes, it was a bad wound, at least I thought so at the time. Why are you asking me this?'

'Phoenicians heal quickly, we don't die very easily either, not like you.' He pauses. 'No like Tartarians and Humans.'

'Okay.' She responds, but she doesn't understand what point he is trying to make.

'When you had that scrape on you knee all those months ago, how long did it take for it to heal?'

'I can't remember, a few days, maybe about a week. It wasn't a very bad scrape. Why Malcom, what are you trying to tell me?' She takes her hand and brushes his face and looks him deeply in the eyes.

'Do you remember what happened today?' He goes on to ask her.

She shakes her head and begins to rub her stomach. 'I can feel them.' She takes his hand and places it onto her stomach and smiles. He can hear and fell them. She wants to change the subject, but he won't allow it.

'Bonnie what happened today?' He presses her gently.

'What do you mean?' She is getting irritated now. 'Nothing happened, I wanted to visit Henry, but you said no. I just sat around and waited for you. I did hope you would change your mind though, but you didn't. Oh, and I went down to the underneath to explore, but there was nothing in there, nothing at all.' She starts to play with his hair, she is happy again and the irritation is gone. 'My name is actually Daphne.' She smiles. 'But I like Bonnie too.' She kisses him and her hands are all over him. He doesn't stop her this time, he likes her *wanting* him.

They lie in front of the warm fire, their bodies intertwined and she remembers seeing the scar on his back.

'What happened to you?' She pauses and decides to rephrase the question. 'What I mean is, you have a big scar along your spine, how did you get that?'

'My mother.' He clenches his jaw. 'My real mother did this to me, she tried to kill me.'

'What!?' She cries out in horror. 'How could she do that? Why would she do that?'

'I am an abomination. She never wanted me; she was forced to have me Bonnie.' He kisses her shoulder and she can feel his warm and tender breath all over her neck. 'Just like you are forced to have my abominations,' he carries on. 'So, she gave birth to me and then she tried to kill me, but what she didn't know was that, we don't die so easily. In fact, we heal very quickly and there is only way to kill our kind. But she didn't know that, no one did at the time.'

He pulls her in close and it is as if he is talking to himself. 'She left me to die, but I didn't.'

There is a moment of awkward silence and then he breaks it.

'Azrael punished her fairly for what she did and hung her shortly thereafter in the city square, as a warning to the others. I will show you one of these days if you would like?' His voice is calm and collected and it creeps Bonnie out.

'How do you know all of this, I mean you were just a baby?' She asks.

'We remember everything from the moment we are born, just like you.' He catches himself and wants to change the subject.

'I am sorry, she must have not seen any other way out.' She touches his face and kisses him gently.

'Now will you tell me why they chose to conquer us? Why us and not another race?'

'No, I can't Bonnie. You are not my equal and you just can't know these things.' He gives her a soft kiss, but his lips barely touch her skin. 'I am sorry.'

She is disappointed and she doesn't hide it, but she accepts what he tells her calmly.

He holds her tight in his arms and lets her fall asleep, while he wonders why she healed the way she did. It bothers him, even scares him, because it is not natural. He will be visiting with Azrael later this month and he will ask him about it then.

Things carry on as normal, she enjoys her reading lessons and his company a lot more. He makes an effort to not be as controlling and she appreciates it.

It is Sunday, late afternoon, and she is asleep on the bed. He looks over at her and he starts to pack his things for his trip to New York, to visit father. Something is bothering him, he isn't sure what it is, but he doesn't like the thought of leaving her behind and he decides to take her with him, last minute. She is excited, she has always wanted to see more of the country and this will finally give her the opportunity to do so. Malcom is happy that she agreed to come with him and it puts his mind at ease. He didn't even have to convince her, she jumped at the opportunity to come with.

He tells her this is a work trip and mentions nothing about Azrael, she can't know anything about him, it would be the death of her *and him*. She can't know who he is, no one can. Men like him stay hidden, that is how they want it. They control others and their hands never get dirty. When things go wrong, there will always be someone to take the blame, money can buy you that kind of power.

Azrael owns or at least co-owns all the press, the banks and even the farms. No one truly owns anything in reality, but they just think they do. That is the beauty of the tax system he created. The Humans work for a living wage, but pay 50% of it to the State through taxes. They think it is fair and don't question it. They are taught to accept many things from the age of three years old, why would they question anything? Azrael is an ugly being, all Heaven Bearers are clumsy looking creatures. But he is by far the ugliest of them all.

Once they choose a host country, they take on the hosts form, in this case, the Tartarian form. They can never match the Tartarians true beauty or elegance, no matter how hard they try, nor can they achieve the pure blonde hair and blue eyes. But they are cunning, evil and devious, which makes them smarter than a Tartarian. They hate anything good, pure and perfect. Their biggest satisfaction was having the Tartarian women bear their mongrel children and pollute their pure bloodlines. They didn't expect to create another perfect, yet subservient, master race on equal footing to the Tartarians.

The trip is very long, but there is so much to see and Malcom makes the effort to tell her a little bit about his childhood along the way, which made time pass by faster.

She thinks about when she arrived in the Americas almost a year ago and she can't believe how much her life has changed since then. She is happy now, happier than she ever was in the Foundling Home, despite her circumstances not being that, which she ever wanted.

'When I arrived in New York, I remember seeing this lady statue with something on her head, a think it is a crown or something like that?' She says as she stares out of the window.

'That is the Lady of Liberty statue, it was a gift from...' he pauses and for a moment he tries to think of the right name. 'It was a gift from France.'

'France?'

'It is a country in Europe, not from where you come from,' he replies softly.

'You don't have to be so nervous you know; I won't say anything about what you tell me or what you need to do here.' She says and winks at him, then lays her hand softly onto his.

'Say anything about what?' He replies and can't help but notice that she is acting weird and he can't shake it.

'Who you are going to see, I can sense it on you, smell it even.' She turns her back to him and stares out of the window and watches everything as they pass by.

They arrive in New York and he drops her off at the hotel.

'Get some rest, for all three of you.' He kisses her on the cheek and walks two blocks to meet with Azrael. He is wearing a navy-blue suit, with silver buttons and brown leather shoes. He sits with his left-hand placed on the table and he is wearing a chunky gold ring on his ring finger. It signifies his importance to the brotherhood; each Heaven Bearer wears one.

'Malcom,' he says and takes a long drag of his cigar. He blows the smoke out slowly and watches the smoke dissipate as it mixes with the air. He checks his gold watch and grins arrogantly.

'You are thirty seconds late, what did I teach you about always being on time?'

Malcom ignores him and pulls out a folder containing the information he is here to discuss with him and sits down.

Azrael watches him carefully and puts out his cigar. 'You smell of her, that Tartarian wife of yours.'

Azrael pulls a disgusted face.

'I brought her with me.' He replies in a nonchalant manner and doesn't make eye contact with him. He starts going through the numbers on the page in front of him in an orderly fashion and there is no more small talk.

They discuss a few things related to the repurposed buildings and how many Humans were born in total over the last year in North America.

'This is not enough!' He snaps and slams his hand hard on the table. The glasses bounce and clink against each other, but no one stares, not here.

His voice is rough and very deep; he is clearly angry and on edge. 'We need more progress Malcom; we need at least five times this rate!' He pauses for a moment and starts to lick his lips incessantly.

'We need to change the policy. This isn't working as efficiently as we planned. I will have to give it some thought.' He finally replies and signals that he wants another drink.

He sips his cognac and stares at Malcom's face. 'You remind me of that thing, especially in moments like this. The girl is making you soft. Remember what she is, she is a means to an end. After the baby is born, get rid of her,' he orders and lights another cigar.

Malcom shakes his head in agreement and decides not to ask him about the odd things that have happened over the last few days with Bonnie. I will figure it out myself, he tells himself and blocks the thought immediately.

'How is the World Fair coming along?' Malcom enquires and tries to change the subject.

'It is coming slowly, we hit a snag in the official story, but we have figured out a way to plug a few holes. We might even have electricity by the end of the month. Some of these Humans are intelligent enough to figure it out, it just takes a little bit longer. It isn't free like I hoped, so the profit margin isn't as big, but we have time to figure that all out. We need electricity and we can charge a fair penny for that and it will create more industry. You just make sure these Tartarians have more babies, we need more workers!' He snaps and orders another drink.

Malcom orders one too and finishes it in one greedy gulp. Azrael's tone is harsh and it is in that moment, that Malcom realises just how much more like the Tartarians he actually is.

They go through the last few figures and Malcom explains how well the creation of the religion has worked.

'This is good. I hear this has caught on well in South America and Europe too. I have commissioned a few men to write more stories for the book, as we have discussed. It will give these useless and pathetic Humans something to believe in and keep them docile and willing to work.'

Azrael sits back in his chair, with the cigar in his mouth and is enjoying the moment. Religion was one of the harder aspects to achieve, that and the repurposing of some of the buildings.

'Did Samira mention the trouble they had with that virus that killed all the new-borns yet?' Malcom asks and closes the folder that he had brought with him.

'She mentioned it, but has assured me that she has is under control. Is it under control Malcom?'

'I am not sure; I'm having someone look into as we speak. I don't think she is telling us the whole story. Truth is, I am worried. I have noticed the trend that some Tartarians...well they don't mix well with some of the Phoenicians, genetically speaking.'

'Oh? What have you heard?' He asks and hie ears pricks up, this news surprises him.

'There have been major deformities. Some babies are born without vital organs, limbs, that sort of thing. It is happening more often and I see it becoming a problem for us in the future. Also, it means less healthy Humans to be put to work, which slows down your plans.'

Azrael knows he is right. 'We need to isolate these cases then and get rid of that genetic pool, from the Phoenician side. Quietly, understand?'

Malcom nods his head and is reminded that he is his fathers' son. He knows "him dealing with it" will mean he will have to put to death over a thousand Phoenicians in the next month and he feels nothing, no shame and no guilt. He thinks about letting her go in a few months' time and he feels *that* pain again. He shakes it off immediately. Why does her leaving hurt him, but killing his own kind not? He immediately wipes the thought from his mind, before Azrael picks up on it.

He knows he is Azrael's right-hand man, but that is all. There is no other allegiance or *family bond* and if he gets in his way or falls for the Tartarian girl, he will be put to death without a second thought.

'Everyone serves a certain purpose and once that purpose is fulfilled, you get rid of that person.' This is Azrael's motto and Malcom knows to never forget it.

'That reminds me, once the report about the deformed babies comes through, you will need to have a word with Samira, we both know I am no match for her, especially on her own territory. And she will never allow me to do what needs to be done, at least not without a little push from your side.'

'I will handle Samira. You make sure to handle things diligently on your end. No mistakes, we can't afford to have things go wrong Malcom!' His eyes wonder to the corner of the room and he excuses himself and leaves.

The meeting went well, Azrael was his usual self and he is very glad that he has his support regarding the problem with Samira. He is usually *protective* of her, in his own strange way, but he understands that this needs to be done in order to achieve their goals.

Malcom decides to drop by an old childhood friend, before he returns to the hotel. He walks another few blocks down the street and enters a twenty-five-story building, covered with antiquitech on its roof and he is surprised that they haven't removed this yet. He needs to have a word with Rune about it, he reminds himself as he walks inside the building.

'Rune, it is great to see you!' He shakes his hand firmly and is genuinely happy to see him. 'It has been a while, how have you been?

'Malcom? I don't remember you saying you were coming into town?' He replies all surprised, but he is happy to see him too. He gives him a pat on the back and a toothy grin.

'That is because, I didn't old friend.'

'Please take a seat.' He gestures warmly for him to sit down.

Rune is the senior editor at the prominent New York Newspaper. His job is to tell the public what they must believe and know, rather than what is the truth. He is older than Malcom, by four years and is also a Phoenician. He is very different to most of others, he is happily married to a Phoenician woman and they live a quiet life. They have no children, nor do they want any. Rune never married a Tartarian wife, but he did contribute to society and had gotten six Tartarian girls pregnant over the years. Malcom on the other hand wasn't so lucky, not until now. Malcom had the choice, like Rune, to marry a Phoenician woman, but he never met one he liked enough to have around him permanently. He anyway preferred the beauty of the Tartarian women.

Rune's passion and purpose is propaganda and he thoroughly enjoys what he does, just like all other Phoenicians, he has no moral compass and merely follows orders without questioning them.

He gets up to ask his Tartarian secretary for some coffee and closes his office door.

'I take it you are here on official business?' He asks and closes up the file on his desk.

Malcom nods firmly. 'I even brought the wife along.' He smiles sarcastically.

'I heard you managed to do what so few of us can these days, except for me. Congratulations!' He teases.

Malcom smiles and wonders if he should elaborate and decides he wants to talk about what is on his mind and about Bonnie.

'I hear two heart beats, is such a thing even possible?' He asks and taps the table gently with his index finger.

Rune is about to speak, but pauses while his secretary puts down the coffee down next to Malcom. Rune waits for her to leave and close the door behind her and then starts pouring them each a cup.

'I supposes so, but I haven't heard about it. Actually, that isn't true, I heard rumours about it in Africa, two or so years ago. I never got to confirm them and I literally just brushed the thought away, figured it wasn't true. It will make one heck of a story, you know, bring hope to the rest of us if it is true.'

He takes a healthy sip of his coffee and smiles at the news.

'Azrael is slowly losing patience; he is thinking about encouraging more Tartarian births to make up for the shortfall of Humans. But we need to find a better way to control them, dumb them down, make them more complacent, if that is the case. The Tartarians are just not that easy to control.' He says and watches Rune's reaction to his statement. Rune listens carefully to what he has to say, but his expression gives nothing away.

Malcom suddenly gets very stern and places his hands on the desk in front of him. 'I need this to stay between us, otherwise there will be consequences, you understand?'
Rune changes his posture into a submissive one and immediately focuses his full attention on him. 'Of course, Malcom.'

'The girl, my wife...she...Is it possible that she could gain certain abilities from the babies?'

'What kind of abilities?' He is genuinely intrigued by what Malcom has to say and his eyes glimmer.

'Our kind of abilities. She had a bad head wound, there was a lot of blood and it should have killed her, but it didn't.

She lay there bleeding for hours before I found her and her body temperature was very low, she looked dead. But I could hear her heart beat, the babies' heartbeat and her wound, it was almost healed by the time I found her. I don't know how many hours she lay there for, but it wasn't more than eight or nine in total.' He rubs the tip of his index finger over his lips like he is thinking.

'I need you to put some feelers out, someone wanted her dead, which I presume includes the death of the babies. And I really want to know, if through the pregnancy, she is able to gain certain abilities, like us? She seems more like us these than a Tartarian, that is for sure.'

Rune takes a deep breath and runs his fingers through his dark black hair. What Malcom is thinking is a lot to take in, but it excites him and he can't help hide his toothy grin. 'The only people who would want a pregnant Tartarian girl dead is her fellow Tartarians, now that she is expecting. You will have to organise someone to watch her at all times, especially since she is unique and carrying twins. What did Azrael have to say?'

'He was pleased, but I didn't mention the possibility of twins, not until I know for sure. He seemed distracted and agitated anyway, there is something else going on that he hasn't told me about yet.' He replies suddenly distracted and looks at his watch to see what the time is. He has been there an hour already and knows he needs to head back to the hotel soon.

'I have heard, and let me make it clear that, so far is it merely rumours. But I hear that there are problems with Baird and his leadership. You didn't hear that from me. I am sure it will play itself out eventually, but in the meantime, there is definitely tension between the two of them.'

His reply surprises Malcom, well not the reply itself, but the fact that he hadn't heard about the rumour yet. He usually hears about these things very quickly. Have I been too distracted with Bonnie, he wonders?

'Baird and Azrael never did see eye to eye. If it gets ugly Kismet will step in and resolve things, he always does.' Malcom stands up from his chair and seems much more relaxed. 'I need to leave Rune and check up on a few other things, how about dinner tonight?'

'Sure, Aara will enjoy the Tartarian,' he teases and shakes his hand firmly. 'See you at seven at our usual spot.' He watches his friend leave his office and immediately makes a note on small piece of paper and hides it between two files in the filing cabinet.

Malcom had someone at the Newspaper send a message to Bonnie to be ready for dinner at seven pm, while he finished up his day.

Bonnie wears her peach-pink gown, with lace, something Jane insisted that she buys, which she didn't understand at the time. She is glad now that she agreed to buy it and looks forward to meeting Malcom's good friend and his wife. She doesn't have any friends at home, except for Henry, but she isn't sure she is allowed to count him as a friend. She is nervous and paces up and down the bedroom waiting for Malcom to come back.

He enters the room and changes his clothes quickly and snaps at her to meet him downstairs. She does as he asks, but he doesn't come. Eventually, she grows tired and takes a seat in the lobby of the hotel and lets her eyes wander around the room. She watches all the people, there are many Phoenicians, but no Tartarians, except for the few that work in the hotel itself. She spots a couple of Humans and admires their features. She has seen the Human children that live in her street, but she hasn't come across many adult Humans and she wonders where they all are?

Humans are unique, they come in different shades of skin colour. There are some with dark skin and some with very pale skin and all the shades in between. Most have dark hair, some even a red or reddish blonde hair, very unique and completely different to both the Tartarians and Phoenicians. She spots a tall man; he must be at least two metres tall, with orange-red hair and a full beard. He makes eye contact with her, after he notices her staring at him and she starts to blush. The moment is interrupted by a hand on her shoulder, it is Malcom and he is gesturing for her to get up so that they can leave.

They exit the hotel hastily and walk down the street for no more than ten minutes until they reach a very nice restaurant. She hears music coming from inside and grabs onto Malcom's arm with excitement.

'Where is that music coming from?' She asks with a big and happy smile on her face. He takes a look at her and can't help but think she is so beautiful, but he won't tell her that, not tonight and not here.

'From the band, there is a live band inside.' He answers and gives her a soft smile, only to suddenly change his expression back to a cold and mean one.

'Malcom, don't we all have impeccable timing?' A very posh voice sounds out of nowhere and it startles Bonnie.

A tall, slender and very elegant lady walks over to Malcom and gives him a kiss on each cheek.

Bonnie stares at her and can't help but think that she looks familiar. She has bright red lips and they are very distracting, even for Bonnie.

The lady's eyes wander over to her and she briefly makes eye contact with her and Bonnie notices a slight purple in her eyes, before they change back to intense green. She is wearing a full length, somewhat tight-fitting black dress, with a bright red belt and red high heels. She is arrogant and stunning at the same time and Bonnie suddenly feels very underdressed and out of place.

They start to enter the restaurant when it suddenly hits her and she knows where she has seen this lady before. Is it her, the lady Malcom was with at the café the day she met Mrs Wentworth and asked about the mud flood. She is his lover?

CHAPTER TEN

They take a seat at a medium sized, perfectly square table. There are two orange candles on beautiful, glass candle stick holders in the centre of the table and they smell like citrus. The table cloth is black and it has an orange stitching all around the edges, which is so subtle, that it is almost unnoticeable. Bonnie looks around and realises that they have the best spot in the restaurant. She has a full view of the live band and she starts to hum along softly to the song, even though she doesn't know the music. She only realises then, that she has hardly heard any kind of music at all and she doesn't even know what kind of music she is listening to. It has a fun beat and it makes her want to dance. She is tapping her right foot to the beat of the music and gently sways her body to the right and the left. She is happy and enjoying herself. Malcom, Rune and Aara are having a conversation amongst each other, they don't include her and it is obvious that this is done on purpose. In fact, she shouldn't even be with them in the restaurant. Everyone is staring at her and she wants to leave. She looks over at Malcom and gives him a coy smile and he completely ignores her.

She stands up and excuses herself and walks over to the

balcony for some fresh air. She is the only Tartarian girl seated as a guest and she realises how hated her kind really is. She never felt this disdain for her kind in Montreal, oddly enough, and she wonders why it is so different here in New York?

The breeze is cool and refreshing. She can hear a girl giggling in the distance and her eyes search for her in the distance. She is young, Tartarian and she has her arms wrapped around a Phoenician man. They sound happy and in love and she feels a sudden glimmer of hope that Malcom and her can be happy. She can't help but smile at the sight of them and she thinks about the few good moments her and Malcom have shared over the last couple of weeks. The girl giggles some more and her voice and tone are familiar. She takes a few steps closer to get a better look at her, because she realises that she actually knows her.

'Stacy?' She calls out surprised to even be saying that name out loud. She skips a breath when she gets close enough to see that it is her. 'Stacy, is that you? It is you!' She hurries up to her and gives her a big hug.

Stacy is caught off guard and completely by surprise. She pushes her away and takes a good look at her. 'Bonnie? What on earth are you doing here?' Her tone is unfriendly and belittling.

'I'm here with Malcom, my husband.' She is confused and looks over at the man she is with. He is Phoenician, but she can sense the tension between them all of a sudden and she knows he is not her husband. The atmosphere is awkward and no one says anything, until Stacy notices her stomach.

'You got pregnant?' She scoffs in anger. 'Of course, you did! That was supposed to be me!' Her tone is sour and harsh and she pulls a face that reveals her jealousy.

Life hadn't been kind to her and Bonnie can see the anger and hurt in her eyes. She backs up slowly and walks away and back towards the restaurant, without saying another word to her. She isn't sure what just happened and her mind is still processing the sequence of events, trying to make sense of it all.

'I'm sorry Stacy,' she whispers under breath and wipes away the warm tear that rolls down her cheek.

She sits back down at the table in the restaurant and the three of them are still talking like they were when she left. Her body fills with emotion and she can't contain it, she stands up again and begins to cry. She is embarrassed and tries to look for somewhere to go, somewhere to hide. She accidentally bumps into the waitress and knocks over her entire tray of wine glasses and the red wine spills out of them and splashes all over her and the floor. This only makes her cry harder and she suddenly can't breathe. Everything spins and she feels sick and naked and alone.

She feels a tight grip on her wrist and she is being dragged to the end of the room.

'Stop making a scene!' Aara scolds her and is taking her to the restroom. Her pale face is full of anger and she throws a white hand towel at her.

'He should never have brought you here! You are all the same. Clean yourself up and stop looking for attention, silly girl! You are a Tartarian girl, start acting like one.' She shakes her head, quickly checks her hair and make-up and while she stares in the mirror, she mutters at Bonnie.

'Listen to me and listen carefully. When you get back to Montreal, pack your things and head West, as far West as you can get. Take the train to Edmonton, if you can.' Her eyes go purple and she blinks hard. 'Don't look back and be careful. Cover your hair and act like you are travelling for business.'

She walks out like nothing happened and nothing was said.

Bonnie washes her face, catches her breath and as she is about to walk back to the table, she decides to just go back to the hotel and go to bed. Malcom didn't take her with for her company, he doesn't even want her here and he really won't care that she left. She asks the friendly lady at the reception to please give him the message that she left and she strolls the ten minutes back to the hotel, trying to think about all the positive things in her life. The entire street is lit up with lanterns and it is more beautiful than what she has experienced back home in Montreal.

She thinks about what Aara just said and she knows she is right. It wasn't that long ago when she was thinking about leaving and not knowing where to go. At least she has an idea now, Edmonton. Except, she can't be completely sure that Aara isn't sending her into danger. Why Edmonton?

Malcom cares for her, even if it is only a little, she knows he does, she can sense and feel it. He can't fake that and it would devastate him if she just left him. She is confused and sad and angry. What do I do, she wonders and her head is spinning?
She walks up the stairs and as she reaches her room, she notices the door is open slightly. She pushes it open all the way and there is a man inside, patiently sitting on the leather chair with a glass of whiskey in his hand.

'Bonnie!' he gets up to embrace her.

She stands at the door confused and puts her hand up instinctively, almost to stop him from coming closer to her. 'I am sorry, Mr, but I don't think we have met. You have me confused with someone else and you don't belong here.' She looks at him carefully and her body cringes. 'Please leave!' She says, as firmly as she can, but he scares her.

He smells like old, dusty clothes and he doesn't wear the smile on his face well, it is creepy and very out of place. Something tells her to look at his shoes and she notices the same shiny, black, leather shoes that she saw that day at the mansion and her heart sinks. She swallows hard and knows she needs to run and get away from him as fast as she can.

Her body is frozen in time, yet it is moving and she is running out of the room and down the stairs. She almost loses her balance and tumbles down the entire staircase, but the man, with the orange-red hair catches her and helps her back onto her feet.

His face is kind and soft and Human. 'Careful now miss!' He doesn't notice the panic in her eyes and she quickly pulls away from him and hurries out of the hotel and out into the street. She wants to scream, but who will want to help a Tartarian girl? She spins around thinking about where to go, while keeping an eye on the main entrance for that man that is coming for her.

She doesn't know what to do and starts to jog down the road towards the restaurant to look for Malcom. He is still in there seated at the same table, but not with Rune and Aara, but with someone else. It is a man and he is tall, with long black hair and he is wearing a navy-blue suit. He is wearing a big, obnoxious looking gold ring on his left hand and she is drawn to it. She wants to go inside, but something stops her. She looks behind her and there is no one around and she hopes that man from the hotel is gone. *What does he want?*

The man seated in front of Malcom has noticed her and automatically makes direct eye contact with her. He is so intense that it makes her puke on the side walk. She can feel her throat close up and she can't breathe suddenly. She fights for air, but she can't get any. She drops to the ground and gasps in horror, her face is turning a purplish blue and she can see her mother's face smiling at her.

'Daphne, breathe baby, breathe!' She can hear her mother shout and she walks over to the man sitting next to Malcom. She stops when she is standing next to the man and she looks afraid, then nods at Bonnie. She is trying to tell her something and her face is stern.

Bonnie knows she needs to fight harder and she presses her hands hard against the cobble floor. And with all that she has, she takes the biggest, deepest breath that she can and, in that moment, everything stops moving. Every table and chair, every patron, both Tartarian and Phoenician suddenly levitates off of the ground and the sky above her turns bright blue.

She can feel her lungs fill with air and the air is sweet and warm. Everything and everyone crash back to the floor and her face regains its colour and people start to scream in terror. She quickly gets up onto her feet and she notices that the man that was sitting with Malcom is suddenly gone. She scans the restaurant for him, but he is nowhere.

Malcom is still seated at the table with his back turned towards her. He gets up calmly, takes his coat from the back of the chair and walks up to her with fear on his face. He grabs her by the arm and pulls her along with him, as he rushes down the street. His grip is tight and rough and he doesn't care that he is hurting her slightly.

'We need to go right now Bonnie.' He is in a rush and he walks straight past the hotel without stepping a foot inside it.

They walk for a long time until they reach a big park. She is tired and breathing heavily, while Malcom is anxious and fidgety. He looks around him and then at his watch and then back around the park.

'What was that Bonnie?' He grabs her and shakes her hard. 'What did you do?' He is terrified for her and this time he can't hide the emotions on his face or the fear in his voice.

'I don't know!' She shouts back. 'I don't understand what is going on. That man, who was he?'

'None of your business!' He snaps!

'He is pure evil; I could feel it and he tried to kill me! I walked back to the hotel and the man with the shiny black shoes was there. He is ugly, scary looking, something is wrong with his face. His eyes are small and white, grey actually, with yellow.' She is mumbling. 'He was there that day when I was exploring the underneath floor of the mansion, the man with the top hat that has been following me.'

She is now remembering what happened that day. 'He tried to grab me the first time, but I hid, then Henry found me. The second time, I had found something, a metal shaft with engravings of the old Tartarian language on it. He must have taken it. Who is he?'

Malcom is confused and for the first time, he doesn't have the answer.

'What happened at the restaurant? And remember I can sense when you are lying!' He is warning her and she knows what is happening is serious and dangerous.

'That man that was sitting in front of you, he saw me and

his gaze was so intense I started to puke. Then next thing I know I couldn't breathe. I could feel his hands around my neck and he was squeezing so hard I thought he might break it.' She starts shaking uncontrollably at the thought. 'I saw my mother and she told me to breathe, so I fought as hard as I could to take just one breath. I don't remember what happened after that. I could just feel the air enter my lungs.'

There is a moment of silence and Malcom uses it to gather his thoughts.

'You levitated everything Bonnie, you levitated the entire restaurant.' He calmly tells her and holds her hands to stop them from shaking. He looks at her carefully and still can't believe what just happened. For the first time he is in shock and doesn't know how to handle it or respond to the situation.

'Tartarians don't have powers!' He mutters. 'How do you have these powers?'

Her hand moves to her stomach and it hits her. 'No, Tartarians don't, but Phoenicians do and I am carrying two of them.' She replies and holds her stomach.

'Bonnie, Phoenicians have abilities, we can heal, we are strong and fast and we can sense things, like if you are lying by the way the body reacts. But we can't levitate things! Abilities are not powers! I don't even think Heaven Bearers can do what you just did!'

He runs his hands through his hair out of frustration, he doesn't want to accept her explanation and he can feel the hair on his neck stand up. He is here! His eyes flash purple and he knows he needs to protect her.

'Run!' He shouts and postures his body ready for a confrontation.

Her legs start moving before her brain understands his command and she doesn't look back.

'Malcom, my boy! You didn't mention that was your wife. Pretty girl I have to admit and pregnant. I guess congratulations are in order!' He is angry and sarcastic and Malcom knows there is no way he is getting out of this situation alive.

'I had heard about a special bloodline and I assumed it was hers, but she proved to be useless, no powers whatsoever. It clearly wasn't her bloodline, but his and passed down to the girl through the sister.' Azrael is talking to himself and carefully piecing the story together in his head.

'Who exactly is *she* supposed to be?' Malcom snaps at him and is surprised by how he is reacting. He wants to keep Azrael away from her as long as he can, so that she has a proper chance to run as far away as she can. I hope you are running Bonnie; he thinks to himself and takes a step closer towards Azrael.

'Queen Arielle.' He hisses in his creature voice and licks his lips viciously! His face starts to twitch awkwardly and he has to adjust himself in his hosts body.

'These Tartarians sure like to fight back,' he chuckles and for the first time Malcom feels uncomfortable around him. King Finn is still there, unlike the General, he never admitted defeat and for the last seventeen years, he has been fighting Azrael trying to regain control of his body.

'Your wife is the niece of the beloved King. I thought she died in the mud flood, at least that is what I was told. The rest of her family did, well except for the father, I took care of him myself.' He laughs and feels his face as if to make sure it is fitting correctly over his enlarged and scaly head.

'This body can sense her, in fact it sensed who she was before I did,' he finally replies.

A man suddenly appears out of nowhere and Malcom can smell old rags and he notices that his eyes don't suit his head, they are too small. He glances down at his shoes and they are shiny, black leather shoes. They are so shiny that he can almost see his reflection in them and he knows then, that he is the same man Bonnie had described to him earlier.

'The man with the top hat,' he mutters and he shakes his head in disbelief. 'You knew who she was for months and had her followed?'

'I suspected I knew who she was, I had to be sure, so yes

I had her followed. It is my right after all or have you forgotten who I am Malcom!?' He is starting to lose his temper. 'I want that girl Malcom. I want her dead!' He hisses at him and his saliva sprays out if his mouth.

'No!' He shouts back at him and swallows hard. Azrael could walk up to him and kill him within a split second and with one swift movement, but Malcom has to stand his ground. *For her and for his babies.*

'Not yet, I want those babies!' He replies and tries to downplay the fact that he cares for her.

'Babies?' Azrael's interest is peeked. 'That is not possible! I have never heard about them having twins! Are you sure?'

'I hear two heartbeats.' His face is stern, he didn't want him to know, but he knows he doesn't have the strength to lie this time. He also knows the news will distract him, which will give Bonnie more time to get away.

'Hmmm, this is very interesting, but still, they are just Humans, I'm willing to sacrifice them.' He leans over to the man by his side. 'Find her!' He barks and he relishes the thought of her dying.

The man immediately nods in acknowledgment and Malcom can see he is going to enjoy killing her, just as much as Azrael will enjoy hearing about her death.

'Now, where did she go?' He asks nicely and tries to read Malcom's thoughts, but they are blank.

Malcom nods and looks in the opposite direction that she went. 'Back to the hotel, perhaps? Or to the train station, I am not sure.' He looks Azrael dead in the eye and can sense that he believes him and this astounds him.

'Right, well you go back to your duties, I will handle the girl. You can find another wife, you have already done it twice,' he mocks him and walks away into the shadows and Malcom loses sight of him completely.

Bonnie runs as fast as her legs can take her. She takes long, deep breaths and holds her stomach as she runs down the long, open street. She is almost six months pregnant and she can feel she is getting tired.

'Come on babies, don't give up on me now, we have made it this far.' She still seems to be under the impression that the babies are the ones giving her the powers and not that it is in *her bloodline*. She has no idea *who* she really is.

She sees lights in the far distance and knows this is where she needs to head. She can feel a rush of warmth flow over her body and it gives her the strength to keep going. She runs for another couple of minutes and smells the air turning musty and damp. It reminds her of old linen, that has been sitting in a cupboard for too long and she know he is here.

She stops and looks around, turning around in a full circle. The sweat is running down her face and her heart is thumping hard in her chest. She slows her breathing down and lets her eyes search for him. The smell is getting stronger, which means he must be close. He is hunting her and she is terrified. He can smell her fear in every drop of sweat that runs down her face and arms and he can't wait to taste it.

She turns around thinking he is there, but there is just darkness all around her. She turns back around and he is suddenly standing there grinning from ear to ear, his eyes are red with bloodlust and in his hand, he is clutching a silver and gold pocket knife. He charges at her with the knife pointed at her chest and time stands still, giving her enough time to react and take a step away from him. She puts her hands up in the air, with her palms facing him and she screams out as loud as she can.

'No!'

Her eyes flash gold briefly and the cobble stones start to vibrate next to each other.

A blue energy emits from her hands and she can feel him fight her. She stands her ground and her whole body begins to light up with the same blue energy. The ground starts to vibrate harder and the knife in his hand crumbles into powder and falls to the ground. She closes her eyes and imagines pushing him away and when she opens them again, she sees that he is slumped over on his knees. He is slowly turning into dust, just like the knife did, and what is left of him blows away with the slight breeze. She stands there with her adrenaline pumping and watches him disappear before her eyes. She is astounded by what she has just witnessed, but knows she needs to keep moving ahead. All that remains are his clothes and those shiny black shoes.

She starts to shake, *what are these things growing inside of me?*

CHAPTER ELEVEN

Malcom walks back to the hotel and he can't help but regret taking her with him to New York. He is angry and starts to blame himself for what happened. He shakes his head and realises she would be dead if he hadn't taken her with and kept her close. The man in the top hat would have found her there alone and killed her. He wonders why it took Azrael so long to be sure about who she is? Why kill her now? He runs his fingers down his face and he wants to punch a wall out of frustration! How did Azrael know about her, he himself admitted he thought she was dead, which means he wasn't even out looking for her? Neither Bonnie, nor he knew who she really was. Someone must have tipped him off, but who, he wonders? He can hear laughter and it snaps him back to reality. I need to get back to the Hotel, he tells himself and hurries back.

He stops in the lobby at the sight of her. Aara is standing there waiting for him and her face is filled with sorrow.

'Aara, what is going on? Did something happen to Rune?' He knows something terrible happened and immediately walks up to her.

She sheds a single tear and wipes it away and regains her

cold demeanour. She clears her throat and her eyes turn cold.

'He is dead!' Her voice is loud, but he can only hear a slight whisper leave her perfect, red lips.

Malcom isn't sure that he heard what she said. He takes her by the arm and walks with her to the side of the room and leans her up against the wall. 'What did you just say?' This time his voice is mean and cruel.

'He is dead Malcom! Azrael was waiting for us when we got home. We were no match for him, you know that!' She is angry, she loved Rune, in her own, cold way. Her eyes scan his face. He is pale with shock; his forehead is frowning and his hands are balled into fists. 'Malcom, there is nothing you can do about it...' She stops mid-sentence and realises Bonnie isn't with him.

'Where is Bonnie. Please tell me he didn't get to her too?'

'I don't know, I told her to run...' He stares into her eyes and they go purple. He allows her to read his mind, including all of his memories, thoughts, wants and needs, which he has never before done and she understands what is happening.

'What did Rune know?' He proceeds to ask her.

She shakes her head. 'Nothing. Nothing that I know about. I told the girl to head to Edmonton and if she really has these powers, she will make it. She will know what to do when she gets there, but I will try get word out.'

Malcom grabs her by the neck in a sudden rage. 'What did you just say?' He pauses and tightens his grip and watches the fear grow in her eyes. 'Try get word out?' He lets go of her and takes a step back and he knows she is a traitor!

'You are working for the resistance?' He can't believe what he is hearing, how could she betray Rune like that!? He feels a rage enter him and he wants to kill her and she knows it.

'You will thank me one day Malcom. I know you love her, perhaps your love for her will save us all.' She walks away knowing this will be the last thing she will ever say to him. Malcom stares at the wall in front of him and it feels like his whole world is collapsing all around him. He starts to punch the wall as hard as he can, hoping he will feel something other than the pain he is feeling in that moment. He eventually stops and looks at the wall. There are bricks that are missing and the skin on his hands is gone, exposing bone and raw flesh.

Aara needs to figure out what Rune was up to or what he knew. He had no idea that she was feeding the resistance information, at least she doesn't think so. Azrael must have known about the resistance somehow and perhaps assumed it was Rune who was betraying him? She can feel death in the air and she knows she doesn't have long until she will join Rune in the Canopy of the Tree of Life. She thinks about seeing him up there and she isn't afraid. They will be at peace and most importantly, they will be able to spend all of eternity together. She walks into Runes office and starts to ruffle through his files, only to notice that there are many lying on the floor already and she knows Azrael has already found what he was looking for. The room gets ice cold and she can feel her heart turn rock hard and she falls, head first, into the file cabinet in front of her and she closes her eyes.

Malcom, meanwhile, walks back into his room and paces up and down. He isn't sure what to do next. He wants to find her, but he knows he can't protect her, not from Azrael. He sits down on the bed, takes a swig of whiskey and decides to play along and go back to Montreal, as instructed. He is no use to her dead and he knows it.

Bonnie finds her way to the train station and decides to book a ticket to Edmonton, or at least to a city close by, except she realises she has no money with her. They will be waiting for her at the train station, she tells herself and she isn't sure what to do next. She sits down, about a hundred metres from the entrance and waits there until she figures out what to do. In the meantime, she just watches the people hurry in and out and can't help but think that they look like the ants she used to watch at the Foundling Home. They have no real purpose other than to run around all day doing menial tasks.

'Are you alright miss? A male voice startles her and she looks up at him from where she is sitting.

There is an elderly Tartarian man and his wife standing with their dog. Bonnie has never seen Tartarians this old before and she stares at them awkwardly for a minute. She catches herself and realises they are staring awkwardly back at her. Her dress is covered in red wine and she must look terrible. She did have a terrible night and she grins coyly. Malcom? She suddenly wonders what has happened to him, but she can somehow feel that he is unharmed and she knows she needs to carry on with her journey.

She explains to the elderly couple that she lost her purse and is on her way to Edmonton to be with her husband, but isn't sure how to get there without any money.

'We are headed in that direction; we are happy to have you travel with us, if you would like?' He asks and she stares at him, trying to establish his true intentions. His face is wrinkled from the sun and he looks like he has had a hard life.

'Thank you, that is very kind of you.' She is surprised that they didn't question her story at all. She would have, had she been in their position.

She walks with them to their horse and carriage and climbs in next to his wife. She knows this will be a very long trip, but no one will find her this way and it is her best chance at getting to Edmonton alive.

'Where exactly are the two of you headed?' She asks politely and quickly fixes her hair.

'Quebec City.' His voice is relaxed and he looks straight ahead.

'No, but that is in the opposite direction to Edmonton, I need to go to Edmonton.' She gets up wanting to get out.

'Quebec City is a big city, it will be easier for you to get to Edmonton that way, trust me.' He gives her a soft smile and places his hand on hers. 'Time to get some rest dear, it has been quite an evening for you, hasn't it?'

She wants to ask them who they are, but decides to let it be for now. She is exhausted and closes her eyes for a little while. She wakes up to the glaring sun on her face and it is warm, too warm. She opens her eyes and tries to orientate herself.

'Good morning dear, I hope you slept well.' The old man asks and grins at her.

'Where –' She clears her throat and rubs her neck, it is stiff and sore. 'How long have we been on the road for?'

'Long, you slept the entire day and night. It's about eight am now, judging by the angle of the sun. Us peasant people don't have the luxury of owning watches.' He replies sarcastically and he takes a look at the fancy ring on her finger and she feels ashamed and guilty. She looks around her and all she can see is farmland. It is beautiful and peaceful here and she feels calm, relaxed and well rested.

He looks directly ahead and his wife is holding out a big, red apple for her.

She takes it and immediately eats it. She is so hungry; she is pregnant with twins after all. It is juicy and sweet and quenches both her appetite and thirst.

'Who are you exactly?' She asks and takes another bite of her apple. 'I didn't know there were some older Tartarians. What I mean is that, most died before the mud flood happened, didn't they?' She catches herself and decides not to carry on. 'I'm sorry, that was insensitive.'

'That is alright dear, we understand what you mean.'

Bonnie leans over to the wife and gives her a warm smile. 'Thank you so much for the apple, it is delicious.'

The old lady nods twice and smiles.

'Is she shy or afraid of me? Why doesn't she talk?' She asks the old man softly.

He frowns gently and looks at her with stern and sad eyes. 'She has no tongue, they cut it out fifteen years ago!'

Bonnie flinches at the thought and gets angry by what has happened to her people. She wants to kill them all! 'I am so sorry!' She can't hide the horror on her face or the sadness in her eyes.

'We will continue on this path until sunset, thereafter you are on your own dear. We won't go any further, we have sacrificed enough in our lifetime.'

She nods in agreement and lets her eyes wander off into the far distance. *Malcom, I hope you are okay, wherever you might be?*

Her cheeks quickly fill with some colour and they feel warm and she knows he is okay, that he made it home safely and alive.

Another ten hours pass by and they finally stop the cart and ask her politely to climb off. She is grateful to be on her feet again, but knows the walk ahead of her will be long. She thanks them both and they hand her some water, bread and another apple.

'Take care dear and if you ever meet a Cassiel, which I believe you will, tell him we helped you, will you?' The old man gives her a little wink and carries on slowly down the road.

'Of course, I will,' she mutters under her breath and waves good bye.

She walks for hours and her feet start to hurt. She has no idea where she is going, she just knows she must keep walking. She thinks about Malcom and her heart misses him, every inch of her misses him. She thinks about the "abominations" in her belly and wonders what will happen when she arrives at her destination?

Will they accept me? Will they accept me and the babies? She isn't sure, but she knows she must try.

She walks for three days straight and finally spots a creek. She takes off her boots and flinches with pain. Her feet are raw and she has blisters all over them. She sits a while and the breeze is cooling and calming as it brushes over her wounds and she stares up into the sky. She squints her eyes and can swear she can see the canopy of a tree, or at least the shadows of it and she wonders what is up there? Who is up there? Where did all the dead Tartarians go or do they merely cease to exist? She ponders that thought for a while and shakes her head. No, they must go somewhere, they have to, she tells herself. After all she still sees her mother in her dreams, so she can't merely cease to exist.

She looks around and knows she needs to find another way to get to Edmonton, she can't walk all this way on foot. She puts her boots back on and carries on with her journey slowly. She is hungry and tells herself she needs to find a small town and somewhere to rest for a few days. She hears a train in the distance and she thinks she can see a town. She picks up her pace and hurries along. She is about a mile away and she can definitely see a town and is relieved.

It is a small town, but big enough to have accommodation and she looks for a small hotel or restaurant. There is a Human sitting on the sidewalk polishing a pair of shoes and she is distracted by him. He looks like he is about thirteen years of age, he has brown hair and little brown spots on his cheeks and nose. She can't help but smile at his cute appearance.

'Excuse me? I am sorry to bother you, but I am looking for a restaurant or hotel. Can you tell me where you mother is?'

'Can I help you?' A voice disturbs her and she turns towards the voice and sees a Tartarian man standing with a blade in his one hand and a cloth in the other. She looks at him carefully and feels relived at the sight of him.

'Yes, hello, my name is Bonnie. I am in desperate need of a place to stay and something to eat.' She pauses and looks down at her hands in shame. 'I have no money.'

'Can't help you then, sorry.' He turns to walk away.

'No, wait, please. Can you not help a fellow Tartarian, please I have a long journey ahead of me?'

'What did you say your name was?' His eyes move and notice her big belly.

'Bonnie, my name is Bonnie.'

He begins to walk away.

'Daphne, my real name is Daphne!' She says out loud hoping this will get his attention.

The man stops in his track and takes a moment to gather himself.

'Mikkel, go find your mother, quickly!' He orders. The teenage boy runs off in a hurry and the man gestures for her to follow him down the little pathway.

He takes her to a small wooden house, with a bright blue door. There is laundry hanging on the washing line and the wind starts to pick up. He walks up to a small stone well and hands her some water. She is grateful and gulps it down as quickly as she can. She wipes her mouth and already feels better.

'I can't say I expected you, but I did hear about the prophesy.' He pulls a face as he glares into the sun and sips some water and pours the rest of over his head to cool down. The metal cup in his hand reflects the sunlight onto the ground and she follows it with her eyes, while she listens to him talk.

A woman comes running over and she smells like honey and flour.

'Hello.' She takes a good look at Bonnie. 'What is your name dear?'

'My assigned name is Bonnie, but my real name is Daphne.' She takes a deep breath. 'Don't even try and hurt me, I have powers, or rather abilities, so you leave me be!' She warns them.

The woman laughs softly and looks over at the man. 'My name is Jenae and this is my brother Keena, we welcome you to our home.' She stretches out her hand and gives Bonnie a soft hug and helps her inside of the house.

Malcom spends the next week pretending nothing is wrong and throws himself into his work. Jane is hovering and he doesn't trust her like he used to. He doesn't trust anyone these days and he feels like someone is constantly watching him.

Her reaction to the news that Bonnie had run off was sinister in itself and there is something about her that seems very wrong, even dangerous. She tends to his every need and he distracts himself with work. He starts to work on the plan on how to handle the situation with Samira and the genetically inferior Phoenicians. He will send one of his men with a letter to Asia and see how she will respond, if favourably he will plan his trip for the very next day and assess the situation in person. He has never enjoyed ordering the death of his fellow Phoenicians, but it was simply the order of things, a kind of sacrifice to the Heaven Bearers, at least that is how he saw it.

"There needs to be death in order to make room for new life." That is what Leesa used to always say and he can't help but remember that. He thinks about his childhood and the hair on his arms stands up with the thought that someone like her could raise his children, his two sons.

Sons? He laughs out, he has no idea what gender they are and he misses Bonnie. He even misses getting angry with her. He quickly erases her from his thoughts and begins to draft the letter to Samira.

He hands the letter to Jane and asks her to post it immediately. Little does she know that he plans to send another copy of that letter himself. She grabs her coat and immediately hurries off and he follows her. She walks down the end of the road and turns in the opposite direction of the post office and he follows her all the way to the opera house. Harlow is waiting there for her and she hands the letter to him. Harlow? Of all people, he is very surprised to see Harlow. Perhaps Azrael has asked him to keep an eye on him, in case he goes looking for Bonnie perhaps?

He posts the letter and then walks back to the house slowly; he has nothing to go home to and for the first time he feels empty inside.

Two days later he receives the news that Aara killed herself and that she left a note explaining how she couldn't live anymore after having to endure the tragic death of Rune. Malcom knew she cared for him in her own way, but not enough to die for him. He figured they got what ever they could get out of her and then killed her. He isn't sure if he feels bad that she is dead, but he knows he will miss seeing her and Rune when he goes to New York in the future.

He sits back in his leather chair and wonders what she knew, what she told them and how long she has been working with the resistance for? More importantly, he wants to know why? He would never have guessed this, he never even sensed this and it bothers him tremendously.

He is suddenly sad that she is dead and can't help but question if she deserved it? He shakes the thought and distracts himself with the fact that he will have to kill the Phoenicians in Asian soon.

It isn't easy to kill a Phoenician, at least not for another Phoenician, a Tartarian or a Human.

Phoenicians need to feel fear and only once they have felt a sufficient amount of fear, will they reveal their biggest weakness. It is in this moment that one must strike, as this is when their heart opens up and is exposed. Their hearts need to be punctured or ripped out of their chest in order for them to die. He has heard about other ways, but as far as he knows they are just myths. Stabbing them is the least messy means to kill them, as they don't bleed much from their hearts this way. Although, it is very time consuming, especially to get some of them to *feel fear*.

His orders over the years have resulted in many deaths. He has never bothered to count just how many, but if he had to guess, he would assume that both directly and indirectly he has been responsible for the deaths of at least ten thousand people, both Tartarians and Phoenicians. But he has not yet killed a Human. He stops for a moment and realises this for the first time. He doesn't like what is happening to him, she has made *me soft.*

CHAPTER TWELVE

Jenae is a kind lady. She is tall and skinny, very skinny and she has lightly tanned arms. She must work outside a lot; Bonnie thinks to herself and wonders what her story is. *Every Tartarian has one.*

'I was married off to one of them, just like you.' She points to the big diamond ring on Bonnies finger and her face cringes. She closes her eyes and tries to regain her composure. 'But I'm sure you guessed that already with Barnabas over there?' She continues. 'I love my boy, but it doesn't change the fact that he is half *them*.' She pulls a face of disgust and grabs a glass jar with white powder in it.

Bonnie sips her water and doesn't say anything. She doesn't want to pry and ask her about anything personal, although she is curious about her situation. She wants to know where the Tartarian husband is? Or perhaps he didn't marry her and they had a set up like Rune had with the Tartarian women? Bonnie looks down at her diamond ring and spins it around her finger so that the stone is no longer facing the top of her hand. She takes a good look at her hand and imagines she had something plainer and simpler.

'It is a beautiful ring dear, you don't need to hide it,' she says as she finishes mixing the bread dough and puts it to the side of the long table.

'My husband, he wasn't bad to me. He is a mean man, but he never hurt me.' Bonnie says as she turns the stone back to the top of her finger and reluctantly makes eye contact with Jenae.

Bonnie feels embarrassed that she is in love with a Phoenician man, especially because deep down inside, she hates everything that they represent.

'What are you making?' Bonnie asks and attempts to change the subject, while she takes a good look at what Jenae is busy doing.

'I am making a stew, a rabbit stew. It is my mother's recipe, well, it was passed down from generation to generation. I have no doubt that you will like it dear. Vi takker deg morens natur for dine velsignelser.'

Bonnie feels mesmerized all of a sudden and can't help but stare at her in awe.

'I understand what you are saying, but have no idea what you said.' She mumbles and snaps out of what feels like a daze and sits down clumsily. She instinctively rubs her stomach and looks towards her. 'They give me abilities or something like that and I don't understand why? Did you have the same thing when you were pregnant with your son?'

'No, I did not, but then again, the Phoenician is the son of Queen Ariella and you are the niece of the King. Legend has it, the King's bloodline contains some kind of powers that are passed down, but not to every generation it would seem. The Queen, on the other hand, well, she had abilities like many Tartarians back then. The re-education camps made sure our kind no longer know how to use them.' She starts to chop some carrots and she slams the knife down hard onto the chopping board. 'They start with removing your language and then your culture. Once a people lose that, they lose their entire identity!' She lays down the knife and her hand is trembling with anger. She shakes her hand hard and quick and carries on chopping the vegetables for the stew.

Bonnie sits there with big and bright eyes and it takes her a moment before she can formulate a response.

'I am the niece of King Finn? How...how did you know my husband is the son of the Queen, I never mentioned that?' She begins to feel nervous and she looks around the room cautiously.

'The legend says so dear. Just like you are pregnant, the legend explained that a young, pregnant Tartarian girl would stop them and restore the Empire. You are supposed save us all. But by the look of you, I am not so sure. You seem...you seem too soft and sweet somehow.'

She turns her back towards Bonnie and starts to wash the big, cast iron pot that she will cook the stew in.

'Did you know them? Did you know the King and Queen?' She asks nervously and plays with her hands like she is a little girl that is in trouble.

'No.' She shrugs her shoulders and wipes her forehead with the back of her right hand. 'I was only ten years old when it happened. I have seen them in pictures and heard all about them. I never did meet them. I hear she was wonderful though, really kind and good to her people.' Her voice is heavy and nostalgic and she clears her throats softly, so as not to draw attention to her emotions.

'What about King Finn?' Bonnie presses her.

She smiles. 'And perhaps you would like to know if I met your mother too? I am sorry, I don't know them, but I know they were wonderful, they ruled fairly and were good to mother nature.'

She takes out a big knife and starts to gut the rabbit. The sight makes Bonnie feel nauseous and she turns her head away and covers her mouth in disgust.

'I'm sorry dear, but this is part of cooking rabbit stew. How about you wait outside until I am done?' She smiles and Bonnie can't wait to get outside and breathe in the fresh air. She has been staying with them for two days now and is ready to leave, but she has this nagging voice telling her she hasn't found what she is looking for just yet.

'What do I need to find?' She starts talking to herself and goes for a walk towards the little creek.
Barnabas is busy fishing, with a make-shift rod he made himself, and she sits down next to him. She just wants to enjoy his company for a short while and to not think about anything. Most of all, she doesn't want to have to worry about anything.

'My mom killed my dad! Did she tell you that?' He stares straight ahead at the water and his face doesn't change with any emotion.

Bonnie suspected as much, but she didn't want to actually know the truth. She can't imagine ever killing Malcom, even if he did take her babies away from her and let them become slaves. Perhaps she could, she really isn't sure. She gives her stomach a quick rub and realises that the walk has been strenuous on her and she still has a long way to go. She thinks about what Jenae said about her bloodline and she isn't sure now where she has her *powers* from?

'Do you wish she hadn't killed him?' She asks and looks at him with tender and motherly eyes.

He shrugs his shoulders. 'Sometimes. I think I would have liked him to teach me how to fish and hunt.' He replies happily and she rubs his head gently and giggles along with him.

'I need to go soon...' She isn't talking to him, but rather to the universe or mother nature or to her ancestors, she isn't sure. She stares out at the water and just watches it flow and her mind is completely blank.

They spend the remaining hour and a half out by the creek before the sun starts to set and neither one of them says another word. Bonnie stares at the sunset and it is solemn today. The colour is brighter and darker than normal and it she feels a pit in her stomach.

'We need to walk back now Barnabas.' She holds out her hand and helps him onto his feet.

They eat the rabbit stew greedily. It is tender and full of flavour and Bonnie dishes up second helping for herself.

'Can I ask something and please be honest? In fact, I might even know if you are lying to me.' She eats her last spoonful of the stew and pusher her bowl away. Jenae gives her a subtle look and she knows that they all know that she is the girl from the prophesy. 'What is going to happen when I get there? Will they take me and my babies in or will they kill my babies?'

'I don't know.' Keena answers this time and he keeps his eyes on his bowl. He doesn't want to make eye contact with her and it is obvious and strange.

'They are an abomination!' Jenae snaps and gets up from the table. There is not a single ounce of love in her heart and she looks over at Barnabas while he licks his bowl clean.

Bonnie swallows hard and feels uncomfortable. *I need to leave here and soon.*

There is a heavy and loud knock on the door and Keena orders whoever is outside to enter. He still doesn't make eye contact with Bonnie and an ice-cold shiver runs down her spine. She grabs her spoon and stands to face whoever is about to walk through the door.

Two enormous, two and a half metre-tall Phoenician men, walk inside the small house and stand solidly in front of her. A dark-skinned Human, that is much smaller, follows them inside and grins at the sight of her. He has pearly white teeth and sick looking eyes. There is bloodlust in the air and it is making the Human vicious.

'Get back!' She orders them with an authoritative voice and points the spoon at them. But her hand is shaking and they start to laugh at her. The sound of them snickering makes her angry and the spoon bends between her fingers.

'Keena, what have you done!' Jenae cries out in anger and grabs Barnabas and hides in the corner clutching on to him.

'Come with me little girl.' The Human has a deep voice and dark, black eyes that pierce her soul. She looks away, before she gets sucked into the black abyss that they represent.

'I am afraid I can't do that.' She replies and turns her head back towards them. 'Get out at once!' She shouts, but her voice isn't very authoritative.

They look at each other and start to snicker like rabid dogs. The Human starts to approach her and she knows she must act quickly. 'Barnabas, cover your ears and think about fishing.' She shouts at him and he does exactly as she asks.

She takes a deep breath, closes her eyes tight and when she opens them again, she can see them coming for her. Time immediately slows down like it did in New Work, her eyes shine a luminous blue and she screams as loud and as hard as she can.

The little wooden house shakes violently and then splinters into a million sharp pieces, but the pieces don't go far, they remain in a fixed ball around her. She can see the confidence and bloodlust in their eyes change to fear and this time, she starts to grin. She grabs a long, sharp piece of the wood that floats towards her and she stabs each of them men in the heart with a swift and almost practiced motion. They fall to the ground and turn to dust, just like the man in the top hat did. Except for the Human, his body lies motionless on the floor and dark, red blood gushes from his lifeless body and stains the wooden planks.

She drops the piece of wood in her hand and all the remaining pieces fall to the ground shortly thereafter.

She glances towards Barnabas and his mother. They are huddled in the corner with their heads covered and are alive and well. Keena, on the other hand, he is standing in the same spot he was in when the men first entered. His eyes are completely white and she can see her reflection in them. Mother nature as punished him for his betrayal and he shall never lay his eyes upon anything again. Bonnie walks up to him and puts her hand gently onto the side of his face. 'You will find peace soon.' Her thumbs traces down his cheek gently and his skin is soft, but leathery. 'Take care Jenae and thank you for your help,' she says as she grabs a piece of bread off the floor and sets out to continue her long and dreaded journey.

Malcom has had his hands full on the other side of the Earth. Samira refuses to consent to putting, just over a thousand of *her* Phoenicians, to death. She is a proud and an unreasonable woman and this is precisely why Azrael is so fond of her. Malcom knows he needs to pack his bags and make the long journey over to Asia to try and convince Samira that the decision has already been made for her and that she doesn't actually have any say in the matter. Azrael has the final say, he is their unelected leader and no-one has ever questioned this. He arrives in Asia and arranges to meet with her in Hong Kong, immediately upon his arrival. The day isn't warm, but the sun is shining bright and he knows the day will end bitterly. He waits for a horse-drawn carriage to pass him and he walks towards the town square. He can see her standing by the majestic fountain in the middle of the square and approaches her carefully.

'You see this half man, half fish being?' She asks as he walks up behind her and she points to the statue in the middle of the fountain.

'The Tartarians that live here claim that he would stroll around the town square late at night and bless the water. He did this out the goodness of his heart, apparently to make sure that anyone who had any pain, sickness or ailment would take a sip and be forever healed.'

She spits into the water and laughs. Her voice reminds him of that shrieking owl that would wake Bonnie up in the middle of the night, back home and he cringes slightly.

She is wearing a bright red dress and the hem is covered in mud. There is a small tear on the side of her dress and he can't help but wonder what she has been doing that morning?

'They are all so pathetic, don't you think Malcom?' She turns around to face him and her eyes are as black as the night sky in mid-winter. She licks her lips and her eyes search his body. She looks him over thoroughly — 'I forget how handsome you are, the prodigal son of Azrael the great,' she mocks him and gives him a teasing wink. 'I am not putting *my* people to death! You tell him that and leave my city at once!' She orders him sternly.

'Samira, we both know I am not leaving. Azrael won't accept that.' He takes a cautious step closer. 'We need to resolve the problem here and now –'

'Why?' She interrupts him and plays with the water. 'We already dealt with the deformed babies, a sacrifice to the fish god,' her tone is proud and sarcastic.

She turns around and walks up to him, gives him a greedy smooch and whispers into his ear. 'What exactly are you planning on doing about it?' She looks into his eyes and he can't keep her out of his head. There is no mind Samira can't read, this is her particular talent and he knows that she knows *everything.*

'How sweet, the prodigal son fell in love with a Tartarian!' She begins to laugh uncontrollably and places her hand on her chest as if she needs to catch her breath, but she is just mocking him. She is never serious, everything is a game to her, a *sick game.*

'Figure out another way to deal with my little problem or I will tell him!' She threatens him firmly and skips back towards the fountain like a little girl.

Malcom doesn't say anything more and leaves the town square feeling defeated.

He orders his men to round up the genetically impure Phoenician men and knows he will need to channel Azrael's power in order to finish the task.

He stands upright, with his hands firmly by his side, at the entrance of an empty warehouse. It is just outside of the big city like and he feels like a dictator. He explains why this needs to happen to the one thousand and eighty-one Phoenician men, standing in neat rows in front of him and he has no emotions, nor do they.

'Your sacrifice is appreciated and mother nature thanks you for your contribution. The Heaven Bearers, your creator Samira, thank you for your service, but you are defective and perfection is expected.'

Samira unexpectantly appears next to him with a cheeky smile on her face and she leans in to lick the side of his face. 'I warned you Malcom.' She scoffs softly and she has a sadistic aura around her.

She stares at the ornamental dagger hanging on the wall and blinks at it. It flies off the wall where it was mounted and flies towards Malcom, directly for his heart. Just as it is about to reach him, it changes direction and heads in the direction of the Phoenicians lined up patiently and waiting to die. One by one, they drop to the floor and turn to dust as the dagger punctures each one in the heart quickly and painlessly.

Samira loses the cheeky smile on her face, drops to knees and screams out in anger!

'Azrael! No!' Her voice echoes throughout the entire warehouse and bounces back off of the walls.

It takes no more than five minutes and all of the Phoenicians are dead and their souls drift up to the Canopy, where they will find everlasting peace. Malcom waits for the last man to drop to the floor and turn to dust. He takes a good look around to make sure the space is empty, turns around swiftly and prepares to take the long trip back home. His job here is done.

Bonnie eventually reaches a bigger city, called Sudbury. She stops and sits down on a large flat rock for a moment, to catch her breath. She is grateful that she can now take a train the rest of the way to Edmonton. The fact that she has no money doesn't even concern her anymore, not after what has happened over the last few weeks. She enters the train station and walks straight up to the counter and asks for a ticket to Edmonton. The Tartarian lady at the other end of the ticket counter smiles and immediately issues her a ticket and doesn't even ask her for payment. Bonnie is radiating a mesmerising aura and she can feel the way the people are reacting around her. They can't help but notice her, but no one dares to stare.

Her smile is contagious, everywhere she goes and everyone she smiles at, lights up with a grin that stretches from ear to ear. She enjoys the sight of seeing so many happy souls in one space and relishes the moment.

The train arrives twenty minutes later and she boards it, takes a seat at the far end and goes to sleep. Her dreams are getting more vivid with each passing day. They are intense, unfiltered and almost a history lesson of what happened when the Heaven Bearers first slipped through the crack in the firmament and arrived here on earth.

Last night she dreamt she saw the firmament crack open violently and she watched as seven hideous creatures entered and landed on the Tree of Life. Ice cold shrieks radiated down from the Canopy and made all the Tartarians drop what they were doing and look up into the sky with fear in their hearts. They moved around like leeches, looking for a host and after a while they decided to rest and regain their strength. Each one carved a hole into the bark of the Tree of Life and stayed hidden for six days and six nights. On the seventh day they started to drain her of her energy and mother nature called out in pain and the Tartarians came to her aid.

The Heaven Bearers waited for them in the Canopy, completely naked, exposing their crusty reptilian skin and long claws. Their eyes were a mixture of orange with a purple hue and a bright red ring around the pupil. The mere sight of their eyes makes Bonnies body tense up in fear, as she sleeps on the train, but it does not wake her up.

They had destroyed their last host, the entire body of earth and all of its inhabitants. They had mined every last resource that could be found and this depletion and destruction of everything good and pure, caused mother nature to become sick. It didn't take very long until she died and with her death, the Tree of Life died too. Their death resulted in famine and all of the water dried up at once. It was a slow and excruciating death for the lifeforms that lived there on Plerth. Plerth no longer exists and that same fate awaits Earth and her inhabitants unless someone, unless *Bonnie*, can find a way to expel the Heaven Bearers and end their rule once and for all.

The air in the train becomes ice cold. She can feel her breathing slow down, but she isn't ready to wake up. Her hand clutches the side of the trains seat and she knows treachery will follow soon.

She can see the King put on his white and silver robe, followed by his armour and take the metal pole she found underneath the mansion; he is holding it proudly. The fourteen blue stones light up, one by one, and emit a bright, blue haze that is so bright she needs to adjust her eyes in order to look directly at it.

The Tartarian army is on standby all over the Earth and it waits in anticipation. King Finn, along with his General and two thousand men. elevate themselves into the Canopy and approach these creatures cautiously. There is a rotting stench in the air and the smell intensifies as they get closer to the creatures. The King stops at once and can feel death in the air and he tells his men to get into position.

'My name is King Finn, the ruler and guardian of the Tartarian Empire. Identify yourselves at once!' He orders and holds the staff of the magical bloodline with a tight and firm grip.

Azrael licks his lip and a helpless smile appears on his face. He takes a few steps forward and approaches King Finn slowly, with his arms raised up.

'My name is Azrael and we come in *peace.*'

CHAPTER THIRTEEN

'Please, we are the only survivors of Plerth and we bow down to you, you are our masters. We are exhausted and hungry and are merely looking for kindness and a helping hand.' Azrael can sense the kindness in the Tartarians and he knows they will be easy to conquer. The best way to collapse a mighty empire is from the inside, he tells himself.

The Tartarians clothe and feed them, tend to their wounds and make them feel at home. It doesn't take them a month before they try to over throw King Finn, by trying to bribe the General with endless riches.

'Tartarians have no want or need for riches, Sir! Now go back to your quarters and prepare for your departure, you have overstayed your welcome.' General Jokkiel is angry at their lack of respect for their new host country and wants to expel them at once.

The Earth Bearers know they cannot over throw the entire Tartarian empire on their own. Their army expands the entire Earth and consists of one billion, fighting age men. These men are fully armed and have been in training from the tender age of ten years. The Earth Bearers are no match for them and they know that they need to infiltrate their ranks and over thrown them if they are to gain control of Earth and the Empire.

Infiltrating the Tartarians proves to be very difficult. King Finn and General Jokkiel do not trust them and won't let them out of their sight. They also cannot leave Earth and look for another host country, because the crack in the firmament is no longer open and there is no means to open it.

King Finn endeavours to have a word with mother nature, he needs to explain to her what is happening and that they are all in grave danger. Only she can open the firmament and expel their common enemy.

He climbs the Tree of Life with Queen Ariella and they reach the Canopy with warm and open hearts.

The air is thin and cold up here, but it is peaceful and the only sound is that of mother nature contemplating their visit.

'Have we not agreed that I cannot open the firmament. It is not for me to do. My only purpose is to keep the Earth healthy and strong, as I have done for thousands of years.

Queen Ariella moves away from King Finn and bows down on one knee as a sign of respect and to show how serious the situations truly is.

'The creatures, we fear that they cannot be trusted and will destroy the harmony, the trust that we have shared with one another for over a thousand of years. They do not belong here; they do not come in peace, I can feel it.' She says and hopes mother nature will understand.

'Queen Ariella, you have always been such a kind and forgiving soul, do you not perhaps think you are over reacting? These creatures are refugees, they have nowhere to go and have lost all they once had. This is their new home now and we ought to welcome them openly.'

King Finn wants to argue, but the Queen grabs his hand and gives it a gentle squeeze.

'Very well mother nature, we will return to the ground at once and make our guests feel welcome and integrate them into their new home.'

Ariella knows this is a mistake, but what other choice do they have? Mother nature will not open the firmament and this is the only way out for any living soul living on Earth.
The King and Queen make their way down to the ground and can't help but know something sinister is being planned behind their backs and they know they don't have long now until they will need to fight.

King Finn needs to speak to General Jokkiel immediately upon his return to inform him about what was discussed with mother nature.

'A war is coming and we need to prepare! Mother nature can't, she won't open the firmament and these disgusting creatures will destroy everything we have worked so hard to preserve. We can't let that happen!' He says and his face is strained.
General Jokkiel sits in his big, beige leather chair, dressed in his war attire and licks his lips.

'What a pity, it looks like we will have to go to war then, my King,' he says sarcastically and starts picking at the leather on the chair with his fingers.

'I don't want war! I will not put my men in harms way without at least considering an alternative. I task you with talking to these creatures and finding a calm and fair way forward.' King Finn looks around the room, he feels the hair on his neck stand up and he knows something is wrong.

'As you wish my King,' Jokkiel replies and waits for the King to leave the room.
The King leaves the room at once and in a hurry and rushes back to his home to check on his family. He rips open the door and calls out for Ariella.

'Get the children, we need to leave at once!' He shouts and his voice carries into every room.

There is no response and he walks towards the kitchen and looks inside, but it is empty and he proceeds to check the lounge.

'Ariella?' He calls and checks each and every room in the

house.
It is too quiet. Where is everyone, where is the laughter of the girls, he wonders? He sees a note on the floor and he picks it up and takes a deep breath before he reads it.

We are out of time

He hears footsteps approach him and he turns around thinking it might be Ariella, but it is not.

It is Azrael and he is boastful and grinning. He looks around the house and his eyes admire the workmanship and detail put into its construction.

'King Finn, I am so sorry to inform you, but your dear wife Ariella is dead. You see, she had a little accident –' He says, as runs his fingers over the wall as he walks around the room, making sure to keep his distance from the King.
King Finn raises his staff and activates its energy and postures himself in a battle-ready position.

'My wife is not dead; I can still feel her. Now, take me to her at once you wretched creature!' He commands and raises his staff up high as a sign of authority.
Azrael reaches for the staff and to his shock and amazement manages to rip it out of his hand and he throws it to the floor. The blue light immediately disappears and the King knows his time has arrived.

'How?' The King is on his knees and is begging for his life and that of his family.
Azrael leans over and whispers into his ear. 'You can thank mother nature,' he says and as he breathes heavily into his face. King Finn pulls his face away from the angel of death and stares at the portrait of his beautiful family, knowing that one day they will be reunited.
Azrael slowly walks up to the King, relishing every moment, now that he is the alpha dog and takes his crusty hand, forces into the Kings mouth and forcefully climbs into his new host.

The body of the King falls to the floor and starts to convulse uncontrollably, then it is suddenly still. He sits up and looks around the room to orientate himself. He licks his lips and can still taste the fear on them from the King and adjusts himself gently inside his new body.

This is a great fit, he thinks to himself, although the host is quite feisty and he walks over to the mirror to look at his new reflection. He adjusts the belt on his attire slightly and admires himself.

'This is your best look yet! Samira says as he walks out of the former home of King Finn and she is smiling eagerly in her new body.

Azrael grins and breathes in the fresh air. He feels strong and powerful and he can't wait to conquer them all.

'These Tartarians are no longer a fighting force and this Earth is now ours. Round up the dissidents and let us have some fun,' he says and they begin to laugh sadistically in unison.

Bonnie hears her name and awakens from her intense dream. She has tears in her eyes and wipes them away with the back of her hand.

'Bonnie!' She hears her name again and looks towards the back of the train. She doesn't see anyone she recognises. She tells herself she is merely imagining it and looks out of the window feeling an immense sorrow for her people and what was done to them. How could mother nature betray them so easily and for creatures she did not even know?

'Bonnie!'

She hears her name again. This time the voice is louder and she looks towards the back of the train and she sees a hand sticking up from around the corner waving at her and trying to get her attention.

She gets up cautiously from her seat and takes a deep breath. 'This could be dangerous, be on your guard,' she tells herself as she slowly walks down the aisle.

She slowly peeks around the corner and is surprised by who she sees hiding with a coat covering his face.

'Henry?' She says, with big eyes and surprise on her face and immediately drops down next to him.

'Shh, be quiet and don't call me that.' He looks around the room and moves his old blue coat back over his face.

'What is going on and why are you here? Are you following me?' She watches his eyes carefully. 'Just know there is no point in lying to me, I can do things now.'

'I know, I have heard! You have become a monster Bonnie!' He snaps and immediately regrets what he just said.

Her eyes move down and look at her feet in shame. 'I had no choice; it was me or them Henry.'

'I know Bonnie, I am sorry, that is not what I meant,' he replies and gives her hand a gentle squeeze.

'Anyway, I am headed to Edmonton, to join the resistance. Jane sold out, she...I don't know exactly, but she can't be trusted. Malcom went to Asia, apparently to slaughter a whole bunch of Samira's Phoenicians. I don't know the full story, but things are getting out of control. We need to put a stop to them!'

'How?' There is nothing we can do. They overthrew the entire Tartarian Empire, in case you have forgotten?'

'I know,' he sighs and starts to cough. 'We need to be extra careful now Bonnie, there are very few we can trust, you understand what I am saying?'

She nods and pulls the coat from his face. 'When last have you eaten Henry? I know I am hungry and you look just as hungry?' She can tell by his lack of an answer that it has been a while.

'Stay here, I am going to get us some food.' She gets up slowly and starts to walk through each aisle looking for someone with water and food.

It is a cool Sunday afternoon, the bedroom window is open and the curtains are swaying gently from the breeze. He can hear the golden clock above the fireplace tick and he finds it relaxing. He found it in a severely, mud flood affected mansion,

in Paris eight years ago and brought it home with him. The mansion was exquisite, but it had to unfortunately, be demolished. There was too much damage caused by the mud flood and nothing could be done to restore it. He always wondered who lived in it, the family had wonderful taste and he would have liked to meet them. The weight of the mud had unfortunately made it structurally unsound, but he remembers that day well. He met Aara that day, she was just walking around the streets and got terribly lost. It was him who introduced her to Rune.
There is a soft knock at the door and it interrupts his thought.

'Yes Jane?'

'I apologise for the intrusion Mr Harrington, Mr and Mrs Harrington are downstairs in the sun room.'

He sits up on the bed all surprised. 'Was I expecting them?' He asks.

'No, they arrived unannounced,' she answers coyly.

'Well in that case –' He wants her to tell them to leave, but he reminds himself he needs to act natural, as if Bonnie running away isn't bothering him in the least. 'Tell them I will be right down, thank you Jane.'

Jane is secretly meeting up with Harlow, Leesa and Waal show up unannounced? Coincidence, he wonders? He shakes his head, gets up from the bed and fixes his hair.

'There is no such thing as a coincidence,' he mutters and wishes that, in that very moment, Bonnie was lying naked on his bed. He imagines walking up to her, tickling her back and giving her soft kisses, while she lies there with a big smile on her face.

He splashes some water onto his face and it brings him back to reality. He stands in front of his mirror for a few seconds and practices his nonchalant smile and then hurries downstairs.

'Leesa and Waal, what a surprise!?' He says and greets each of them like he always does.

'A good one I hope.' She smiles and watches his expression carefully.

'Of course, I am always happy to see my parents!' He gives

her a soft smile back and exposes his teeth just slightly.

Jane walks in and brings them all some coffee and shortbread biscuits.

'I apologise for the lack of cake today Mr Harrington.'

He grabs a biscuit and ignores her. 'So, how are things in Philadelphia?' Malcom asks and leans back into his chair with his usual amount of arrogance.

'Great, we were just thinking we haven't been here in a while, we heard about Bonnie running off. It was such a shock to us all!' She places her hand over her chest and tries her hardest to be genuine.

'I don't know where she is and as you can see, I am not out looking for her. I will find another one. Make sure to tell him that.' He takes a sip of his coffee and his eyes are burning a fierce green. He would much rather leap over the table and snap her neck with that arrogant little grin she has permanently plastered to her face. It won't kill her, but she will know just how much he really doesn't like her. She is his mother on paper, someone had to take care of him and Azrael was not going to, but she has always hated him deep down inside her. Harlow was the preferred choice.

'What does Azrael want to know?' He asks and takes another biscuit from the table.

William puts his hand on her shoulder as a gesture for him to take over the conversation.

'Where do you think the girl went? Did you know about Rune and Aara?' He asks and watches him cautiously, knowing full well that it is impossible to read his mind.

'Azrael already knows the answer to both of those questions, I didn't hide my thoughts from him. So, on whose behalf are you asking? It is clearly not his.' He replies sarcastically.

Waal is startled by how he is able to sense the situation so well and realises it is better that they leave, immediately.

'You know what, it is not important. He quickly helps Leesa up and tries to leave the room.'

Malcom walks up to them and places his hand across the

door frame. 'Answer my question Waal!'

Malcom is stronger than either of them *and* both of them. He is the son of Queen Ariella and the angel of death, their only child and *son*.

'Kismet and Samira, they want to know. I don't know why.' He says reluctantly and keeps his eyes fixed on the way out of the room and away from Malcom.

Malcom drops his arm and lets them hurry out the front door, they almost trip over one another in absolute fear of their son.

'Kismet and Samira? What on earth do they want?' He is talking to himself and can see Jane hiding behind the door, eaves dropping again, like she normally does.

'Jane, please come here.' His voice is calm and relaxed. He enjoyed scaring Waal and Leesa and it makes him oddly happy inside.

Jane hurries inside with an awkward smile on her face. 'Yes Mr Harrington?'

'What does Harlow want? The same thing as Leesa and Waal perhaps?'
She wants to lie, but knows there is no point. 'Yes. I think, and this is purely speculation, but I think they want to over throw Azrael. He has become too powerful and they know if they don't stop him soon, he will take over their countries too. He will become the new and sole ruler of the great Tartarian Empire.'

'You are probably right, but no one can stop him, not me, not them, not even all six of them together.' He pauses briefly and glares at her. 'They know they are not strong enough, so what do they have planned?'

'The girl?' She catches herself and blushes in shame for her lack of respect. 'What I mean, is Bonnie perhaps?' She asks timidly.

He pauses and looks at her. 'The girl?' He gives off a sarcastic and defeated-like laugh. 'You think Bonnie can stop him?' He starts to laugh harder. 'Now this is even more absurd than the six of them potentially stopping him. Evil like him doesn't die

Jane.' He sits down and feels defeated and lost.

He wonders where she is. He has tried to hear her, see her in his mind, but she has blocked him out. It is probably for the best; he can't risk knowing where she is.

'I think it is best you stay away from Harlow from now on or you will join Henry and the rest of your brethren in the Underneath. I want you to write to Ms Estes tomorrow, I need another wife.'

She found some food, there was a lady with a loaf of bread and she asked her for it. The lady didn't even hesitate and handed the loaf to her with a big grin. People just don't seem to want to say no to her and she is enjoying every minute of it. *I could get used to this.*

She walks back to where Henry is hiding and she gives him a piece. He eats it greedily; he almost swallows the piece whole.

'Slow down, you are going to choke.' She admonishes him and hands him another piece.

'Tell me what happened, why did you all of a sudden leave Montreal?'

'Kismet and Samira, they are planning on over throwing Azrael, everything points towards it. It's not official, but it is what Jane and I think is happening. If this happens, a lot of us will die. I don't plan on sticking around for that.' He says while he chews his bread and he is visibly shaken.

She is taken aback by his answer, she initially thought he had done something that was considered a crime or knew something he shouldn't know. But he isn't lying to her and he is genuinely frightened.

'I don't understand, why do they suddenly want to overthrow him?'

Henry shrugs his shoulders and begins to eat slower. 'I have no idea, perhaps his greed?'

'But Azrael wants me dead?' She says confused. 'He tried to kill me in New York. Is that the reason why they want to stop him? I mean I know I have these abilities, but I am sure they are only temporary. Once the babies are born, I will be completely powerless, won't I?'

'Who says he wants you dead? Maybe he wants you and your powers. Maybe you are very powerful, have you ever considered that? Maybe, that is why Malcom saved you, you are special and he knows it?'

'Are you saying that Azrael knows the others want to overthrow him and he wants me, because I am powerful? He wants me to stop them?' She asks confused and shakes her head at the mere thought.

Henry doesn't answer her.

She leans back against the side of the train and eats a piece of bread slowly. The babies, can they help over throw Azrael? Is this really why he wants her dead and he doesn't want the babies to be born at all, she wonders? They sit in silence and both ponder about the way things are what they will find when they reach Edmonton.

Eventually, she tires herself out with all the over thinking and starts to yawn. She wiggles herself in closer to Henry and covers her face with her own coat and falls asleep.

CHAPTER FOURTEEN

There is screaming everywhere, Tartarian women are being slaughtered in the streets, while the men are hanging by ropes in the city squares. Children are forcefully removed from their mother's arms, kicking and screaming, and are being rounded up and put into wagons. There is so much fear and pain in the air that Bonnie can't breathe. She covers her mouth with her hands and tells herself to wake up!

She opens her eyes again and she realises she can't leave. She needs to witness this and understand what happened. *You wanted to know what happened*, she reminds herself.

General Jokkiel orders the army to take everyone hostage and kill all who disobey or try to fight back. Baird has taken over his body and the General is trying hard to regain control and is trying to expel him, but he can't. He calls out to mother nature to give him the strength to fight, but she ignores him and watches from atop the Canopy.

'You betrayed me Jokkiel, you lied and you were making me sick all this time.' She says as she closes her eyes to the pain and death that is taking place below her on the ground.

Jokkiel is confused and doesn't understand what she is telling him.

She shows him what she means in a vision, that was given to her by Azrael and Jokkiel realises that she was tricked. Azrael made her believe that they decimated entire forests, purposely destroyed ecosystems, polluted rivers and killed the animals for sport. They broke the covenant and this is the price they must pay for their betrayal.

'You really thought you could hide this from me? We made a deal; you live in harmony with what I offer. You broke your promise and now you will pay the ultimate price and your Empire will fall!'

There is no reasoning with her, she believes what the Heaven Bearers have told her and the great Tartarian Empire is now no more. He allows his mind and body to go limp and Baird consumes him completely.

The Tartarian army doesn't question their General and follow his every command, no matter how wrong and cruel it is perceived to be. They take out the prominent Tartarian men first and capture their women. Bonnie's father is one of them and he is murdered in cold blood. He tried to protect his family, but it was all in vain. She watches him die in horror and his eyes turn stone cold.

'Father!' She cries out and tries to reach him, but he fades away before she can touch him.

She is suddenly standing in the middle of all the chaos and she is looking for her mother and older sister.

'Mother?' She calls and knows this is useless, she can't hear her. She looks around anyway and tries to spot her. Where is she?

She sees him, Azrael, and watches how he sits there and watches all the death and destruction from the balcony of a Tartarian bathhouse in King Finns body.

'You have no right!' She screams in his direction, knowing he can't hear her, nor would he care if he could.

He turns his head suddenly in her direction and their eyes

meet. She can feel him in her head. He is looking for something and she can't pull away from him. She starts to fight him off, but he is strong, very strong! He is looking through her memories, memories she didn't even know she had. They flash before her eyes and she can see her mother clutching her in her arms and running for dear life. She can feel her fear, hear her heartbeat and taste her salty sweat in her mouth. She falls to the ground unexpectedly and she loses grip of Bonnie.

King Finn is standing in front of her, he is kneeling down with his hand stretched out towards her.

'Take my hand child.' He says with a smile and his face is warm and trusting.

'No!' Bonnie shouts. 'Get away from him!'

Adult Bonnie knows that this isn't the real King Finn, but baby Bonnie doesn't and she stretches out her little hand and lets him take hold of her. As their two hands touch, she takes a deep breath and everything goes silent. He tries to pull away, but she tightens her grip.

His eyes open wide and she can see the monster that he is. 'It is not possible!' He shouts and pulls his hand away from her, as if she is toxic waste.

She lets out a deep breath and every grain of loose sand lifts up from the ground and pushes up into the air. It stays elevated there, just hovering in place, while the sky opens up and it starts to rain and it doesn't stop raining.

Mud starts to form and the force of the rushing water falling from the Canopy pushes it to every corner of the Earth. People start running and screaming, but it covers them and buries them alive, houses and buildings are destroyed, while only a few survive.

She awakens with a shock and her face is wet. She has been crying silently. Henry is still asleep and she looks at her hands. *They are shaking.* I did this, I destroyed the Empire and killed these people. I created the mud flood! She feels eyes staring at her and she notices a single man sitting at the far end of the train and he is watching her. Their eyes meet and he quickly pulls his contact away from her and proceeds to stare out of the window, pretending to mind his own business. She gets up and walks over to him. He is Phoenician and he pretends to not notice her standing there. She sits down next to him and puts her hand on his. He pulls away and his eyes turn a bright, algae green.

'Who are you Sir?' She asks politely and runs her finger over his shoulder and down his arm in a flirty manner.

Her touch reveals to him that he can't lie to her and that it would be counterproductive to try.

'I don't know you, but I am drawn to you. I know your babies are Human and I curious about you. I can feel your energy.' He replies and he is suddenly very shy.

'What is your name?' She responds, she is curious about this man too.

'Ziekiel.'

'Ziekiel? The name sounds familiar, yet I don't know who you are? Do you know Malcom Harrington by any chance?'

He nods, he is surprised by her question. She leans into him and gives him a very soft kiss, barely touching his lips. His eyes flash purple and then go back to their original colour.

'It was great meeting you Ziekiel.' She pushes herself up from the seat and his hand automatically helps her up. She smiles, blushes and walks back to Henry.

'Henry.' She shakes him roughly. 'Henry, wake up, we need to go now.'

They have arrived at their destination and she is suddenly nervous. Now what? She never thought about what to do when they finally arrived in Edmonton. The only thing she worried about was getting to this point.

'Where do we go from here?' Henry asks while staring at all the people. 'Where are they all going?' There are about a hundred Humans and they are dressed in rags and barefoot. They range from all ages, young and old, some even look to be only children and she is left speechless by what she sees. They are carrying pickaxes, spades and other tools. There are Phoenicians on horseback patrolling them with whips in their hands and the Humans are terrified, cold and hungry. She wants to kill them all and let these people go immediately.

'It is premature Bonnie, keep your calm and find Cassiel.' It is her mother's voice in her head and she knows she is right. She grabs Henry by the hand and they start walking in the opposite direction.

'We need to find a place to stay, I need to take a bath and I need some proper food.' She says as she marches away from the train station with Henry battling to keep up with her fast pace.

They walk around until she finds a fancy looking hotel.

'This place is perfect.' She starts to walk towards the hotel, but Henry stops her.

'We have no money Bonnie.' He is defeated and drained, his journey must have been really difficult and she can see the exhaustion on his face now.

'Trust me Henry, I have made it this far with luck on my side. You need to have a little faith in me.'

He reluctantly follows her inside. And sits down in the lobby chair. Everyone who walks by stares at him and he knows he doesn't belong here. He wants to get up and leave, but Bonnie gestures for him to stay where he is.

There is a young Tartarian man behind the front desk and she musters up friendly smile and approaches him.

'Good Day Sir, I am looking for a room, with two double beds please.'

'Sure madam, I will need to speak to your husband.' He pauses and looks over at Henry. 'We are not that kind of establishment, you understand?'

She smiles, but she doesn't understand why he is not mesmerised by her like the rest of them? She takes a step back and rubs her stomach so that he can see she is pregnant, but this doesn't make a difference.

'Please come back with your husband, otherwise I can't help you Madam,' he says rudely and looks down at the desk.

He is wearing something on a silver chain around his neck

and she wonders what it is.

'Madam, please, I have other customers.' He is visibly irritated with her and she rolls her eyes at him. Why isn't he helping her, she wonders? She walks over to Henry and takes a seat next to him and sighs out in full defeat, while she thinks about another way.

She starts to day dream about Malcom and the mansion and how she wishes she was home right now. She is tired and hungry and for the first time she doesn't want to carry on with the journey.

'Henry, stand up and come with me.' She suddenly latches onto his arm, tight like a vicious dog and drags him along while she walks back to the reception desk.

'Here is my husband, now can I have a room?' She asks the man angrily.

'I am sorry Madam, we don't cater to Tartarian men. Phoenician men only and of course their wives of any kind.' He replies sternly.

'Listen here...what is your name?' She snaps and her eyes start turning bright blue.

'Deezil,' he replies cautiously and is very unsure of himself suddenly.

'What is around your neck Deezil?' Her eyes go darker and she starts to intimidate him so he instinctively grabs hold of whatever is underneath his shirt.

'I want a room, for my friend and I, and I won't be paying for it. Bill my husband when I leave,' she commands him and is not willing to take no for an answer.

She grabs the fountain pen from his hand, dips the tip carefully into the black ink and writes something on a piece of paper, then hands it to him.

Cassiel

She hands him the note and he pretends he doesn't know what

to do with it. She stretches out her hand and glances at him and he immediately hands her a set of keys.

'Enjoy Madam.' He is still clutching onto the object and is visibly unnerved.

'Thank you Deezil, I really do appreciate you helping a fellow Tartarian,' she snaps sarcastically and gives him a funny and mean look.

He waits for her to leave and asks his colleague to cover for him. He rushes out the back of the hotel, as fast as he can and almost trips over the sidewalk. His legs feel like jelly and his heart is beating like he is running for his life. It is her, he thinks to himself and can feel a sense of relief rush over him and it fills him with hope. He walks two and a half miles until he arrives at an old pub. He stops at the entrance and looks for someone inside, his eyes scan the room, but he is not here. He turns around and clutches the object around his neck and is about to leave when he hears his name.

'Deezil, my boy! Aren't you supposed to be at work?'

A man in his early thirties walks up to him with a half-smile. He has long blonde hair, that is tied in a ponytail and his pants are torn and too big for his small frame.

'I have news.' He hands him the note that Bonnie had written and given to him at the Hotel.

'Where did you get this?' His gaze is automatically strong and serious and he clutches the piece of paper like it is a sheet of gold paper and he wants to keep it close to him.

'A woman gave it to me just now, her eyes were as blue as the ocean and she tried to read my thoughts, she was Tartarian and pregnant, very pregnant.' His voice starts to shake, he is visibly perturbed by what he experienced.

'Go find Aaden. Hurry!' He barks and Deezil runs off.

He sniffs the piece of paper and can smell her on it. She is *Tartarian*, but there is something else that he can smell and he doesn't recognise it.

A short while later Aaden hurries up the street towards him. Aaden is elderly, one of the few very old Tartarians who survived the mud flood. He lost his entire family to the flood and he himself, barely survived it.

'The boy told me! Can it...can it really be true?' He needs to catch his breath and leans onto the wall beside them for support.

'Tell me what you are thinking?' He asks, unsure of what is happening.

Aaden looks around and wipes his mouth with a piece of cloth and he coughs loudly until he catches his breath. 'We need to go inside; she is on her way.' He looks up at the Canopy and knows the time for change has arrived, finally.

They walk inside and wait in a separate room to the other patrons. They order some ale and fresh bread and eat it contently, but don't speak to one another.

There is knock on the door and Aaden grips his knife tightly. 'Who is there?'

'It is me Rieva.' Replies a soft voice from behind the door. The door handle turns and Aaden relaxes his grip.

'Come inside quickly!' He barks in excitement and places his hands flat onto the table and grins with joy and hope fills his eyes.

She takes a seat across from him and she is also wearing an object around her neck that has the same shape as the one the young man from the hotel wore. It consists of six triangles that are all attached to a small circle in the centre. It is made of a type of stone, light blue and grey in colour and it glimmers when the sun touches it just right.

'Hand me the piece of paper Beert,' Aaden asks with an undertone of irritation and he hands it politely to Rieva.

Beert does as he is asked and the three of them stare at the single name written on it.

'She is Tartarian, I can smell it, but there is something else there too.' Beert says. He is proud of his observation and takes his last sip of ale.

'I can't smell anything,' Rieva replies confused and looks

over at Beert and then Aaden. 'Can you smell something else Aaden?'

He nods that that he does not and balls his hands into fists and slams them playfully on the table and stares at Rieva. 'I don't think it is her!'

Beert cries out in frustration, crumbles the now, seemingly worthless piece of paper up in his hand and throws it to the corner of the room. 'How much longer must we wait?' He gets up and leaves the pub in anger.

Rieva and Aaden remain seated at the table in complete silence and individually contemplate what to do next. Each of them is smiling and happy, genuinely *happy*.

'It is her, isn't it?' Rieva looks over at Aaden, just to make sure she isn't making a very false assumption.

He fingers the dent on the table and his expression tell her all she needs to know.

'We need to alert Cassiel at once,' he says and his eyes glimmer with hope for the first time in seventeen years.

Aaden stands up and places his hand on her shoulder. 'The prophesy is starting to ring true, every single bit of it. We need to find this girl at once!' He stares intensely at the wall and he recalls the horrors he experienced all those years ago. His eyes tear up and fill his old and weary eyes. 'I will be coming to fetch you later, you understand?' He says, but he isn't talking to Rieva, rather to someone from his memory.

She sits quietly at the table and watches him leave. She knows what happened to him, who he lost and assumes he was talking to his deceased wife, Magda.

Everyone lost someone they loved during the mud flood. How any Tartarians survived at all, was a miracle in itself. She was only a small girl, but she remembers seeing some of the damage. The mud lay all over the place, pushed up against the buildings, it turned hard and started to smell of rotting earth mixed with food and sour milk. She escaped with her older brother to the mountains and they lived there for ten years before they ventured back closer to the city.

The New World Order they call it, except the Earth is the same, the only difference is that there is no more peace, happiness or joy. There is only suffering now.

'We need to get her out that hotel and fast, they will know she is here!' She mutters to herself and leaves the room to find her brother.

She finds him chopping wood in the forest and tells him what has happened. He can see the worry on her face.

'She made it this far by herself and she is powerful, you don't need to worry so much sister,' he says as he slams the axe down hard onto a piece of wood, it breaks into two pieces and they fall to each side of the axe.

'We need to wait for the signal, then you will go to the hotel.'

Bonnie orders them a full meal, roast duck, mash potatoes, green beans and a light pea soup. She orders a sweet pie for dessert, as a surprise for Henry, something to keep his spirits strong. Henry eats most of the duck and she doesn't try to stop him. She is grateful for the room and the meal and knows they don't have long here.

'Henry, I am going to take a bath, when I am done you need to do the same and then we must leave. Try get some sleep while I'm in the bath,' she says as she licks the mash off of her finger and wipes her mouth.

He nods that he understands and finishes off his slice of strawberry pie and wraps up the rest in a napkin for them to take with. He walks to the window and lifts up the white sheer curtain, gently, to peek outside. The street is still bustling with people and he finds it comforting. He lies down on the bed without taking off his dirty boots and waits for her to wake him.

'Wake up Henry!' He opens his eyes and looks around the room. There is no one in the room and Bonnie is still in the bath. He gets up, rubs the sleep out of his eyes and stumbles towards the window. It is getting dark already and he realises he has been sleeping for much longer than it should take for her to bath. He yawns and knocks on the bathroom door, but there is no answer.

'Bonnie, are you okay in there?'

There is no answer and he tries to turn the door handle. The door is locked and he calls out for her again. 'Bonnie, you need to open the door!'

There is still no answer and he starts to worry. He kicks the door, to try and break it open, but he can't. He isn't strong enough. He takes the small wooden chair that matches the writing desk and uses it to break down the door. He takes a big swing and just before he hits it into the door, he realises the door has changed its form. It is no longer the wooden hotel door, but it is a ten-centimetre-thick, grey metal door with no door handle and an oddly placed key hole.

The only way to open it is from the inside. He starts to panic, he knows he needs to get to her, she is in trouble, but he can't get through the door!

He feels a warm and soft hand on his face and opens his eyes. It is Bonnie and to his amazement she is smiling with an infectious sparkle in her eyes.

'Everything is ok, you were just dreaming Henry.' She says and her voice is filled with love and she smells like fresh roses.

He wipes the sweat from his forehead and gets up slowly. 'It all felt so real,' he says and looks around the room and at the bathroom door.

'I know, I have been dreaming a lot too lately. You need to go and freshen up now. They are coming for us. Be quick, but don't rush.'

His face goes pale and he watches her move over to the hotel window and peek outside, just as he had done in his dream. 'Who is coming Bonnie?' He clears his throat and again looks at the bathroom door to make sure he isn't dreaming. 'Are we going to die here tonight?' He asks and his voice is shaking, it is as timid as if he was a five-year-old boy.

'You are not going to die Henry, not here and not until you are an old man, of that I am sure.' She smiles and he pretends to eat it up completely. Although her voice is firm and convincing, he isn't quite sure she has *that* ability, to predict the future, and he closes the door gently behind him, but doesn't lock it.

CHAPTER FIFTEEN

'She is on her way Mr Harrington and will be here by this afternoon. Shall I arrange the proceedings and the union for this evening or tomorrow evening?'

'This evening is fine Jane, thank you,' he responds cold and disinterested as he puts on his coat and notices a single strand of her blonde hair on the sleeve of it. He clenches his jaw and gently lets it fall to the ground.

She nods in agreement and leaves him to stare at the door in front of him with his hand firmly on the doorknob.

Ms Estes has arranged another girl for him already and he can't help but think about Bonnie and the first time he laid eyes on her. He was completely astonished by her and her smile and he realises now, that was the first time he felt some kind of *emotion*.

She was the most beautiful Tartarian he had ever seen. She was small, but not short, she had light pink, luscious lips and luminous blue eyes. He could see a gold flare in them when she was happy, which wasn't often, but it made his heart stop beating for just one single moment when he was lucky enough to see it. He begins to frown and doesn't like *feeling* for her. He opens the door and thinks about the discussion he needs to have with the new engineer and marches down the street with his head down and his hands in his pockets.

It doesn't take long for his mind to jump back to her and he thinks about the first time she enjoyed him touching her in front of the fireplace. He had just washed the blood from her head and when she woke up all she could do is want him. He stops in the middle of the sidewalk and shakes his head at the thought and rubs his hands over his face. He wants to scream and punch something, but not because he is angry, this time he feels sad and lonely. He misses her tremendously and just can't shake the feeling.

Where are you Bonnie? He closes his eyes and searches for her in his mind. He knows that if he finds her, they will find her too. He opens them eyes quickly and continues to walk down the street at his usual, uptight pace and doesn't greet anyone he passes. He is focused on not thinking about her and this takes his full concentration.

He hears the laughter of children crossing the street, they are on their way to the compulsory state education system. He doesn't feel guilty for any of them and they mean nothing to him.

'They are necessary for them, the Heaven Bearers, to achieve their goal,' he mutters as if he needs to convince himself of something and he again shakes his head and realises what he is saying. If they achieve their goals, this Earth will be destroyed completely too, just like all the others before. Heaven Bearers destroy all that they touch, which means *she* will die. He looks up into the sky, directly at the sun and it hurts his eyes. He is having a clash of conscience and he can't control it.

He enters Old-brooks and looks for Sven, the new engineer.

'Good morning Mr Harrington, can I help you with something?' The elderly Tartarian man who works there asks kindly. Malcom realises that he doesn't even know his name, he has never bothered to asked him what it is and suddenly feels guilty.

'It isn't important, thank you.' He is tongue tied and he feels like he is losing his mind. He walks back outside and leans up against the wall. He doesn't like thinking about the true state of affairs and realises then and there just how brainwashed he is. He believed that what he is doing is *good* and he never bothered to question any policy, rule or law. It was decreed and will therefore be enforced as is.

For the first time in his life, he feels a sense of shame fill his body, his mind and soul. He tries to shake it off, but he just can't. It is more powerful than he is and he knows what he needs to do, for her, for them all.

He doesn't go back to the office or continue to look for Sven. He changes his direction and walks towards the grand station. I need to find her!

Bonnie is sitting on the hotel bed. It is soft and comfortable; the sheets are made from silk and cotton and she can't help but want to lie down on it and close her eyes.

'Now is not the time, snap out of it!' She mutters and lets her eyes wander around the room. She stares at the fireplace and can't help think it looks out of place. She walks up towards it and traces her fingers over the edge. Someone has changed the design of this fireplace and she can see the workmanship isn't of the same quality. There was an organ structure above it, there is a faint trace of it on the wall and even with a fresh coat of paint, they can't hide it. She sniffs the wall and doesn't know what she was expecting to smell, pulls back away from it and crinkles her nose.

'Everything was free?' She says out loud as she tries to piece it all together. 'Free energy?' There must have been free energy, in fact there was no money and everyone had a purpose and followed their passion.

Since the Heaven Bearers took over the planet, there has been no energy, she realises. We have to use oil lanterns to light up the darkness, we are all so primitive compared to those great people!

She starts to laugh, but it is a spiteful laugh. The *almighty* Heaven Bearers don't know how to re-create certain things, they can't even replicate the buildings the Tartarians built. The knowledge was lost due to the re-education programmes and very few can read the old books. More importantly, even if they could they wouldn't know what they are reading or at least pretend they don't. We would have electricity by now if the Heaven Bearers had gotten their way.

Her mind suddenly jumps to King Finn, her eyes flash a slight gold and she blinks heavily. She is all of a sudden angry and balls her hand into a fist and gently bangs it on the wall.

The bathroom door swings open and she turns towards Henry.

'My mother was King Finn's sister! Did you know that?'

'No,' he replies, but he isn't shocked by what she tells him. He walks over to the window and stares outside again and rubs a hand towel over his wet hair to dry it. 'There is an old legend, it was around before the mud flood even happened. It was so outrageous, it was disregarded as crazy talk. People generally didn't talk about it.'

'Go on...' She prompts him, her face is inquisitive and he can't help but want to stare at her face for all eternity.

'The great Empire of Tartaria would be invaded by some evil creatures one day. I don't' know all the details, but I know that there would be this girl, a Tartarian girl with abilities.' He pauses and thinks about a better word. 'She would have *powers* and she would completely destroy the Tartarian Empire.'

'Destroy the Empire?' Her face is filled with shock. 'Why would she destroy it, she is meant to save it, save her people?'

'There is no saving it Bonnie –'

She looks away from him in shame, she recalls the fact that she is already responsible for killing millions of her own people by creating the mud flood. She might have seen it in a dream, a vision of the past and she was only a baby, but she knows what she did. She was responsible for what happened.

'It was me you know. I caused the mud flood,' she says and

the words don't penetrate his ears. What she is saying doesn't make any sense and it can't be true.

There is a sudden knock on the door and she walks to open it, without finishing what she wanted to tell Henry.

'No stop!' He shouts and starts to approach her in a protective manner.

She smiles at him and opens the door before he reaches her.

Her heart is filled with joy at the sight of him. She throws her arms around his neck and kisses him passionately; her lips are full of longing, want and need.

She pulls away to catch her breath and kisses him again, this time slowly and she touches the tip of her nose against his, softly, then closes her eyes to take him all in. He smells like she remembers and her fingers move slowly thought his hair and over his neck.

His face is expressionless, but she can hear his heart beating and she knows he feels the same. He isn't used to feeling, he didn't even know that it was possible. Phoenicians aren't capable of feeling anything! This is what they are taught. She however, knows differently and she will show him.

'Mr Harrington!' Henry calls out, but his voice is unsure and nervous.

Bonnie takes Malcom by the hand and leads him inside the room. Henry didn't expect to see him and stands there in utter shock. He wants to greet him properly, respectfully, but his mind is stuck on pause and he doesn't know what to say.

'Mr Harrington,' he mutters again, opens his mouth and then closes it abruptly. Eventually, he finds the right words.

'Bonnie, he is the enemy, he is...Azrael is his creator.' He swallows hard and looks at her hoping she understands what he is telling her. He quickly puffs himself up and tries to be the alpha male and protect her.

'Henry, this is not the time or place,' she says softly. She doesn't want to hurt him, but she wants him to stop this silly posturing. She says nothing more and then asks them both to take a seat. 'We have company.'

Henry's eyes move to the door and notices there are two figures standing at the open door. He didn't hear them arrive and has no idea how long they have been standing there for.

'Come in,' she instructs and has her eyes locked on their every movement as they enter the room.

It is a man and women, both are Tartarian. The man is old, very old and has a missing eye. The woman is much younger and reminds her of Stacy, except she has something wild about her. She doesn't seem to fit the style of clothing she is wearing and belongs in the wilderness.

'We are here about the note you left at the front desk at the hotel,' the old man says carefully, not to reveal more details and he watches her reaction carefully. Rieva is postured in a fighting position and Bonnie notices the symbol hanging from her neck and realises it is the same as the one the young man at the reception desk was wearing. They must all know each other, she tells herself.

'Yes –' She looks over at Malcom and his eyes are bright green and she motions him to calm down.

'I would like you to take me to Cassiel please.'

The woman grins and walks up to her slowly. 'Cassiel? Who is that exactly?'

She circles her, watching her every expression, taking in her scent and wondering what she is thinking.

'You don't trust him, do you?' Bonnie replies.

'Trust who, young girl?' She hisses like a snake.

The man approaches her this time. 'Who don't we trust?' He asks and gestures for Rieva to take a step back.

'The man that has been following you, the one from the pub,' she responds and squints her eyes at him.

'We need to leave at once!' He shouts. His hands are sweaty and he is visibly scared. 'You need to leave them both behind, I am sorry, but we can only take you to him.'

'No!' she calmly rejects his offer.

'But It has been prophesised!' He continues surprised and is slightly angered by her defiance.

She rudely interrupts him and her voice is harsh and angry. 'The prophesy is wrong. Now take me to Cassiel at once or I shall find him myself!'

Aaden and Rieva aren't sure what to do. She leans up to him and whispers, while clutching the object around her neck. 'This is not how it is supposed to go. She is too young; it can't be her!'

'It's her.' He glances over at Malcom and back at her. 'I never expected to see the day when a Phoenician would fall in love with a Tartarian girl, yet here we are.' He pauses and looks directly into Rieva's eyes. 'Miracles do happen.'

He turns around and proceeds to walk out the door. Rivera doesn't move from the spot where she is standing, she is angry and she doesn't want to accept what Aaden just told her.

'The entire Phoenician race will be destroyed,' she barks at Bonnie, then shrugs her shoulders and follows Aaden out of the room.

The night air is cold and it gives her the shivers. Malcom takes off his black coat and hands it to her. He is holding the metal staff from the mansion and she wants to ask him why, but she is distracted by his presence. She takes the coat gracefully and can feel his warmth, smell his cologne and it gives her a rush of hope.

'I need to destroy the Earth in order to save my people. That is what has been prophesised. How does that make any sense? You know I could never do that!'

He smiles and takes her hand in his.

'The prophesy said nothing about a Phoenician finding humility and falling in love with a Tartarian either and look at where we are,' he says and she can't believe what he just told her.

'You fell in love with a Tartarian? Never!?' She teases him and he pulls her in close and kisses her. For that moment and only for that short moment, they forget about all their problems and the imminent war that they can all feel is on the horizon.

She pulls away and touches his face.

'It was me you know? I created the mud flood and killed billions of Tartarians!' She turns her head away in shame and doesn't want him touching her any more.

He is surprised by what she tells him and lets her pull away from him. He watches her and tries to get a feel of what is going on in her mind.

'No, that was mother nature,' he replies confidently, only to notice her cheeks go flush and he knows he is wrong.

He steps away from her and turns around to catch himself. He can't believe what she just said and can't stop the emotions he is feeling. He has a pit in his stomach and it hurts! He starts to laugh out loud at the fact that he can understand her now, why she would just stand there in the mansion and start crying. What is happening to me, he wonders? Why must I feel emotions now suddenly?

'Your emotions will inspire the others and together you can stop them.' He hears a female voice echo in his head and he looks around to see where it came from. He doesn't recognise it and he wonders if he just imagined it.

'I am something more, our reality is more than we know. Something important is missing and I don't know what it is,' she says and interrupts his thoughts and he tries to ignore her for a second so that he can hear *that* voice again.

'Something is definitely missing. None of it makes sense.' He finally responds and feels uncomfortable. 'Let us go, we can ask Cassiel when we find him,' he says but she can see his mind is elsewhere. She can't read his expression and he grabs her by the hand and pulls her after him. She duly follows and wonders what he is thinking about and why he is upset with her.

'Malcom, if you pull any harder, my arm might just detach from my body!' She stops and tugs her arm away from him. 'You are hurting me! What is the matter with you?'

He slows his pace and tries to grab her hand again, but she pulls away. They walk in silence for the next hour and eventually stop on the outskirts of town.

'We can't just find Cassiel. Truth is we don't know where he is. We are merely meant to fulfil a particular purpose and that is to find the pregnant girl and bring her to this place,' Aaden says as he looks around and notices there is nothing here. Bonnie can sense his mood and looks towards the East. She can see the mountains in the distance and she feels a warm breeze pass over her.

'Is there a star fort nearby? Perhaps in the mountains over there?' She points in the direction of the East.

Everyone looks at her in confusion and no one answers her question.

'I need to get to the star fort,' she continues and crinkles her nose at the dumb expressions that are staring back at her.

'Bonnie, star forts are just empty forts, they have no purpose. The stories are all based on myth.' Henry eventually says and tries to break the awkward atmosphere.

Bonnie shakes her head and gives him a silly smile. 'Henry, there is a reason why there are thousands of them all over the earth and it is not because they were used to ward off enemies. She pauses and can see he thinks she is crazy.

'What I am saying is, that these forts were built for a reason and is it not just a coincidence that they are scattered all over the Earth. There is no such thing as a coincidence.' Malcom is completely ignoring her and Henry is scratching the tip of his boot into the ground. Aaden is facing the East and staring out into the dark and she approaches him.

'We need to head towards the mountains, find me that start fort!' She says out loud and they reluctantly comply with her orders.

It takes them three and a half hours, but they eventually find a small star fort next to a semi-dry lake. The water is crystal clear and smells sweet, but no one dares touch it. The light pink colour is disturbing to look at. The star fort is covered by bushes and broken branches and there are chunks or old rock scattered all around it.

'It doesn't seem like it has been used since the mud flood, yet it is not covered by any mud?' She says and finds it weird that the entire area seems relatively unaffected. The trees are big and old and the air around them has a different feel and smell.

She starts to clear away some of the plants that are blocking the entrance to the star fort and notices old engravings carved into the rock.

'Can anyone here read Tartarian?' She asks and pushes her finger into the grooves.

Henry walks over and takes a good look and scratches his head.

'I know a few words, the first word is "The" and – I'm sorry, but I can't read the rest,' he answers and plonks himself down on the floor. He fiddles with some dry twigs and she knows they need to figure this out soon.

Aaden and Rieva also attempt to read it, but neither can figure out what it says.

'How old are you Aaden?' She asks and stares obnoxiously at his missing eye.

Her question surprises them all.

'I am seventy-one years old, what does my age matter dear girl?' He is truly surprised by her question and his expression shows her that he thinks she is going mad.

'If you are seventy-one years old, you should be able to read Tartarian, surely? Or is losing the ability to understand a language a natural phenomenon?' She asks sarcastically. Her tones snaps Malcom back to reality and he knows something is wrong.

The breeze stops suddenly and she can hear an owl screech in the background. Henry starts to panic and comes closer towards her. Malcom has his fists clenched tight and has his eyes locked onto Aaden.

Rieva walks up to him and wants to place her hand on his shoulder, but before she can do so Aaden spins around and snaps her neck. Her limp body falls to the ground with a thump and Henry cries out in horror and fear!

'What is your name you wretched creature?' Bonnies eyes turn bright blue and she locks eyes with it.

Aaden twitches and licks his lips nervously, but doesn't respond to her question.

Malcom steps forward, his foot steps are hard and firm and she can hear every crack the branches make as he steps closer to the Heaven Bearer. He takes a good look at Aaden and his smile indicates he recognises it.

'Kismet? Hmmm now I didn't expect it to be you. I haven't seen you since I was a child, but I do remember that you smelled like rotting fish.'

Kismet laughs out loud and lunges for Malcom, but he can't move from where he is standing. There are vines that have attached themselves to his feet and they are holding him into position. Bonnie moves forward and Malcom tries to stop her by placing his hand out gently. She gives him *that* look and he backs down immediately.

'You made a mistake creature, this is holy Tartarian land. The trees that you see all around you made a covenant a long time ago with the Tartarians and they do not answer to mother nature. There is a power here that you couldn't even begin to comprehend!' She stands and speaks with unimaginable authority, like a true ruler and Malcom can feel goose bumps form all over his body at the magical sight of her.

She bends down and takes a handful of the reddish-brown soil and blows it into his face.

He starts to scream in agony and the vines and roots that have taken hold of him earlier start to tangle their way up his entire body and slowly pull him into the Earth.

The wind picks up and it is warm and it smells sweet, like the pink water in the lake.

'The forest is talking to us,' she says as she notices a bright blue light radiate from the star fort and the staff that Malcom is holding starts to light up as well.

'The metal...the staff! Look!' She says and takes it from

Malcom before he drops it.
She hears a voice radiating from the star fort and it sucks her in slowly and starts to consume her mind. She walks up to it and glances at the writing again. This time she knows what it says.

'Malcom, Henry, come here please.' She stretches out her hands to both of them and holds onto them tight. She gives Malcom a loving smile and her eyes flash gold.

'Freedom and peace for all or for none at all,' she says and the blue light intensifies. It takes only seconds until the entire forest is illuminated by it.

Malcom squeezes her hand tight and his eyes turn from green to purple and their feet gently lift off from the stone floor.

CHAPTER SIXTEEN

It feels as if there is no gravity and she is floating endlessly in a place with no sense of time. She is still in the forest and she can feel neither warm nor cold. Her heart is racing, but she can't hear or feel it. Everything is blue, every shade of blue, from light to dark, that she could ever imagine.

Nothing makes sense, yet it is all familiar to her. She looks around and can see beams of light, shapes of objects, fauna and flora, everything is glowing and following a predetermined script that was written hundreds of thousands of years ago. Nothing is out of place, not one branch or leaf, animal or droplet of water.

The Old World? Was this how it was in the Old World, she wonders?

'Daphne –'

She can hear a voice, it is neither loud nor soft, but it blocks out every other thought she has and her mind is completely blank, like a canvas waiting for the artist to fill it with colour and purpose.

'Daphne –' The voice calls her again. It is a soft whisper, but it is coming from every direction.

'Yes, I am here, I can hear you,' she replies and her eyes look everywhere for a face to put to the voice.

She can feel the soft touch of woman's hand on her face and it excites her skin and senses. She looks over at Malcom, but he is gone and she quickly turns to see if Henry is gone too. There is no one there, only her. Where did they go?

'They were just here,' she mutters and it bothers her that they are gone.

'Daphne, listen to my voice.'

Her eyes continue to scan the area for the source of this voice and then she hears *that* tune.

'Ladida dada di lala.'

'Mother? Is that you mother?' She asks this place with excitement.

A woman walks up to her and her face is young, gentle and kind. She is wearing a golden butterfly in her hair and she can smell her scent. It is the same scent of those colourful flowers in the field she dreamt she saw her mother in, playing with her older sister, when she was just a baby.

'Who are you?' She pauses and tries to think. 'I know you, but I don't know if we have met. Have we met?'

The lady suddenly turns into a little girl and she giggles and covers her mouth with her little hand.

'It is me Cassidy, you big sister silly!' She giggles some more and then abruptly stops and becomes an adult again.

'Mother is disappointed in you. You are the chosen one, yet you didn't do as you were told. You should have listened Daphne!' She scolds her and starts to giggle again. 'Mother won't understand, but I do. I understand sister.'

'Did you know that I created the mud flood? I killed our people, I let them starve and suffer terribly?' She asks and wants to cry, but no tears fill her eyes. She wipes at them, but they are bone dry. She knows she is sad, but has no emotion at all.

'Why can't I feel anything, it is as if time has stopped and I ceased to exist?'

Cassidy laughs and plays with her hair. 'No one ever said it would be easy Daphne, you are crossing over to the Underneath. You might never go back and you might never see them again!' Her giggles turn to sarcastic and sadistic screeches and Bonnie can feel someone is in her head.

'Them, who do you mean? Malcom? But he was just next to me, where did he go? I want him to come with me! I need him, please!' She pleads, but it falls on deaf ears.

'I don't make the rules –' The voice starts to fade and her sister is a little girl again.

'Wait, I don't want to go to the Underneath, I am meant to find Cassiel and the resistance. Why am I going to the Underneath, what is waiting for me there?' She calls out to the voice, but she gets no response.

Cassidy skips off into the distance and hums along to that song, that she knows and it fills her with belonging, which quickly turns to anger and frustration.

'Cassidy! Wait, where are you going? Cassidy, please come back here!' She shouts, but she is once again completely alone in a place that is confusing and she doesn't know where she is.

The blue light fades and the colours return to normal, but she isn't in the forest anymore. She is Underground and she can hear a river flowing, it is not far from where she is standing. She follows the sound and the current is strong and loud. There are fish swimming in it. They are gold in colour, with bright red fins and they are fighting against the flow of the crystal-clear water, trying to get back upstream. She bends down to take a sip, but the water slides off of her hand, just as water separates from oil. She pulls her hand away and gently runs the fingers of her other hand over her palm to feel if there is something on her hand.

My hand feels normal, there is nothing there? She is confused and sticks her hand back into the water, but the water is repulsed by her. She jumps into the river and the water lifts up to either side of the river bank, in the shape of a circle so that she is surrounded by it, but it doesn't touch her. She can feel the white and grey pebbles underneath her feat and she walks through the river all the way upstream until, she reaches its source.

'The Underneath?' She mutters to herself and wonders why she is here?

She looks out ahead and there is a massive body of water, but it is not blue, it is not any colour at all. How can this be? She climbs out of the river and picks up a pebble and throws it into the body of water and it dries up suddenly, leaving millions of these golden fish to wriggle in agony on the river bed. She picks up a single fish and takes a good look at it.

'Take your friends and swim downstream,' she orders it and one by one the fish push themselves along the dry ground towards the river and throw themselves back into the clear water.

She doesn't understand what is happening, but she isn't afraid.

'Ladida dada lala...' She starts to hum along to the tune and strolls over the dry lake floor. The dry pieces of sand crunch under her weight and she enjoys the sound they make.

She has only been walking for a few minutes, but she has already reached the opposite side of the lake and she stares back to where she started and it looks to be over a mile away. Everything that is happening around here is defying logic and makes no sense. She looks around and then decides to carry on walking but she suddenly can't go any further. There is nothing but a big, stone wall, with rough edges, right up in front of her and it appeared out of nowhere. She can't go back; the walk is too far and the wall is too high. She doesn't know what to do or where to go and she is running out of patience.

'I am getting tired of the games!' She shouts across the vast nothingness and hears how her voice echoes all around her. 'What is expected of me? Someone just tell me so I can do it. I'd like to get back to my husband now.'

There is no answer and she stomps her foot hard on the ground and sighs out loud!

The earth begins to shake violently and black roots force their way up from the ground and grab hold of her legs and she cries out in pain as they grab hold of her. I feel this, why can I suddenly feel pain? She reaches down and tries to free herself from the stronghold that they have, but she can't hold onto them. They slip out of her hands like jelly. She clenches her fists as tight as he can and she screams.

'Enough!'

Everything goes quiet, the roots disappear and snow falls from the sky with just a single snow flake landing on her outstretched hand. She carefully places the snowflake onto her tongue and she is transported to the flower field that she sees in her dreams.

Cassidy is there and her mother is braiding her hair, while she is telling her a story about how the Tartarians joined forced with an evil race, called the Phoenicians, in order to over throw their one *true enemy.*

'But mommy, why must we hate them so, if their hearts are so pure?' Cassidy asks confused and pulls the petals off a dainty purple flower.

'I don't know sweetheart, we are just told to hate them and we don't question what we are told. Why would we? Our leaders only want the best for us, they would never lie to us?' She answers robotically.

Her response seems rehearsed and it bothers Bonnie. Why don't they question anything? Everything should be questioned, this is the only way to ensure you always know the truth, she thinks to herself.

Father walks up to them and hands them each a bunch of freshly picked flowers.

'Wow, these are gorgeous Geenly, thank you.' She says and finishes braiding Cassidy's hair.

He sits down in front of Cassidy and touches her soft and sweet face with his big, protective hands.

'We don't hate them, at least not for long, your sister will unite us and she will save us all.' He looks over in the direction where Bonnie is standing and she stretches her hand out to him, her finger tips longing to feel him for just a short moment. He smiles at her and blows her a kiss.

'Go now child, we don't have much time!' He says to her, but not with his mouth through words, rather with his thoughts. Bonnie is conflicted, she doesn't want to leave them, her heart tells her to stay, but her mind knows she must leave.

A tsunami of emotion floods over her and she is gasping for air. She calms her thoughts and she is suddenly back in the river and the water is touching her this time. She swims along with the current until she sees Malcom waiting at the edge of the river for her. The golden fish reappear and swim happily around her and help guide her to where she needs to go and she reaches out her hand for him to grab hold of her.

His grip is strong and he yanks her hard and out of the water. He pulls her up close to him and holds her in his arms. She is cold and completely naked he and tries to cover her with his arms as best he can.

She looks up into his eyes and they are hollow. It is not Malcom, but merely a shell of him, his soul – *he is missing.*

'Malcom!' She pushes him away from her and he crumbles into a heap of dust in front of her, exactly the way he is supposed to if she killed him.

Bonnie is growing tired of the games and she lays her hands on her stomach and she can feel her babies growing weary and impatient too. She knows she has to leave this place and find Cassiel, but how? She calls out to the universe or mother nature, to anyone that will just listen and let her leave the Underneath and get back to Malcom and Henry.

'I come in peace! You can sense my true intentions, please show me the way and let me leave. I need to find Cassiel, will you show me?' There is nothing, but more silence. 'Please!' She whispers.

She looks around and everything has gone completely pitch black. A single blue butterfly appears suddenly, flies up to her and lands on her shoulder. It makes a sound that she doesn't understand, but it sounds like a trumpet of hope and power.

It grows large suddenly, three times the size of her and she climbs on to. She is no longer naked, but wearing a tight-fitting blue dress, with long sleeves and golden coat.

'The colours of the Tartarian Empire,' the butterfly proudly announces and takes off, while the sun starts to rise and the sky turns a soft blue.

They are not moving, but the breeze on her face tells her that they are and millions of small blue butterflies appear all around her. She looks down at her arms and she is holding her two new born babies. They are each wrapped in golden blankets and are fast asleep. *They are perfect.*

'I name you Amile and Amelia.' She says and smiles, with her heart bursting with pride.

They arrive at the top of a snowy mountain and the butterfly sets her down gently. It hovers for a moment and then it flies away, together with all the others butterflies in perfect harmony.

'Mother, where are we going?' A timid little voice asks. Startled and confused, Bonnie looks down and realises that she is holding each of their little hands in hers. They are already five years old and she wonders where the time has gone? They look like her, their hair is golden blonde, with small curls and their eyes are as blue at the bluest ocean.

'Malcom, where is Malcom?' She asks the universe in that moment and she can feel a presence behind her. Her body doesn't tense up and she knows it is not an enemy, but a friend, a lost soul that she needs to reunite with.

'Cassiel?'

She turns around to face him and fate shows her what was supposed to be. She was supposed to be *his.*

She is dressed in a gold-coloured gown, which is covered in crystals and pearls and she sees him waiting for her with his hand stretched out.

'Come.' He says gently and she follows the sound of his voice without any doubt or concern. He is standing in front of the Tree of Life and she knows her destiny was him. He was to be her husband and they were to rule the Empire together, after King Finn and Queen Ariella. She smiles at him, but stops walking down the aisle.

'I am sorry Cassiel. This was destiny, but it is no more,' she tells him and slips the ring off of her finger and lays it down gently onto the floor, at her feet.

He smiles that he understands, nods in approval and she runs as fast as she can to go and find Malcom.

She arrives in a medium-sized town, walks straight into the town square and there are thousands of people gathered waiting for *her*. She walks up the stairs to balcony and gazes at the view of all the Tartarians who came to see *her*.

'My name is Daphne and I am looking for my husband. Where is he?' She asks the crowd.

A man appears from the middle of the crowd and stops in front of the balcony and looks up towards her. He looks like Malcom and starts to grin at the sight of her.

'I am your true husband, according to destiny,' he replies, but his eyes are not green, they are hazel brown.

She walks down towards him and touches his face. 'Destiny abandoned us a very long time ago, now take me to him,' she orders.

He leads her into a city of over a million people, that is just down the valley from the town she was in. They have built this city in the middle of uninhabitable plain of ice and snow and it defies all logic. There is a big star fort at the entrance and free energy flows around them and lights up the entire area. It is freezing cold and there is ice and thick snow everywhere, but she is warm.

'Is this what is what like before they came? Is this the Old World?' Her eyes trace his in awe and amazement.

'Yes, many of us have retained our way of life here and they can't find or harm us. The snow hides us well and protects us,' he replies.

'But they will find you eventually, you can't hide for ever!' She replies and bends down to touch the snow. It is cold to the touch, but she can hold it, without it hurting her hand.

'Yes, at some point our luck with run out, but it won't be today.' He says and guides her to a red face-brick, five-story building. It reminds her of the hotel she stayed in when she was in New York with Malcom. It has the same fine details and she can appreciate and admire the superb workmanship of those who built it.

It is just as breath-taking inside, as it is on the outside. It is decorated with gold ornaments and the staircase is made out of marble.

'This is how we conduct the free energy that we harness from mother nature,' he says and points to the gold ornaments that are strategically places above them on the ceiling and roof. There is an organ above a fireplace and she chuckles at the sight of it.

'That metal thing, with all the pipes, what is that?' She asks eagerly and her eyes burn with fire.

'We use that to harness the free energy. Everything has a frequency, it is what gives everything its shape, just like a snow-flake. Change the frequency and the shape will change too. The organ sends out the right frequency for all the different types of free energy. For example, there is a certain energy that will create electricity, but we use a completely different one for heat and to regulate the temperature. Do you understand?' He asks her.

'Yes, it is amazing. I didn't realise how complex it all is. What I don't understand is why mother nature just gave up on us like that? She chose the Heaven Bearers over us and it makes no sense!' She pauses briefly and anger runs through her like a flooded river. 'She deserves to die for her betrayal!'

'Do you think you deserve to die for causing the mud flood?' He replies and give her a soft smile.

She goes pale white and doesn't say a word. 'How?' She clears her throat. 'How do you know about that?' She asks and her eyes fill with tears. She wipes them away and notices a silhouette of a man in the corner of her eye.

'Father!' Amile cries out and together with Amelia runs towards him and he embraces them gently.

He hasn't aged a single day; he looks exactly the same as she remembers him and this confuses her. It has been five years. She sees a mirror and looks at her own reflection, touching her face to make sure it is real.

'You haven't aged a day either Bonnie,' he says, but she doesn't go towards him yet. She notices Henry and he is standing at the edge of the staircase with a smile on his face and he is holding a baby in his arms. His young Tartarian wife is standing by his side and Bonnie is happy for him.

She feels the peace and harmony all around her, every single person here is living in equilibrium with mother nature and there is only happiness.

She runs up to Malcom and finally embraces him. 'I have missed you so much!' She tells him and kisses him passionately, but his lips seem strange.

She looks at his face and he is grinning. She pulls away from him suddenly and he starts to twitch and lick his lips and she knows it isn't Malcom. Bonnie rolls her eyes and starts to laugh out sarcastically. There is an undertone of anger in her laugh and everything around her fades away into fine, white dust and blows away with the wind.

'Nice try Azrael, but I am more powerful than you think!' She closes her eyes tight and tells herself that it is now time to get back to the others. She focuses on Malcom and attempts to spot him in her mind. It takes her a while until she can hear his voice, but she can sense that he is close. She locks onto his aura and holds onto it as hard as she can. She finally opens her eyes and she is standing in front of an ocean. It is cold and she has Malcom and Henry standing next to her. She is still pregnant and she has no idea where she is, but she knows she is far away from *Tartaria.*

'Where are we?' She asks and grabs hold of Malcom's hand.

CHAPTER SEVENTEEN

'I am exhausted, can we find somewhere to rest?' She asks them and Malcom can see the exhaustion on her face.

Bonnie isn't sure where she was or why she experienced what she did, but it made her feel uneasy and worried for the first time. She was gone for four hours and had Malcom and Henry absolutely frantic with worry. Both Malcom and Henry arrived in this place at the same time, but she was nowhere to be seen. They searched everywhere for her and eventually didn't know what else to do but wait. Malcom knew she would show up eventually and she did.

'I don't know what to expect, but I'm worried Malcom.' Her eyes reflect her worry and pain and the bright blue colour is cold and faded. 'We need to head to the mountains tomorrow, I can feel a storm is coming and it will be a bad one.'

There is a crackling cold in the air and she huddles up closer to him, hoping his warmth will keep her from feeling so cold and alone.

Her shoulders are heavy and sore, she has been carrying this intense weight of having created the mud flood, of killing all the Tartarians and she can't do anything about it. Will saving them now somehow be her redemption?

Her stomach is growling, she is starving with hunger, but there is nothing here to eat. There are no rocks, trees, plants or animals anywhere.

'There is nothing here!' Henry mutters under his breath and glances over at Malcom. 'What are we going to do!? He gets up and starts kicking at the snow on the ground in frustration. 'We are lost Bonnie, you got us lost Bonnie! I thought you were our saviour, where are we?' He is upset and starts to panic and throws himself onto the floor. She crawls over to him and rubs her hand over his back gently and starts to hum *that* lullaby. It calms him and he stops crying and that blue butterfly that she saw earlier lands on her hand that is placed on his back. She carries on humming and watches as more and more butterflies descend down onto them and they light up their surroundings to revealing a hidden door among the vast nothingness.

It is big, at least four-metres high and it has no door handle.

'Henry, get up quickly!' She looks over at Malcom and he is already walking towards it. He runs his hands over it carefully. It emits a pale, blue light and gives him a sharp electric shock.

'Ouch!' He pulls his hand away and rubs the spot where the door shocked him on his hand.

The door is made out of wood, silver in colour and has a soft texture. She sticks out her index finger and traces her finger from the right to the left of it slowly and watches how a drop of blood trickles down it.

'It is soft, but it is sharp, almost like it is covered in a million pieces of broken glass.' She isn't talking to Malcom or Henry, but to herself, almost as if she is thinking out loud. 'What is it that you want from me? Cassiel, we are here, we would like to enter,' she says and continues to inspect it.

'It is tiny pieces of diamond,' Malcom says after taking a good look at the stones.

'What did you say? She asks and glances at him with a

frown.

Malcom's statement has caught her full attention. 'Did you say it is covered in diamonds?'

He nods, but doesn't see the importance in that statement.

'Diamonds, diamonds, diamonds!' She screams and sighs out loud. She is very frustrated now and it feels as if she should know what to do. 'What am I not seeing? I am so tired of all these riddles. Why can't it just open? I am Daphne, the niece of King Finn, it should know this and open the moment it senses my presence!'

She sits down in front of the door and has now too admitted defeat. 'I am out of ideas Malcom.'

The ground starts to tremor and the ice shakes loose to reveal that they are sitting on a frozen lake and she can see the golden fish, with the red fins, glowing and swimming around beneath the water.

'Those fish, I saw them earlier, when I was stuck in that place. What do they mean?' She asks with intrigue as she stares at them. Malcom and Henry look at her perplexed and keep staring at the door to try and figure out a way to open it.

She sees a very big fish, it is at least twice the size of the other fish and it swims towards the door and crashes hard into it.

The earth shakes again and she braces herself against the ice layer on top of the lake.

'Move back!' She screams and kicks her feet up against the door to give herself enough distance from it. And, in that very moment, the heavy right side of the door swings open and crushes the ice in front of it, with the swinging motion of it opening.

This causes a ripple effect and the rest of the ice begins to crack and drop off, piece by piece, into the freezing lake.

'Malcom!' She can feel herself dropping off of a slippery block of ice and she lands into the freezing cold water.

'I can't swim!' She screams and bobs her out of the water

and tries to catch a breath of air, but her dress is heavy, now that it is wet and Malcom can't reach her. She feels the fish swimming all around her and she calls out to them for help. They understand her and work together to push her up and out of the water. This gives her the opportunity to take a deep breath and cough out the water that started to fill up her lungs.

Malcom and Henry dash towards the door. With only a moment to spare, Malcom grabs her by the sleeve of her dress and tugs her up into his arms and almost levitates with her inside. The door slams shut behind them and they fall to the hard ground! They can hear how the rest of the ice crumbles away on the other side and they get up and onto their feet, breathless and in shock at what just transpired.

'Bonnie, look!' Henry shouts and walks ahead of them. She follows his footsteps and realises that they are in paradise.

'Wow! Malcom, I think we made it,' she says as she stares at Henry, he is smiling from ear to ear.

Malcom doesn't share her enthusiasm and isn't smiling. He has a concerned expression on his face and he is analysing his surroundings.

'This can't be real, this doesn't exist,' he mutters to himself and feels a sharp pain suddenly.

He turns to her and reaches for his neck in confusion and blood starts dripping down his neck.

Paradise disappears and she sees Cassiel standing fifty meters away from them, with a bunch of other men. He is standing with is left leg perched up on a rock in front of him and he is holding a round and spikey blade in each hand.

Bonnie understands what is happening and she tries to reach over for Malcom when time suddenly stands still, except *not* for Cassiel. He leaps forward and grabs her by the neck and throws her across the empty space where she was standing. She starts to move uncontrollably in the direction he throws her, only to stop mid air and swing right back at him and she gently lands on her feet. Her eyes turn a dark and luminous blue and she gives off an electric shock that makes Cassiel and his men drop to the floor in agony. Cassiel fights her and she can feel he is strong, but she is stronger and she keeps him pinned down to the ground.

She tries to regain her composure, but she is emotional and Malcom is slowly bleeding out with a gaping hole in his neck. She lunges towards him and tries to stop the bleeding, but there is a lot of blood and she can't save him. He smiles at her and tries to tell her something, but he is choking on the blood that has filled his throat and lungs. He reaches for her and she can *feel* what he is trying to say and she suddenly remembers what he told her. *Phoenicians don't die easily and you have to pierce their heart*, is what he told her. Her body relaxes completely and so does the intensity of the electric current pulsing through her and radiating over the barren plain that they are in.

Cassiel musters up all the strength he has left and reaches up his hand in attempt for her to stop what she is doing.

'Please!' He begs and places his hand back down on the ground and grabs hold of the sand.

She is angry now, he tried to kill Malcom and she focuses her gaze completely onto him. The blue in her eyes changes and it becomes ice cold and dreary.

'Bonnie, stop!' Malcom suddenly grabs her by her shoulders and shakes her roughly to get her to snap out of it. 'This isn't you, you are not a killer, stop this now!'

Her eyes don't change colour and he can feel her body tense up more. He gives her a big kiss and tries to penetrate her mind with his. 'Remember who you are Bonnie and what you came here for!'

She bites his lip and tries to push him away. She wants to kill Cassiel, she can't stop her rage and her body is on autopilot.

'Bonnie stop!' Malcom tries one more time to reach her with his mind and get her to realise what she is doing.

Her eyes flash gold and she suddenly snaps out of her rage and looks down at the floor.

'My water just broke!'

Cassiel and his men slowly get up and cautiously move towards her to take a look at the Tartarian girl that is going to save them and restore the Tartarian Empire to its former glory.

'Welcome Daphne, I apologise for our initial introduction, but I had to be sure. You are not the first to try and fulfil the prophesy,' he says as he glances over her and avoids the Phoenician that is holding her hand. He can see they love each other and he can't bear the sight and turns his head away in disgust.

starts panting and clutches onto Malcom. 'They are coming! She cries out while laughing and her grip is so strong, it would crush a steal pipe.

The birthing process is quick and she is in labour for only a few minutes. The sound of the crying babies, a girl and a boy, cause the sky to turn dark and a single powerful lighting strike lands just metres away from where they are gathered. It strikes the ground hard and causes a slight shock wave, that causes the air to turn bright red.

'It has begun!' Cassiel looks out into the distance with a grave look and knows that there is no turning back now.

'What has begun?' Malcom asks concerned.

'Our final struggle for survival! Amile and Amelia are our only hope and we need to make sure to keep them safe.

'You have already named them?' He snaps and grabs onto Cassiel. Malcom is surprised and instantly jealous. These Humans are his and he will name them, not some Tartarian! He feels Bonnie's gaze on him and his anger subsides.

Cassiel gently takes Malcom's clenched hand off of his arm and smiles.

'No, I did not name them, but she did.' He looks at Bonnie and Malcom follows his gaze and notices her smile. It is warm and infectious and he knows everything was prewritten by the universe. He helps her onto her feet and they walk the three miles back to the *city* of the resistance. It is a long walk, but Bonnie is walking on air. Every step she takes, feels as if she is floating. She has a bounce in her step and she is not wanting or needing anything anymore, *she has it all.*

Amelia is staring at him and he can't pull his gaze away from her. She has deep-blue eyes like her mother, with a light purple halo around them. They remind him of Rune's eyes, even though his were green.

'I wonder if I will still have these powers now that I have given birth? I mean I am sure it was them that gave me the ability to do the things I did? I would have noticed if I had powers at the Foundling Home, if they were truly mine.' She is almost talking to herself, but her expression tells him she wants him to answer her.

'I really don't know, you weren't supposed to have any powers in the first place. Tartarians don't have powers, but you think you caused the mud flood, so I really can't say. Time will tell –' He pauses suddenly. 'I wouldn't have loved you any less, if that is your concern?'

'No, it is not. But how?' She pauses and isn't quite sure how to phrase what she wants to say. 'How can I protect them now if I don't have any powers? Perhaps they have powers?' She turns her head towards him and crinkles her nose, then pouts her lips and he can't help but love her madly in this moment.

It is my job to protect you and that is what I will be doing from now on. Can you trust in that, in us?' He asks and gives her an intense kiss that immediately reassures her completely that she is safe with him.

'Yes. Would you like to take her? I can tell you really want to?'

He laughs. 'Are you reading my mind, by any chance?' He asks jokingly, while she shrugs and hands him Amelia.

They reach the settlement and it is bigger than either of them could have imagined.

'There must be over a hundred thousand people here?' She is perplexed and Cassiel decides to explain what happened.

'Many Tartarians fled after the Heaven Bearers took control of Earth. Queen Ariella tried to get word out that there were a few prominent families that made it all the way out here. We, my family was one of the families she managed to reach before she was taken prisoner and murdered in cold blood.' He pauses and can't help but show his disdain for the Phoenician race, Malcom in particular, since he is her bastard child. He catches himself and carries on with his story. 'Anyway, over the years more people showed up here and they kept coming and coming. We could not, we had no right to turn anyone away and so we didn't. But as we got bigger in size, it became more difficult to hide. We had to get creative and well, I have some abilities, albeit not quite like yours.' He admits and gives her an envious smile.

'What? I thought that only King Finn's bloodline contained special powers?' Malcom asks surprised.

'Not completely, his bloodline is the most powerful, but there are others.' He replies and exudes arrogance.

Malcom watches him carefully and notices the way he looks at Bonnie, the way his eyes light up when he speaks to her. He knows that destiny would have brought them together and he can't help but wonder if destiny will prevail at some point in the future? What needs to happen in order for Bonnie to be with Cassiel, he wonders? He knows the answer to this and realises, in that moment, that it is inevitable, he will die in the coming war.

A middle-aged woman is walking down the road in the far distance. She is carrying an empty wicker basket and Bonnie imagines it is filled with some purple flowers and thinks about her mother. She drops the basket at the sight of Bonnie and comes running down the hill, as fast as her feet can take her!

'Daphne!' She calls at the top of her lungs. 'Daphne, is that you!?'

Bonnie is drawn to her, she hands Amile to Henry and runs to meet this lady half way. They stop and take a good look at each other before she takes Bonnie into her full embrace.

'My darling girl!' She takes another look at her. 'I knew I would see you again, I just knew it!'

She takes her hand in hers, gives it a soft kiss and they

walk hand in hand back to Cassiel and his men.

'Cassiel, did I not say this day would come?' She says and her eyes are filled to the brim with joy.

'Yes, you did Mira. You kept a lot to yourself, however.' He reprimands her gently and doesn't elaborate further.

She doesn't know what he means, but understands when she sees Malcom standing there with a new born baby in his arms and she immediately pulls out a dagger and tries to stab him in the heart.

Bonnie merely raises her index finger in defiance and the dagger drops out of hand and falls to the floor, as if she was a glowing, hot stone.

Mira looks over at Bonnie in horror!

'No, Daphne no! They are, he is an abomination, you need to let me do this!' She shouts at her and her eyes are wild with hatred.

'No mother, he is not an abomination and neither are my children.' She takes a step closer and looks at her in an intimidating fashion, her eyes flash gold and she watches the expression on her mother's face. She leans into her and places her hand on the side of her face. 'If you ever try to hurt either one of them again, I will kill all of you.' She breaks eye contact with her and can *feel* that Cassiel heard every word that she said and she is glad.

'The Phoenician and the Humans are out of bounds to all of you! Is that understood?' She raises her voice now and she can feel the power running through her veins and it scares her. 'The only way we can take back what is rightly ours is by working with the Phoenicians. Should any of you not agree, then leave now and find your own way!' She commands. Everyone, in the entire camp, can hear what she is saying even though she is far away from some and they drop what they are doing to listen. 'I have heard about the prophesy and I know what was dictated, but the prophesy isn't accurate. I am here and I will die fighting for you, but you need to work with me!'

No one knows what to say in response to her and she eyes

Cassiel sternly. He is their leader now and at some point, he will have to relinquish his leadership, or at the very least, he will have to share his leadership with her, until the war is won. She isn't interested in being a ruler, but she is the chosen one and she can't change that. He makes eye contact with her and then arrogantly takes a step forward to address his people.

'Daphne has spoken and we shall respect her wishes. She is the niece of our beloved King Finn and we shall welcome her as we would have welcomed him. Clearly – 'He pauses and clenches his jaw tightly and quickly tries to adjust his composure. 'There is more to the prophesy than was told to us.' He paces up and down. 'If anyone harms a hair on their heads, and that includes the Phoenician, you will hang like they hung your forefathers. Is that understood?'

'Yes.' The crowd is unanimous and Bonnie is amazed by the respect he holds among these people.

'Thank you Cassiel, now I really need to have a word in private, if you don't mind? And some food for my husband and Henry, would be much appreciated.' She smiles and places her hand softly onto his arm, much to his delight.

'Of course. Tara, please fetch Keera and prepare for them the best of whatever you can find,' he commands and a young girl appears from nowhere and she can't help but stare at him with absolute love and admiration in her eyes. Tara nods happily and marches off to do as he asked.

'You bring these people...you bring us all hope. It hasn't been easy and, well if I am completely honest, I wasn't completely sure that you even existed. But, now that you do, you shock me even more with your ways.' He says that last sentence with such emphasis, that is overpowers the rest of his thoughts in that moment.

He looks uncomfortable, but decides to go ahead and ask her what is on his mind. 'How can you love that creature?' He asks and he can't help but cringe at the very thought of her letting him touch her. 'Your rightful place is with a Tartarian man, you know this Daphne. What you are doing, what you *choose* to do is against our entire way of life. We are proud of *our race.*'

She knows what he is trying to say, she was supposed to be his. That is what destiny wanted, but mother nature changed the order of things when she broke the covenant and let the Heaven Bearers take over Earth.

'As you should be Cassiel.' She goes silent and cold and her eyes lose that sparkle. 'I hated him for some time and then one day I didn't. I didn't make the conscience decision at the time to marry him. I did as I was told and quite frankly, I didn't know any better!' The wind picks up and then immediately dies down again and her eyes turn bright blue. 'You know they can feel emotions just like us,' she replies nonchalantly and then begins to smile. 'They are not all that different from us you know. I mean technically, they are *half us*. We have no right to hate them!' Her reply makes perfect sense and Cassiel looks at her surprised and doesn't believe what she is telling him.

'He is my destiny and no one will change that. With time, you and your people will come to terms with that somehow.' She gives him a small smile, but her statement is a warning to him.

They continue to walk in silence until she stops abruptly and pulls him to the side.

'I have been having these dreams, vivid dreams. It was like I was there when the Heaven Bearers took over Earth. I saw what they did, how they slaughtered our people. Worse, I could literally feel the pain and suffering. Fear was everywhere, it was unbearable!'

He listens carefully, but brushes off what she says as a mere nightmare and carries on walking.

Bonnie remains where she is and he eventually realises this and stops still facing forward.

'Bonnie, you were a child, barely a year old. You couldn't possibly remember –'

'Except I do.' She interrupts him. 'I remember my mom picking flowers with my sister, Cassidy and I remember my father. I remember the mud flood. I remember them.'

He pricks up his ears at the sound of the word *mud flood* and interrupts her immediately. 'What do you know about the mud flood?' He barks and she can see the mere mention of it makes him angry. He is suddenly filled with hate and she flinches slightly.

'I know that I caused it somehow!' She snaps back at him and shows him he can't intimidate her. 'I don't know how, but they were going after my mother and she was screaming and I tried to help and then I did something. I saw how the sand partials started to lift off of the ground, in slow motion and it started to rain and it didn't stop raining.'

Cassiel turns around to face her and he is trying to process what she is telling him. It can't be, he tells himself. But he knows she is powerful and he can't automatically dismiss what she is claiming, not after experiencing what she did earlier.

'Who have you told about this?' He asks and postures himself like this is classified information.

She shrugs. 'Malcom knows of course, but I haven't shouted it from the rooftops for the Earth to hear! I think Azrael knows, that is why he is after me now. He was under the impression I was dead. I don't know why he thought this?'

'What?!' His eyes glimmer with shock and he grabs her by the shoulders. 'Bonnie, you do know who Azrael is, don't you?' His posture changes suddenly and he takes her in his arms.

'Yes, of course, why?' She is pushing him away from her, but he locks eyes with her, hoping this is his way in. His way, to get her to finally *want him.*

'That thing, Malcom, he is Azrael's son. Did you know that?' He is suddenly angry and happy at the same time and his demeanour makes her angry. 'Tell me, how do you think your husband would feel if we killed his creator. His father?' He asks excitedly and he wants to kiss her.

She starts to laugh sarcastically at how pathetic he is behaving. 'I guess we will have to ask him, but I am sure King Finn would very much like his body back!' She responds and he lets go of her immediately. Her response surprises her, just as much as it does him and she is amazed by what she suddenly knows.

'What did you just say?' Cassiel is angry. 'You ought to be careful how you talk about the King!'

'Relax Cassiel, he is my uncle in case you forgot. I can feel him, he still there. Not all of the hosts give up and die. King Finn is still fighting to get rid of Azrael, which will be to our advantage soon.' She replies and is distracted by movement. There is a woman staring at them just above the hill, she is trying to eavesdrop and Bonnie looks over at her.

'Who is that woman over there?'

'That is your sister, now go say hello,' he orders her with a smile and walks back towards the settlement with his hands in his pockets and his head down.

Bonnie told him a lot that he didn't want to hear and it will take some time for him to process all of this new information and truly understand what it is that he is supposed to do. He bears a great burden, he is the leader of almost one hundred thousand people, all of whom look to him for guidance, their safety and survival.

Bonnie watches him walk away from her and for a brief moment, she wonders what life would have been like had destiny prevailed. She thinks about the vision Azrael showed her of Tartaria and her wedding day, the day she was supposed to *marry Cassiel.* She knows he would have been good to her, but she can't bare the thought of not having Malcom in her life.

She squints her eyes and searches for Malcom down the hill in the settlement, she wants to know what he is doing. Her eyes scan the settlement quickly, pacing through all the people and the makeshift-homes, scattered all over the place. The people are hungry and tired. There are holes in their clothing, they are dirty and poor. *Wretched souls*.

They are refugees, with nowhere to go and it makes her blood boil with anger. She can hear babies crying and she thinks about Amile and Amelia and starts to look for them frantically.

She hears happy laughter and *that* voice and she follows it. Malcom and Henry are seated at a small, wooden table, eating some deer stew and are deep in conversation. She doesn't bother listening to what they are talking about, she is merely content that they are getting along and she can hear her babies breathing softly in the small crib beside Malcom.

She closes her eyes and lets the moment of contentment fill her veins, then turns around and prepares to meet her beloved sister.

CHAPTER EIGHTEEN

'Daphne? I can't believe it is you!' She is jumping for joy and gives Bonnie the biggest hug that she has ever received.

'Mother told me stories about you, but they were just stories you know?' She touches her face and gives her cheek a little squeeze. 'I just want to make sure you are real,' she teases.

'How.' She shakes her head in utter disbelief. 'How did you and mother make it here? I thought you were dead?' She replies and crinkles her nose and frowns hard.

Cassidy's voice gets soft and she grabs her by the arm. 'Come with me Daphne, quickly!' She drags Bonnie by the arm and hurries down the back of the hill, without looking back at her once.

They walk a good fifteen minutes from where they were, until she stops and huddles behind some rocks. Sleet starts falling and Bonnie looks up into the sky.

'The clouds are rolling in, are we getting a storm?' She says out loud, but she isn't really asking Cassidy, rather she is talking to herself.

'Much more than that! We don't have long at all; we were desperately waiting for you and now you are finally here!' She looks around her suddenly and feels uncomfortable. 'I'm not sure what is going on, I'm not privy to many things, but I feel like I should warn you. I just don't know what about. Just don't trust anyone okay?' She grabs Bonnie by the arm and squeezes hard. 'I am serious Daphne.'

'Okay, Cassidy!' She replies sternly and lets her mind have a peek at her thoughts. She starts to smile and chuckle, Cassidy has done a lot of eaves dropping over the years. She comes across a memory of Cassiel and her mother. She is busy gathering some wood and, on her way back to the camp, she hears whispering. She puts the wood down quickly and takes a few steps closer, trying her best not to make a sound. To her surprise it is her mother and Cassiel and they are fighting about something.

'She will come Cassiel and she will yours, the prophesy says so!'

'You say this every year!' He barks back at her. 'I am tired of waiting, if she isn't here soon, I will take another and make her my wife. I am Cassiel the Great and I will lead my people back to their former glory!' He says proudly.

Bonnie realises just how arrogant he is and knows that destiny wasn't destiny at all. It was a mere wish. Cassiel was never meant to rule the Kingdom, he has no humility and it would prove to be worthless to a people who choose not to be ruled.

The sleet starts to turn to snow and she can feel the small snowflakes land on her head and gently brush past her face. She looks up at the sky and loses the memory she was watching. She looks for it, she needs to know what happened, but suddenly can't find it among all the rest. She blinks hard and snaps back to reality, to Cassidy.

'Has anyone mentioned anything about me, stuff I should know about myself, but don't?' She asks and realises Cassidy has been staring at her the entire time.

She shakes her head as if confused by her and the question. 'Like what exactly?' She asks and wipes the snow from her hair.

The day of the mud flood bothers Bonnie, she remembers her mom lying on the floor, fighting for her life and she saw Azrael coming towards her and then the mud flood happened. What really happened that day, she wonders?

'Do you know what happened the day of the mud flood?' She asks Cassidy casually.

'No, not really, I just know the usual stories, you know?'

Bonnie shakes her head slowly. 'I'm not sure, maybe tell me quickly?' She prompts her gently and Cassidy takes the bait.

'Okay,' she leans in and gets all excited to tell the story. Bonnie can tell that she has re-told this story or at the very least has heard it, many times. She is curious what she will hear come out of her mouth.

'So mother, well father actually, fought off those wretched creatures as best he could, but there is this one creature, he is stronger than the rest and evil. They call him the angel of death and he is hideous and mean and he has this son, who does his bidding and murders Tartarians for fun. You see he took Queen Ariella as his sex slave and after she had that bastard-killer, he killed her.' She pulls a disgusted face and then her eyes get sad. 'He killed father too. Mother had hidden me along with some other Tartarians fleeing the conflict. She was planning on meeting up with the group later that day, when she was attacked by them. She bravely fought them off, but they snatched you from her arms and she had to let you go.' She places her hand onto Bonnie's cheek and gives her a kiss on the forehead. 'I am sorry Daphne, please don't be mad with mother.'

Cassidy's explanation is all over the place, so it takes a moment for Bonnie to piece it all together properly. She knows a lot more than she realises and it surprises her.

'Oh, dear sister, I always knew I'd see you again. It is written so and I just knew it to be true. I just…'

She looks away and pretends to be distracted by something.

'No please finish.' Bonnie interrupts her and senses something that she doesn't like in her story.

Her happiness quickly disappears and Bonnie realises it was all for show, to distract her, by her playing the loving sister role.

'You won't understand.' She snaps and starts to play with a few pieces of dried wood that she found on the floor and crushes it between her fingers.

'Try me Cassidy. I married a Phoenician, the *bastard-killer*, as you call him. Oh, and I now know that I am the niece of the King and seem to possess powers! Tell me again what I won't understand?' She is getting snappy and irritated by all the games and lack of honestly among these people.

Cassidy isn't completely shocked by what she hears, but she does lean back from her, slightly, as if she is toxic and she doesn't want to risk getting too close to her.

'I have this memory and I never told anyone about it.' She replies quickly and it is obvious now that she is visibly shaken by Bonnie's brutal honesty.

'Go on. I promise I will keep it to myself,' she assures her and relaxes her expression.

'I have this memory of mother and father fighting one night, just before the mud flood happened. They were fighting about you. Father was furious and mother was crying.' She looks unsure of herself, as if perhaps she should stop talking now.

'I'm not father's daughter?' Bonnie guesses and waits for her response.

'Mother was saying that you –' She pauses and wants to leave, but knows she can't. 'You weren't fathers or hers, even though she gave birth to you. She made it sound like she merely carried you in her womb, but that she didn't know who your real parents were. I know it makes no sense.'

Bonnie's face cringes in response to what she is saying and she shakes her head in confusion.

'What? How does that make any sense? What do you think about that story? What does your gut tell you Cassidy? When you look at me, what do you see? Do you see some weird person or do you see your baby sister?' She asks loudly and tries to control the sudden shame and anger that is pulsing through her.

Cassidy crinkles her nose, shrugs her shoulders awkwardly and starts to chew her thumb nail nervously. Bonnie knows what she is thinking and she takes a little peek into her head. Cassidy thinks she is *something else* and she is scared of her.

They sit and stare at the settlement. The wind slowly picks up its pace and it causes the snows to blow in whirlwinds around them. She watches the snow fight the wind and struggle to find a spot to land on the ground and she finds it relaxed and inspiring. Bonnie replays that memory of the fight between her parents in her head and stares blankly at the vast nothingness all around her.

'Where there is a will there is a way! Even the snow manages to land despite knowing the wind is stronger,' she blurts out and Cassidy doesn't know what she should say in response to her statement. She watches Bonnie and can see she is physically present, but not mentally and she just watches her wondering what, who she really is?

Mother is shouting and crying in the vision and she can't catch her breath. She is hysterical and worried and her hands are shaking with panic. 'There is something wrong with her, her eyes change colour, she can read my memories, I can feel it!' She shouts at her husband in absolute horror.

'You are overreacting Mira, she is a baby, our baby. She is no different to her sister sitting in the next room. You need to stop this now! This isn't healthy for anyone.' He replies, trying his very best to calm the situation.

'No! That baby, she is evil, I can't bear to look at her!' The tears have stopped and her eyes turn cold and all the love that was in them disappears.

Father tries to touch her face, but she smacks his hand away. 'Don't touch me!' She wipes her hand over her wet face and looks at him, deeply into his eyes. Her eyes are burning with hatred and she grabs onto his arm. 'We need to get rid of her! We need to do something before people start to notice what she is.' The expression on her face is stern and serious and he can't believe she is willing to abandon her child.

'I will take the child. I will not let you get rid of her; mother nature will never forgive you if you do this! I will never forgive you for this!' He snaps. His eyes are filled with tears and pain, she has made him choose between her and his daughter. He closes his eyes and realises the decision is, in fact, an easy one.

He takes her hand off of his, turns his back on her and walks away to check on Bonnie. She is lying in her crib and she is staring at the ceiling, her eyes are golden in colour and it seems like she is watching something up there. She is giggling and he looks up at the ceiling, but he can't see anything and his heart is filled with love for her. He rubs her little cheek and vows to take care of her, *no matter what.*

Bonnie hears little feet walking away and the memory goes blank. She is saddened by what she just learnt and she doesn't know what to make of it. After all this time she thought her mother loved her dearly and all she ever wanted, wished and hoped for, was to see her mother. *Just one more time,* she used to think and feels so stupid suddenly. It was her father that loved her unconditionally, not her mother.

'We need to head back, I need to check on my children,' she says suddenly and realises that is it snowing a lot harder now.

'You have children? As in children with that –' She catches herself. 'You have Human children?' Cassidy is surprised by this news. 'The prophesy says you would be pregnant but that would it be Cassiel's child,' she replies and emphasises the singular aspect of the word *child.* She proceeds to get up slowly and pulls a confused face.

'The prophesy seems to have gotten many things wrong, or I am not the one,' Bonnie replies and starts to walk back to the settlement.

Cassidy sticks out her tongue to taste a bit of snow and mumbles softly as she watches her walk away. 'No, I know you are the one sister.'

Malcom is waiting for her inside a little cave that they had prepared as best as they could for them, on the far right-hand side of the camp. It is quiet out here and private. Bonnie is grateful for the privacy. There is thin mattress on the floor, made out of some kind of thin plant or bark, she isn't sure and a warm blanket made from different items of clothing sown together.

'This is a far cry from the mansion and what you were able to provide for me.' She pouts and gives out a slight sigh. 'This place is depressing and it is always snowing. I am amazed that they found a way to feed so many people.' She lays down next to him and snuggles up to him. 'I am very glad you are here with me, my life would be worthless without you in it.'

He plays with her hair and looks over at their children and can't help but feel the same as she does.

'I don't like feeling Bonnie. What have you done to me?' He asks her softly and means every word that comes out of his mouth.

'Nothing Malcom, you were always capable of emotions. I just needed to show you how to access them and so I did.' She gives him a long and drawn out kiss and breathes him in.

'I think we should get some rest, I am exhausted,' she says as she closes her eyes tight and places her hand softly onto his chest.

Bonnie sleeps solidly until her body is fully rested. Amile and Amelia are quiet and content and they wait for their mother to wake up before they start to crave her attention. They don't cry or get anxious or even restless, they don't *need* to cry.

Bonnie wakes up and looks over at them. 'Good morning my babies!' She says and sits up with fright once she realises something is wrong with them. She rubs her eyes thinking she only imagined what she just saw and her heart is racing. She looks back over at them and she is speechless and perplexed.

'Malcom, sweetheart?' She calls, with a broken voice. He notices there is panic and worry in it and can't imagine what could be wrong.

'Malcom, please come here!' She shouts more firmly.

There is a shadow at the entrance of the cave and she can feel the freezing cold air come inside, as he enters.

'Something is very wrong with our children,' she says and he can see her hands are trembling and her face is pale white. He walks up closer and dusts off the snow from his hair and shoulders, not taking her particularly seriously.

'What is the problem? Hmm, let us have a little look.' He pauses and stares at Amile and Amelia in utter amazement. He closes his eyes and opens them again and is completely bewildered by what is sitting in front of him.

'How is this possible?' He asks and he tries to make sense of what he is seeing.

'I have no idea, but I am not merely seeing things, am I?' She asks.

'No.' He bends down and strokes Amile on his cheek. 'Is there something about this in the prophesy?' He asks and looks back at her

'I don't know.' She shakes her head. 'To be honest, I am not sure there is such a thing in the prophesy at all, I mean how could there be, this isn't normal!?' Her mind replays that memory from Cassidy that she saw yesterday and she remembers what her mother said. *She isn't normal and is pure evil!*

'What do you mean? Everyone has heard about the prophesy; this must be in it somewhere, surely?' He asks, surprised by her reaction.

'No. I saw a memory from Cassidy and mother was terrified of me. It seems like I had powers as a baby already. The night before the mud flood, my mother wanted to get rid of me and she had a big fight with my father about it. Father naturally refused. But my mother said I was *pure evil!* The morning of the mud flood, she snuck out of the house with me and was preparing to throw me from the Misty Bridge, but she never made it that far. Azrael was suddenly there and I don't know why or what he wanted. I have this memory of her fighting *for me*, but I realise now she was fighting to get away from *them* and fighting for her life. She was not fighting for me at all.' Her tone is soft with the realisation of the ultimate betrayal, something a mother should never do.

'I am sorry Bonnie.' Malcom stands up and gives her a soft kiss and whispers into her ear. 'I will fight for you and them, always. This is a promise I will never break.' He puts his arms around her and they stand staring at their babies.

Amile and Amelia have grown into six-month old babies, even though they are only officially a week old. No one understands why they are growing so fast, in fact, no one has ever experienced such an odd thing and can offer no explanation. Bonnie has no idea either, but her gut tells her that they will help them stop the Heaven Bearers from destroying the Earth and be an important aspect in the coming war.

An entire month goes by and the twins are already five years old. Bonnie is watching them play in the snow and she can't believe what has happened in just one short year. Malcom and Cassiel have become friendly with each other, but they are not friends. They are working with each other to achieve a particular purpose and when that purpose is fulfilled, their friendship will end.

Cassiel has his moments when is angry, envious rather, that he can't have her. She was promised to him and he hasn't come to terms with the fact that this won't happen. Not ever.

Even if Malcom would magically disappear, she has no interest in him and he knows there is nothing he can do that will ever change that. Her heart belongs to a Phoenician and that is the ultimate kick in the teeth. His ego is bruised and he can't shake it, no matter how hard he tries.

'I need to focus on saving my people and killing these wretched leeches for good!' He mutters while he impatiently checks the perimeter around the settlement. 'She will be *mine*!'

He says loudly and looks over at her. It is a warning, not a wish and she knows it.

'Time is getting short; we need to move soon or we will miss our window of opportunity.' He says as Mira picks up some snow and forms it into a snowball. She throws it as far as she can away, from her and they both watch it land and splatter on the floor.

'We have waited this long Cassiel, a few more days won't be the end of us. The twins need to grow still, I don't think she can do it on her own.'

'She?' he snaps! 'She needs me, not those bastard children!' He Scoffs in anger and realises he ought to bite his tongue. He storms off into the deep snow and out of sight.

'She is mine!' He mutters as he walks off into the distance. He knows he needs her, but his ego doesn't want to admit that.

It is late afternoon and the snow has stopped for a short while. Bonnie is resting with the twins inside the cave and she is having another one of her vivid dreams. Except this time, it is not a dream about the past, but about the future and what awaits *them all.*

Something unexpected happens, she is back in the mansion and she returns to her old life. Malcom is in his study preparing his paperwork, while Jane is in the kitchen getting tea and a lemon cream cake ready for afternoon snacks. Amile and Amelia are playing outside in the yard, laughing and mock screaming. Bonnie is standing at the oval shaped window, on the second floor, with the dark blue curtains. She is playing with the tassels on the silver-coloured tie backs, while she watches her children play happily on the neatly mowed lawn. She is pregnant again, with another boy, and he is completely normal and has no powers or special abilities.

The twins no longer possess their powers either and she doesn't know why. They are a normal and happy family, the world did not end and the Tartarian Empire survived the war, just barely. It will take many years in order to repair what was broken, but the Humans, Phoenicians and Tartarians have found a way to co-exist. A new covenant was reached with mother nature and peace and harmony prevails, completely.

She is happy with the ending to the story, but she can never erase that particular day. Their final battle was horrific, in every way, and it cost her so very dearly. She shakes the thought away and tells herself that there is no point in dwelling on it. You can't change the past Bonnie, she tells herself and goes back to watching the twins play. It is summer and the sun is shining, there is a sweetness in the air and the garden is filled with bright, blooming flowers. Malcom walks up behind her and wraps his big and loving arms around her gently, while he kisses the side of her neck.

'Can you believe that they are already three years old?' He asks and kisses her neck some more. His lips are soft and send tiny shock waves through her entire body.

'I am just glad they were lucky enough to have a normal childhood, a clean slate after everything they had to see and do,' she says with a slight undertone of pain in her voice. 'We all lost so much that day.'

'Yes, we did, but look at what we have now.' Malcom moves his hands over her belly and pulls her in closer and up against him. 'How about we head to the bedroom for a few minutes, Jane will keep an eye on them.' He starts kissing her neck more passionately and she can feel the lust in his lips. It is electric and she turns to face him and stares into those luminous green eyes. She starts to kiss him, while her hand wonders down to his belt and she unbuckles it. He pushes her against the wall and lifts her arms above her head. He takes a moment to look at her, just look at her. He finds her so incredibly beautiful, irresistible and he wants her to know this.

'Take me and put me onto the table in the corner of the room,' she orders him.

He picks her up and puts her down on the table gently. Within seconds his hands are under her dress and he can't wait to have her.

She wakes up suddenly to the sound of screeching and she looks around her, forgetting briefly where she is. She listens carefully and lets her eyes scout the settlement to make sure everything is okay. She hears the screeching again and sees that it is merely some boys teasing a young girl with a dead creature they found, buried under the snow. She lies back down and smiles with the knowledge that they will win this war.

'At least I hope so,' she mutters under her breath and pulls the blanket over her head. She doesn't share her dreams with anyone, not even Malcom. The last thing she wants to do is to create false hope and have those she cares about believing in a lie. *It won't do anyone any good*, she tells herself.

Malcom and the twins are still sleeping, so she grabs her coat and walks outside. It is full of holes and only has one button, but it is warm and she likes the colour. It is a soft blue and it reminds her of a clear summer sky.

'We need to have a little chat,' she mutters to no one and walks up towards the mountain. The wind is strong, which makes the thirty-minute walk difficult, but she can't have any prying eyes or ears around. This conversation is private and needs to remain private.

The wind suddenly dies down and with it, a rock with a flat top gets uncovered from the snow, for her to sit down on.

'Thank you.' She takes a seat and rubs her hands together to try and warm them up. 'It is cold and we have hardly any food left, you have provided well, but we need more if we are to wait and survive here longer.'

The air gets very thick and warm suddenly and an old lady appears in front of her. She is neither Tartarian, nor Phoenician. She is also not a Human or Heaven Bearer, she is nothing and no-one. She is the Tree of Life in the form of a Human, something relatable and non-threatening.

Bonnie and the Tree of Life have been meeting up for two weeks now, secretly. Bonnie needs guidance and she is willing to offer it.

'Mother nature was fooled by these creatures. I have tried to show her their evil ways and how they tricked her into believing the Tartarians broke the covenant, but she is stubborn and blind to the truth. This Heaven Bearer, Azrael, has her wrapped around his rotten claw and it sickens me to see this. I am working on a way for us to prove the truth to her, but it won't be easy. In fact, I see only one way and it is very likely we will fail Bonnie.' Her eyes are sad and hollow.

'No. For the sake of my children, for all the children, we will win. I dream about it.'

'Bonnie – ' She interrupts her. 'Those dreams are hopes, they aren't reality and you know this.'

Bonnie nods and a tear rolls down her cheek. 'Yes, but I choose to believe, that is more than what you are willing to do,' she snaps and immediately regrets it. 'I'm sorry.'

'Now, now dear, you are right. It will all be okay in the end. But many will die! This is the only way that we will end the war. *This will be the war to end all wars*.'

The Tree of Life suddenly gets quiet and stares up into the Canopy and cries out in agony! 'Bonnie! It is time, they have figured it out and –' She disappears in an instant and the heavy air drops suddenly, pushing down hard onto Bonnie. The wind gets stronger and the snows falls even harder and settles all around her. She gets up and tries to head back down the mountain, but the wind is blowing up against her and it is too strong and cold. She can't move forward.

She puts her hands in front of her face to block the snow smashing into her face, but it doesn't help, the snow is coming from every direction and she only has her two hands. The wind blows her over and she struggles to get back onto her feet. She closes her eyes and braces the snow and turns her head up in the direction of the Canopy. She opens them again and her eyes turn a deep blue and quickly flash *that* golden colour.

Her mind is scanning, looking for him and what he is doing to make mother nature so angry all of a sudden.

'There he is!' She mutters. She can see him and he is whispering something into her ear and she is angry, very angry! She pricks up her ears and tries to zone into what he is saying. She focuses on his moving mouth and blocks out the howling wind and the crackling in the sky.

'The Tree of Life is working with those who betrayed you, it is time to make an example of her and kill the girl.' His tongue is long, like that of a snake, and his eyes are glowing yellow. He is hideous and she cringes at the sight of him.

Mother nature is unsure and waves him away. 'No, the Tree of Life will not die, not by my hands or yours!' She glances at him. 'She will be punished for her betrayal, I will make sure of it, but without her I cease to exist. We all cease to exists, the Tree of Life is *Earth*,' she says and gazes down below her. She can see Bonnie and zooms in on her face. 'Such a pretty girl, isn't she?'

Azrael doesn't like what he hears and he wishes he could kill mother nature, but he knows he needs her in order to defeat the Tartarian girl. He isn't powerful enough on his own and it bothers him that he has to rely on her.

'Can I kill the girl? You don't need the girl. In fact, she is capable of destroying me and taking over. She can't be trusted!' He says and licks his lips in excitement.

'Yes, she is powerful, stop her now before she gets even more powerful!' She orders and the night sky cracks loudly making every living soul shake with fear.

CHAPTER NINETEEN

The war has started.

It will be bitter and cold and many will die. The mud flood *reset* the entire world and paved a way for a new age, the New World Order. This war, however, has the potential to destroy an entire race of people, erasing history completely and setting the world on fire.

Bonnie knows that this war isn't preventable, but the collateral damage needs to be mitigated as best as possible. Innocent people should never die, but they do. Innocent people always suffer the most during war.

She can feel the weight press down on her shoulders, it will be up to her and the twins, and Cassiel.

'Fight with me Tree of Life! I need you now more than ever, I can't do this on my own!' She shouts out, hoping she will hear her pleas, while she struggles against the snow storm.

She feels the snow start to melt between her fingers and she knows the Tree of Life is still there and able to help her. She feels a sense of relief rush over and her eyes turn the snow bright blue.

She stands up and an invisible sphere forms around her, blocking the wind and snow from touching her body and she takes one giant leap forward. She lands hard on her feet, stumbles forward and lands on her knees. She looks back at the mountain that she just leaped off of and watches the sky turn black.

'Malcom!' She screams as loud as she can and her voice doesn't sound liked hers at all, it is deep and it echoes across the whole plain and strikes the heart of everyone in the settlement. She starts running as fast as she can towards the settlement and watches how the snow around her melts away, making way for a path for her to follow.

'The war has begun,' she mutters under her breath for Malcom and Cassiel to hear. She is terrified and they can feel her fear in those four words.

Cassiel looks out into the distance and can see Bonnie running up towards him. The clouds forming are dark and heavy and the air becomes extremely cold.

Everything starts freezing all around him and he knows the war is already lost, unless Bonnie has a miracle under her sleeve. The ground starts cracking as it freezes over and a woman screams out in pain. He looks in the direction of the scream and it stops suddenly, leaving the lady frozen dead in the very spot where she lay. She didn't even get the chance to run away, it all happed so fast. He tries to stop it, but he can do nothing at all.

Bonnie stops just outside of the settlement and with all her might she slaps her hands together. Nothing happens! She tries again, this time in conjunction with a deep breath and every pain receptor on her body activates at once.

Her hands are on fire, but she isn't burning and she pulls her hands apart and blows the flame over the settlement. The flame forms a burning dome around them, that keeps everything warm, but sets nothing on fire. She can feel the heat radiate from the burning wall of fire and turns around to watch the storm coming. There are giant shadows forming in the distance, the sky starts to crackle and her heart thumps in absolute fear.

'It will alright momma.' A voice startles her and Amile takes hold of her one hand and Amelia takes hold of her other. They are seven years old already and their eyes glisten with the same fighting spirit of their mother. The three of them stare out into the distance and watch closely as evil descends onto the Earth.

Her neck feels warm suddenly and she feels his breath on her. 'You are not alone in this Bonnie.'
Both Malcom and Cassiel are suddenly there behind her and they stand ready to do whatever is necessary. Malcom hands her the metal staff from the mansion and she takes it from him and watches it light up in her hand. She can feel their presence and knows that her entire bloodline and its powers are within her now.

'The shadows, we need to stop them before the reach us and turn into real creatures!' She shouts and starts to throw flames in their direction. The sky flashes bright as the balls of flames pierce the dark sky.

Amile and Amelia fly off and search for the Tree of Life in the Canopy. They need to free her from Azrael, they will need her and her full strength after they defeat these creatures in the sky. They are just the beginning of what is coming.

The creatures hover and hiss up in the dark, black and purple sky. They begin to grunt loudly and this grim sound, that radiates from them, shatters the rocks and ice beneath them as they move over the empty tract of land and fly towards the settlement. They are fierce and blood thirsty and she can feel a droplet of their saliva land on her. She smells the stench as is turns to acid and melts another hole in her already hole-filled coat.

A grunt turns into a loud and frightful screech and the first creature lands down in front of Bonnie and Malcom. The ground shakes like an earthquake struck nearby and a crack forms in the ground and stops just outside the settlement. The creature smells like death and it drools a yellow liquid that turns into an acidic mess around it. She eyes it carefully, trying to figure out what it is and how to kill it. It is covered in scales with sharp, knife like edges and claws that could cut the hardest of rock in half, with ease. It is reptilian, but looks nothing like she has ever heard of or seen.

'The Heaven Bearers would have no powers without mother nature on their side. We need to get to her and talk to her!' Cassiel shouts towards Malcom.

'We need to tell Azrael that the others want to over throw him, perhaps they can kill him for us?' She says and can feel a sharp pain in her heart as she looks over at Malcom, as he gives her a gentle nod and soft smile. She knows what he needs to do and it kills her inside. She gives him a loving smile back and her mind talks to his. 'You come back to me! That is an order Mr Harrington!'

'I love you Bonnie,' he replies and knows she can hear everything he is thinking, including what he isn't saying. He tells her it will all be okay and that he knows what he is doing, but she knows he is no match for Azrael on his own, not even with the Tree of Life helping him. She senses that this will be the last time she is going to see him; she holds back the tears and fights off the thought and feeling. This can't be the last memory he has of her. She walks up to him and gives him *one last kiss* and he heads up to find Azrael in the Canopy.

She scans the Canopy for Amile and Amelia, but they are not there. There is a loud thump next to her suddenly and it is them. They have grown again and are now teenagers, she would guess they are thirteen years old. They stand next to her proudly and she can see why. They have brought the Tree of life with them and she is safe. Bonnie is relieved, they desperately need her to help them convince mother nature of the Heaven Bearers true intentions.

'Malcom will need your help!' She tells them and Amile and Amelia acknowledge her with a simple nod and off they go again.

The Tree of Life follows their lead and walks towards the

settlement and through the flaming dome of fire to guard it from the inside.

Two more shadows land and become real life creatures and all three come charging at her and Cassiel at once.

Bonnie clutches the metal staff in her hand, as hard as she can, and a bright, blue flame emerges from it. Her body lifts from the ground and she circles around them at the speed of sound and cuts a circle into the ground, that turns blue and a dome completely surrounds them. She swoops back towards Cassiel and another dome forms over him, as she lands next to him and gets back into her fighting position. The first creature that landed charges at them and bounces off of the dome that she created and starts to dig with its sharp and stubby claws to get underneath it.

'Cassiel, take this.' She hands him the staff. 'Focus on holding the dome in place and extend it down as far as you can, let them dig!' She is calm and collected and her eyes are looking for something.

Meanwhile, Malcom has reached the Canopy and is waiting for Azrael to come out of hiding and face him like a man. The atmosphere up there is calm, yet there is sorrow and unkindness lurking in the air and it is hot, very hot. Sweat forms on Malcom's brow and he wipes it off with the back of his hand.

'I can smell you father, let us *not* play games today!' He is sarcastic and angry.

Azrael is the master of deception, surprise and as his nickname goes, the angel of death. Every soul he takes results in him getting stronger, more evil and craving more power. His goal is to create a new race of slaves, the Humans, so that he can amass wealth and control. Once he has achieved a certain level of this, he will kill off the other Heaven Bearers, he can't have them challenge him and he is not willing to share. They serve a purpose for now, just like everything and everyone else.

Azrael is different to the other Heaven Bearers. He was the first born of once great lineage of beings called the Heaveners. They were a simple people that lived in the clouds. They had no real purpose; they were created to be a lazy race and they spent most of their days hovering above the Canopy of the different Trees of Life. They would watch the difference races down below thrive and live their lives and their only goal was to maintain the clouds and regulate the rays and heat from the sun. If there weren't enough clouds, or the wrong ones, the suns rays would be too intense and could boil and destroy a planet. Azrael found this job menial and boring. He sat and watched from above, green with envy at the different races and what they had. He saw their riches, their precious stones and metals and he decided he want it all for himself!

He befriended a Wanderer named Azul and together they plotted a way for them to gain control of the galaxy. Their plan was simple, they would start by inhabiting one Tree of Life at a time. They started with Merth, but the Mertheners fought back and killed Azul and Azrael fled for his life. He knew he needed to find another way, a simpler way. He made a pact with the Goddess of the Underneath, named Zaara and she promised him power and his heart's every desire. She was a serpent like creature with six-legs and no eyes. She could not witness true beauty, but she wanted it and in exchange, Azrael promised her copious amounts of it. He wanted power by whatever means necessary and to learn the art of *deception*. He was willing to do whatever it took to achieve this.

'Azrael, it is simple. All you need to do is sacrifice every single one of the Heaveners, the young and the old, to me and send them to the Underneath. If you do this, I promise you can have all that you have ever dreamed of,' She hisses and sniffs his face.

Azrael didn't ask a single question and immediately began devising a plan on how to murder all of his people. It needed to be quick and easy, he told himself. He changed the position of the clouds and let the rays from the sun slowly heat up the top of the Canopies of the different Trees of Life, knowing full well that they will fight back to try and protect their roots. The leaves gave off an oily liquid that would reflect the sun's rays away from them as a defence. Ordinarily, the extra heat would merely evaporate and dissipate into the galaxy. Except, this time Azrael lined the clouds up in such a way that they blocked this heat from escaping into the galaxy and it cooked the Heaveners alive. It melted their skin right off of their bones and they became a thick sludge that cooked away, until there was nothing left of any of them.

After Azrael had killed them all, he returned to see Zaara and accept his powers that she promised him.

'Silly boy, I have no powers to give you!' She proceeds to laugh and then hisses at him. 'I want beauty, I want to be beautiful, but you can't give me that. You never could, so I made you ugly like me.'

He looks down at his hands and in utter disbelief realises he became a scaly monster just like her.

'This was never part of the agreement Zaara, why do I look like this?' He shouts at her and is angry. He doesn't want to accept this reality; he can't accept it.

She laughs at him and licks his face with her bright orange tongue, but she says nothing.

He realises then that he was fooled by her. It was simple and he had not expected it. His shocked expression changes into one of amazement and awe. He wanted to become a master of deception and she had just shown him how easy it was to deceive.

He stayed with Zaara in the Underneath for seventy-three years and he fathered six children, Baird, Kismet, Samira, Enid, Niamh and Ard and called they called themselves the Heaven Bearers. Zaara taught them everything she knew until they were ready to conquer and so they did. For four hundred and fifty years, they went from Tree of Life to Tree of Life and took anything and everything they wanted. They got high off of the fear they created and their greed for beautiful things, including the women, festered.

Sometimes they gained special abilities from the beings

they conquered. They did this through their art of deception and with the promise of safety and security, in exchange. There was, however, never any safety and security. They were cruel and showed no mercy and the more they pillaged and killed the innocent beings, the more they enjoyed it.

Plerth was their third conquest. The galaxy started to notice something was causing planets to combust internally and knew something had to be done to fix the problem. The galaxy didn't realise that it was due to the Heaven Bearers and their pillaging ways. The Heaven Bearers knew they needed to keep their true intentions secret. They devised a plan to find a race of beings that had a King that sat on the Council of the galaxy and the Empire of Tartaria was at the head of this particular table.

Azrael walks out from the shadows and he is in his normal form. This surprises Malcom completely and he can't help but wonder why? His eyes quickly scan the room to see if he can find King Finn's body anywhere, but he doesn't see it.

'You surprise me Azrael. You walk around with such arrogance, even though you know you have met your match with her. She will end your rule!' He pauses briefly, while he takes a good look at him. 'You are uglier than I could have imagined,' he mocks him and gives him a toothy grin.

Azrael laughs out and the other Heaven Bearers suddenly appear next to him in their Tartarian form. 'You forget you are my son Malcom. That means you are half as ugly and evil as I am, you will realise this one day and so will your pretty little Tartarian.' He grins suddenly and gives him a sinister look. 'Or maybe not.'

Malcom can feel his body panic slightly at the sight of is grin and he immediately pushes the thought away.

'You understand what the end goal is here? Don't you?!' He glances at each of the Heaven Bearers, one by one, but they are expressionless and don't react to his words at all.

'This creation of the Human race to be your slaves is a pipe dream, it will never work. You are not getting the birth right that you want, there are not enough of them and the more you allow the Tartarians to reproduce, the more chance they have of over throwing you at some point in the future.' He looks directly at Samira and takes a step closer to her. 'That is if you even manage to live that long. Azrael doesn't like to share, each of you knows this very well. How long do you think it will take until he kills you off, one by one?'

'There has been a new development silly boy.' Samira steps forward and places her hand on Azrael and she smiles cunningly at Malcom.

'The Humans are reproducing in great numbers Malcom, you just don't know about it and your little Tartarian can't stop it, no one can. You can thank mother nature for that.'

He shakes his head in disbelief, he was always the prodigal son and he knew everything there was to know about the breeding programme! He took part in from a young age! He is angry now and reminds himself that Azrael might have the nickname of the angel of death, but his *true gift* is deception. He feels stupid suddenly and wants all of this to end. He doesn't want to fight, but he knows he has to.

'Mother nature will realise that you have deceived her, you can only pull the wool over her eyes for so long. And when she does realise what you have done, she will show no mercy and you will all be killed. This is the last race of beings that you will conquer, but you will *not destroy* them, mark my words.' He warns them gently. His hands are balled into fists and he believes every word that just came out of his mouth. He has to for *her* sake.

'Oh, sweet Malcom, you sure are naïve.' She walks up to him slowly, flirty and rubs her finger over his chest. 'Mother nature has decided she wants to share in the riches.' She flicks his chin with her sharp finger nail and cuts him just enough so that a single drop runs down his chin and neck. He flinches and his eyes flash purple.

She licks his cheek, which is followed by a teasing kiss and she forces her hand into his chest and punctures his heart with the same sharp nail.

His face turns a pale pink, with the sudden realisation of what has just happened and the luminous green fades from his eyes. He falls down to his knees and feels a wave of emotions rush over him.

'Bonnie!' He cries out. He didn't see this coming; he didn't even feel fear. How did she manage to get him to reveal his greatest fear, without him even knowing about it?

The colour completely drains from his face and it hits him suddenly, they are going to try and kill Azrael and they are going to use Bonnie to do it! He takes one last look at Azrael and then at Samira. 'She will kill you for this!' He musters up one last, arrogant grin and with it, releases his last breath and gently slumps over.

Bonnie was wrong. Life doesn't go back to normal and her dream of them watching the twins play outside was just that, a dream.

Azrael, like the coward he is, stands over Malcom's dead body and pushes him over to the floor and looks at his lifeless face with pleasure. 'How are the creatures doing down in Alaska?'

There is silence and no one wants to answer him. He steps away from Malcom and stares down at the ground and he can see the dome of fire and feel her power. It angers him, her power is what he wanted. It was what he will get once he finishes off the competition, he tells himself.

Baird steps forward reluctantly and swallows hard. 'She has them trapped inside some kind of electrical dome.'

'How is that possible?' He shouts and kicks Malcom's lifeless body. 'She is just a silly girl! She doesn't even know what she is or what she is capable of! I want that power!' He hisses and Samira looks away in fear. 'She has found a way to harness the free energy, something we have not yet found a way to do Azrael. And she has the Staff of the Elders.' Samira snaps back at him, carefully. She knows this revelation will anger him and she happily stands her ground, just to see his expression.

Azrael scornfully grabs her by the neck and lifts her off the ground. 'Thank you for the reminder daughter! I want the girl dead, now go and find her, you useless bunch!' He shrieks and lets her drop to the floor.

They do as ordered and make their way down to the settlement, while Azrael walks back to King Finn, who is chained up in the far end of the densest part of the Canopy. His arms are rubbed raw from the chains, that he has been trying in vain to free himself from, and this excites Azrael.

'King Finn, you should know better than that. There is no way you can break those chains, but I do like it that you tried!' He grins and licks his crusty lips. 'Your niece is just about dead, sorry King. It is finally over and she did suffer.' He walks up closer to the King and smells his pain in the air. 'That was the good news. Now for the bad news?' He chuckles sadistically. 'You will create another child, one who is just as powerful as she was, and you will do this *specially for me*!' He turns away and breathes in his own arrogance and pride. 'I will be truly unstoppable then.' He says out loud, talking to himself and then looks back towards the King, only to suddenly frown in confusion.

Something is different from the moment before and his eyes flicker to the right of where he is standing in the Canopy. It takes him only a moment, but it was a moment too long.

'No!' He screams as the realisation hits him like a hard stab to the heart and he lunges forward to grab hold of the King. *But it is too late.*

The Tree of Life has already consumed him and he is gone. She has taken him, with his approval, to become part of the bark and act as a source of nutrients to keep the almighty tree alive.

Azrael screams out in horror and shock! This was not supposed to happen! He needed the King and his powers, he was the last of his kind.

'The girl!' He mutters in anger and he knows he needs to stop the others from killing her at once.

'I need her alive!' He howls from the Canopy for them to

hear him and leaps out towards the ground.

CHAPTER TWENTY

The twins suddenly arrive back on the ground without Malcom.

'Where is your father?' She asks them with a worried look on her face, but she distracted.

Amile shrugs his shoulders. 'I don't know mother, we looked everywhere for him, but he wasn't in the Canopy. There was no one there at all, so we went and scanned over the firmament for a while, thinking he might have gone there, but he wasn't there either. I'm sorry.'

'We thought it best to come back and help you here on the ground?' Amelia says while she gives Amile a kind smile. 'We are stronger together and we will stop them. Father will join us in a little while, I am sure of that!'

There is a loud groan that echoes and makes the ground shake violently. Bonnie is distracted by it and her gaze goes back towards the creatures trying to kill them all.

The creatures are dutifully still digging under the dome and the biggest one has just about made it through.

'I can't extend it any further Bonnie!' Cassiel shouts in

her direction and she can see that he is struggling to wield the power of the shaft. He isn't meant to; he is of the wrong bloodline and they both realise this suddenly.

'Amile and Amelia, take over from Cassiel and expand it down if you can?' She both asks and orders them at the same time. There is no pre-written script, she doesn't know what she must do, but she knows she needs to defeat these creatures and soon.

The twins follow their mother's orders and manage to extend the dome down, just enough to keep the other two creatures from being able to dig through. The third one has already managed to pull its hind legs through and is standing on all fours, frothing at the mouth. It is hungry for blood and it wants *hers*.

Bonnie suddenly thinks about the pain she felt losing her mother for all those years while she lived at the Foundling home and her eyes start to fill with tears. She tries to stop herself, thinking that she has more important things to worry about right now, but her eyes keep filling with tears. The first tear rolls down her cheek and a massive droplet falls inside the dome in which the two creatures are in and are so desperately trying to dig out of. She realises what is happening and allows her emotion to take over and lets her tears fall uncontrollably. She watches the dome start to fill up with water from every direction and waits for it to be three quarters full. She reaches her hand through the blue jelly like substance, that the dome is made of, and gently touches the water with her index finger. The water starts to bubble and turns a bright purple. There is a sudden explosion and everything within the dome burns and becomes a fine, black powder that trickles down like dust after a wind storm, until it settles on the floor. The black powder gently mixes with the last bit of her tears that falls and magically turns into millions of shiny purple stones that litter the entire area. Cassiel, the twins and Bonnie can't help, but stare at them with open mouths and amazement. This is how the amethyst stone was created and it will become a popular and important stone in the future. It will be the stone that will represent the Tartarian Empire and will be worn with pride by every Tartarian, man and woman.

'Bonnie watch out!' Cassiel tries to caution her, but he is too late. The last remaining creature has her pinned to the ground and a single drop of its toxic drool drips onto her in the face.

'Get off!' She shouts and she tries to push its head away from her. She suddenly cries out in absolute pain and she can feel her heart rip out of her chest.

'Malcom!' She starts crying hysterically and tries again to get the creature off, but it won't move. She is exhausted and she reaches for him. The twins come running over to her and Amile takes the shaft and forces it into the creatures' head. Amelia quickly joins him and they use her last bit of strength to force the shaft right through until it hits the ground with a hard bang.

The creature twitches and starts to bleed out a white goo, while still on top of her.

'Get it off of me!' She screams and is in absolute panic. Cassiel runs on over to her and helps the twins get the creature off of her. Her clothes are burnt in patches from its saliva and she is covered in its white blood.

She looks up at the Canopy and immediately gets onto her feet. 'Malcom! I need to find Malcom.' She says and tries to gather her thoughts on how to get to him.

Cassiel tries to stop her and grabs her by the arm, but she pulls away from him and with one swift push she is up in the air and out of sight.

The storm dies down and the fire dome disappears from the settlement. Snow starts to fall again and the resistance starts to cheer in victory. Cassiel looks around and knows their cheers are all in vain. 'This is just the beginning,' he mutters and looks up into the sky. The Heaven Bearers will be on their way soon and the air starts to stink of rotting flesh.

Bonnie arrives in the Canopy and she sees Malcom lying pale and motionless on the floor and there are many small roots creeping all over him. They are trying to consume him and she runs over towards him to stop them.

'Malcom!' She cries out and drops down next to him. She knows he is gone and she is furious and broken. She starts pulling away the roots and more keep replacing the ones that she pulls away and she can't keep up. She drops her hand in defeat and puts her head into her hands.

'I saw it! I saw our lives together!' She is furious and upset and the tears are rolling down her face and she can't contain them, nor does she want to.

She searches his body to see where he is hurt and notices a tiny drop of blood on his shirt near his heart and she knows then, that the prophesy was wrong. She can feel another presence arrive suddenly and sees mother nature appear in front of her. Her eyes turn completely golden and she quickly stands up and grabs her. Her eyes stay that golden colour and the tears stop rolling down her cheeks.

'You did this! How could you be so heartless!? For what?' She is shaking and she is screaming. 'He isn't like the others, he could feel, he cared!' Her voice is filled to the brim with anger and her grip starts to tighten and she wants her to suffer and die.

'Dear girl –' she says and her words hang in the air. Bonnie wants her to say something else, but she doesn't and all she can hear are those two words over and over again.

Mother nature isn't what she expected, she expected her to appear as a small, old and frail lady, just like the Tree of Life. However, she is not. Mother nature is a feeling, a colour, a breeze. She doesn't take on the form of a person, but she speaks like a human. Her voice is soft, like a child and she isn't happy or angry or sad. Her voice is emotionless and it reminds her even more of Malcom and how he was when she first met him.

'This wasn't necessary, you don't even know what you have unleashed upon this Earth! Why do you think they came here? They destroyed their last home and everyone on it and they plan to do the same here!' She screams at the top of her lungs. Her anger begins to scare her, because it takes away her humility.

Mother earth changes from orange to red, to black. Bonnie wonders what this means and guesses that her colour changing signifies her emotions, since she doesn't express them in human form.

'The Earth Bearers, Azrael, they want to destroy the Earth and you are allowing it!' She barks at her and can barely contain her anger or breathe any more. 'How can you be so stupid! How could you allow them to trick you? You had peace with the Tartarians for over a thousand years and these wretched creatures arrive for a few weeks and you take their word over that of King Finn?'

Her hands are shaking, her nose is bleeding and she feels dizzy and she drops to her knees.

'Sit down dear child,' she orders her, then brushes her hair out of her face and whispers ever so softly into her ear.

'It will all become apparent soon, now go and save the resistance and your children. Hurry, before it is too late. Malcom belongs to me now.' She disappears suddenly, with Malcom, and leaves Bonnie standing there all alone. Bonnies eyes change back to their bright blue colour and she realises what is about to happen down on the ground and she darts back to them.

She lands with a thud and loses her balance and crashes to the ground. Her body and mind are filled with anger and frustration. She is tired and weak. She can't bear the thought or come to terms with the loss of her husband and her nose is still bleeding slightly. She sees the twins. Their sweet faces are plastered with fear and worry and she drops down to her knees in defeat. Samira has a knife to Amile's throat and Kismet is holding one to Amelia's.

Rotting flesh and evil fills the air. Azrael walks over towards her and touches her face with his scaly hand and like a reptile lets his tongue search the air to taste her fear and pain. He breathes it all in and lets it consume him completely, while he savers the

moment.
'It didn't have to be like this Bonnie, it still doesn't need to be. All you need to do is submit to me, here and now. End the coming pain and suffering. If not for yourself and the millions of Tartarian men and women, do it for your precious little twins.' He is taunting her and the blood dripping from her nose stops abruptly.

Time slows down and she closes her eyes. She thinks about Malcom and his smile, the way he looked at her, the way he *loved her*.

There is a sudden and loud scream coming from the mountains and it distracts Azrael for brief moment, a mere second of second and she levitates back onto her feet.

'Angel of death! You want power? Come and get it!' She shouts and she watches his eyes fill with rage. He wants to storm at her with his claws, aimed for her face and head so that her can rip it off of her shoulders. But she knows he wants her, needs her this time and *alive!*

Mira and the others from the resistance, with the help of Cassiel, are standing steadfast with the staff among them and it is emitting the free energy that Azrael so desperately wants to monopolise.

He looks over at Bonnie and laughs. 'Do they not know that it is too late?' He scoffs at her, drooling with bloodlust.

'It is never too late!' She replies and looks down at the floor, because it is moving beneath her feet. There is a sudden and bright blue flash and the entire Earth stops spinning on its axis. The flash is so bright, it is visible from the galaxy. Brown-coloured roots shoot out of the ground and wrap themselves around the legs of the Heaven bearers and pin them to the ground.

'I can't hold them for long! Bonnie you need to do something, quickly!' the Tree of Life implores Bonnie urgently.

'Bonnie, Bonnie you need to fight! Sweetheart you can't give up, not yet. He wouldn't want it. Please Bonnie!' Mira is pleading with her too.

Bonnie doesn't move from her spot. She stands completely still, her hands are draped by her sides and she feels a whirlwind form around her, sucking in everything that is less than two-metres away from her. Mira and Cassiel start to back away from her slowly and realise what she is doing. She is self-destructing, which could cause the entire Earth to implode.

'Everyone back up now and head to the mountains, hide wherever you can!' Cassiel shouts to the resistance and they start to panic and run away in fear.

The Heaven Bearers start to feel uneasy and aren't sure if what Cassiel just said is part of the deception or not. Niamh's head starts to shake violently, he is frothing at the mouth and his eyes pop out of his head and spill onto the ground! His Tartarian body falls over and begins to shine, the same way a diamond would when the light hits it, just right and it slowly floats up into the Canopy. His true reptilian-like body remains on the ground where he stood, naked and melts away until it completely dissolves into the ground. Samira and Kismet stand before her with fear in their eyes and for the first time ever, they are terrified of someone other than Azrael. They simultaneously press the blade into the twins' neck but feel bare, skin on skin and realise that the knives that they were holding disintegrated into nothing. They failed miserably and they try to get away from her, but the roots are still holding on tight.

The twins hurry over to Bonnie and stand by her side. 'What do we do next mother?' Amelia asks concerned and is ready to fight alongside her.

'Run!' She shouts and without hesitation they join the others fleeing as fast as they can, away from *her.*

She kneels down onto the floor and the wind that has formed around her has gotten so strong, that the roots holding onto the Heaven Bearers start to rip off and gets sucked into the force of nature she is becoming.

She scratches a circle into the ground with her index finger and says Malcom's name out loud. The ground around them immediately starts to shake violently, reaching the distance of over a mile. Boulders of rocks starts to descend down on them and one crushes Enid right where he is standing.

Samira starts to run and hide, but she trips over her own feet and a rock lands onto her legs, crushing them completely and she is unable to move at all. She is screaming out in pain and it pleases Bonnie. She has lost herself completely and only seeks revenge now.

'Girl, stop this at once!' Azrael shouts at her and dodges the rocks that are aiming for him. Ard starts running for the mountains and Bonnie imagines the earth breaking away right in front of him and hot sap from the Tree of Life filling the crack that opens up. She begins to smile as her imagination turns into reality and she can hear him scream as he burns to death.

'Thank you.' She says calmly and can feel the Tree of Life acknowledge her.

'Get Azrael! I will take care of the Tartarians and keep the mountains at bay,' she hums in the wind for Bonnie to hear.

Bonnie smiles and lets the entire ground, on which she is standing on, crumble away. Rocks crash into each other crush everything in their path. Some rocks shatter into smaller ones, while others turn to powder and mix with the soil and other vegetation around them. Everything is spinning in circles, until they land in the Underneath and then everything stops moving and goes completely quiet. Her eyes are still bright in colour and it lights up this dark and decrepit place.

There is movement in the far end and she glances quickly into that direction, but there is nothing there. She can't see the Heaven Bearers, they are all buried under the rock and soil, but she knows that they are not dead. Samira is still groaning in pain and trying to dig through the sand back up to the surface. She watches the ground move and her hand reaches out in desperation for someone to help her. Bonnie walks up to her and takes her by the hand and pulls her up gently.

Her face is cut up and bruised from the fall and Bonnie

actually feels sorry for her suddenly. She drags her over to a safer corner and takes a good look at her wounds.

'Your legs!' She says and realises then that she will never walk again. Her humility has returned and she wants to help her.

'Tree of Life, can you hear me?' She feels a sudden breeze and her blonde hair starts to sway. 'I need you to take her somewhere safe and tend to her wounds. I want her alive, she will pay for what she has done. Death will be too easy for her.' Bonnie says and she watches how that same big, blue butterfly descends down in front of her and takes Samira away with it.

The ground in the corner of her eye starts to move and she can feel a presence behind her. It his Kismet and he charges at her, swinging a sharp rock in her direction. She ducks down and the rock just barely misses her head. It scrapes the top of it just slightly and she watches as a few strands of her hair land at her feet. Her eyes quickly flash to gold and he knows he has just angered her greatly.

'I'm not going to kill you monster. You will have your day in front of the Council and you will be punished accordingly for your crimes!' She tells him arrogantly and starts to fight him.

CHAPTER TWENTY-ONE

Kismet is physically strong, he is much stronger than Bonnie, but she has the kind of rage that he could never understand. This makes her stronger overall and she knows it. It makes her more confident, which is something that she needs to feel, in order to distract her from reality. He climbs out of his Tartarian body and reveals his true form. He reminds her of Azrael, he has that same look of evil in his eyes, although he is smaller in size and looks more like a snake than a lizard. His eyes are an awful, orange colour and his pupils are very big and as black as a moonless night. She feels sick looking at him and wonders how something so ugly can exist.

'You are no match for me little girl!' He says as he leaps forward and he smacks her around to the ground. She lands awkwardly and he tries to stomp on her head and crush it like a watermelon.

She rolls out of the way and picks up a small piece or rock and hits him perfectly in the right eye.

'Aah!' He groans and starts rubbing his eye. He is big and clumsy and for the first time, this is to his disadvantage. He realises this now, but it is too late for him to change back into the

Tartarian body.

Bonnie is briefly distracted by another patch of moving ground and he manages to get her in a strong choke hold. He lifts her off of the ground and she tries kicking at him, but her legs swing helplessly in the air as she struggles to get away from him. She lets her body go limp and as he tightens his grip, she turns her body 180 degrees and is suddenly facing him full on.

'Hello Beast!' She says with a smile and head butts him hard and sticks her thumbs into his eyes.

He drops her immediately and reaches out his hands to grab at her, but she is too quick this time. She grabs the biggest rock that she is able to lift and she swings it at his head.

There is loud clonks and Kismet is lying motionless on the floor. He lands with his head on a sharp rock and he is knocked-out cold, but he is not dead.

'Tree of Life, I have another one for you,' she says and proceeds to find the next creature behind her. It is Baird and he stays in his Tartarian form. He is filthy and angry and he storms at her like a wild animal. She leaps out of the way, but he manages to grab her by the arm and he breaks it with one easy twist.

She screams out in pain and tries to pull away from him as hard as she can. He pulls her in close, gives her a twisted smile and then lets her go. She falls back quickly and hooks her foot on a rock. She loses her balance completely and hits her head hard against a big boulder, that hadn't broken up into smaller pieces when it fell down, into the Underneath.

She tries to move, but she can't feel her body at all. She can hear footsteps approaching her and a loud rumble. There is dust falling all around her and it makes her cough as it mixes with the little bit of air that is in the Underneath. She closes her eyes suddenly and knows what is happening. The rest of the ground from above has broken loose and is piling down onto them. It gets pitch dark suddenly and she can't breathe at all. Her lungs fill up with sand and she doesn't fight back.

'Malcom!' She thinks and imagines that he can hear her, wherever he is.

Cassiel and Mira manage to lead, almost all of the resistance, to safety. Unfortunately, some fell behind and were swallowed up by the ground as they were trying to escape. Bonnie couldn't stop it and didn't want anyone to die, but there are always casualties in war.

'Something is wrong with mother!' Amile says and he looks into the distance. The mountains start to shake softly and small stones fall down from the top and they cover their heads to shield themselves from getting hurt. A small rock hits Cassiel on the side of his face and he starts to bleed.

'Ouch!' He says and wipes away the blood. 'Can you see anything Amile? Can you see her? He asks genuinely concerned about her.

Amelia starts to cry, while Amile shakes his head in sorrow. 'Father is dead and mother has just joined him.' He says and takes his sister into his embrace.

'It cannot be!' Cassiel walks past them and stares at the massive dust cloud that is present over the gaping hole in the ground. 'The prophesy!? The prophesy was clear, she was going to save us and restore the Tartarian Empire to its former glory!'

'The prophesy is wrong!' Amile shouts back at him. 'Have you really not realised this by now? You were supposed to marry my mother and she was going to bear *your* child. But she didn't, did she?'

He is angry and he lashes out harshly at him.

'I am sorry Cassiel.' He walks over to him and shakes his hand respectfully. 'No one expected this, no one wanted this ending,' he proceeds to say with sorrow and it takes over his entire expression.

Cassiel places his hand on his shoulder, like a father would to his son, and gives it a gentle, but firm squeeze. They share a moment together and the lightning forming and crackling in the sky ends it quickly.

'The war is not over and we will win!' Cassiel says as he throws the staff of the Elders toward Amile and he catches is it, with one easy, swift motion. His pale blue eyes sparkle, but they do not turn bright in colour like that of his mother or father.

Amile looks up towards the Canopy and smiles at the thought of his parents, knowing that they are finally back together and can spend all eternity with one another, exactly as reality, not destiny would have it.

He takes a deep breath and watches the staff light up and stares directly out ahead of him as Azrael appears from the dusty pit in the ground.

'Come on beast, I am ready for you!' He says and both Amelia and Cassiel appear at his side ready for the most intense battle of their lives. It will be up to the three of them to stop him and they know this.

'We need to get closer to the creature, we can't risk him bringing the fight here and hurting our people.' The twins agree and they start to run towards him. He knows what they want to avoid and diverts the lighting strikes towards the people hiding in the mountains.

They can hear screams and know someone is hurt or dead.

Amile leaps up into the air and he uses the full strength of the staff to knock Azrael onto the ground.

'Now we are on a level playing field beast!' Amile is cheeky and arrogant like his father and uses it to his advantage. 'Come on beast, show me what you can do?' He taunts him and Azrael takes the bait.

He stops attacking the mountains and focuses all of his hatred and anger onto Amile!

'You look like him you know and I will enjoy killing you just as much as I enjoyed watching him die.'

Azrael expects to see pain in his eyes, but there isn't any. 'You do understand what I am saying Human? Your father is dead. Oh, and so is your mother.' He thinks they are unaware of their deaths and wants to get under their skin, but this only makes them want to fight harder and better.

Amelia steps forward slowly. 'What are we waiting for? Can will send this best back to where he belongs already? I am tired of these games.'

'I agree, its time to go back to the Underground beast!' Amile scoffs, but is interrupted by Cassiel. Cassiel notices a sudden change in the sky and he grabs hold of the twins. 'Get back to the mountains and hide.' He shouts.

Mother nature has joined in the fight and with her on his side, they stand no chance. Cassiel knows he needs to distract them to give the twins a fighting chance and to get back to the mountains. But deep down inside he also knows that, even if they make it, they cannot hide from mother nature, not for long.

'Stop this!' He calls out to her. 'Can't you see what suffering you are helping to unleash upon this Earth? We had lived for one thousand years in peace and absolute harmony.' He shakes his head in disbelief. 'Look around you, how much better is the Earth now? There is no peace and happiness and only pain and death. Can you really say this is better than what was before?'

He gets down on his knees and bows his head. 'Forgive us if we have wronged you, but this needs to stop, now!' His eyes turn bright blue and he keeps them down on the ground and completely humbles himself before mother nature.

He feels a sudden shock of pain and falls face first onto the ground. He coughs up hot and sour tasting blood and can see reptile-looking feet approach him. It is Azrael and sniffs his chard clothing, then licks the side of his face. 'Mother nature can't hear you anymore, because she chooses not to. She is my little puppet now, you silly Tartarian. You beings never learn and this is why I will win every time. I am the master of deception!' He says and raises his arm up into the air and lets it fall back down again, signally the lightning to finish him off.

She is dreaming, but she is wide awake. Her throat is clogged with mud, but she can breathe. Her fingers start to move and claw the soil and she can feel that it is damp. She isn't sure how she is lying, facedown or up and tries to remember what happened? Her mind is blank and sore. She pushes her body up, but it doesn't move a single inch.

'I could use some help here!' She calls out with her mind for someone to hear and help her, but no one can. 'Amile and Amelia? Can you hear me? Can anyone hear me?' She waits for a few moments and listens carefully, hoping to hear something or someone. There is nothing, but complete silence and she realises she is all alone down there. Her mind feels heavy, even though she can't seem to replay any memories. She can't quite understand what is happening. She can't even feel the twins and it suddenly hits her! *I am dead.*

The thought excites her and she starts to dig to find her way out. If I am dead, I can find him, she tells herself. She digs and digs, but the sand doesn't get any less. An hour passes and she is still stuck in the same place.

'Can someone please help me!? I am completely stuck and I don't know how to get out. Hello?'

There is still no answer and she starts to get frustrated. 'Can someone please help me now?' She shouts and she can feel her body tense up and she starts to dry heave. She pukes up the sand that filled her throat and it feels like it is on fire and it burns. She remembers lying on the floor in the bathroom of the mansion and Malcom standing there, looking down at her with a smile on his face. It was the first time he smiled and she rolls her eyes at the thought of all the grief he gave her then.

'You were such a pain actually. You made me cry many tears, that wasn't fair you know?' She is thinking out loud, even though no one can hear her.

'I am sorry Bonnie! I was very unkind to you and I should never have made you cry as I did.'

She lays there still and wonders if she just imagined this. She tries to turn her head slightly. 'Is someone there?' She mutters into the dirt.

There is no answer and she knows that she is merely losing her mind. She is dead and stuck there, all alone and she doesn't understand why, but she accepts the reality and lies still.

She can feel the weight on top of her, lift slightly and then much more, until suddenly she doesn't feel pinned down at anymore. There is a hazy light around her and she thinks she can see, so she clenches her eyes and then opens them up again. She pushes herself up from where she was lying and she can feel an arm wrap around her waist and pull her upwards. She stands on her feet, but is wobbly and starts to fall over. But the arm catches her gently and pulls her up again and closer against whoever it belongs to.

'I know you!' She says under breath. 'I recognise the way you smell and feel.' She turns around slowly, keeping the arm tightly around her and faces him. 'Malcom!' She says and leans her face up against his chest. 'I wasn't sure you were going to find me, I was calling out for you, but you couldn't hear me and –' She looks up at him and notices that he is wearing a clean black suit, with a white shirt and she realises she is making him dirty. She pulls away from him suddenly and starts to blush. 'I am so sorry! I didn't mean to make your clothes dirty.' She wipes her hand over his white shirt and realises it is completely clean. She looks at her own hand and it too, is spotless.

'Huh?' She mutters out loud and looks back at him, directly into his eyes. 'Why aren't you dirty and where did you get those clothes?' She asks and looks down at her own body. She is also dressed in new clothes and she is clean. Her dress is a simple cotton one with short sleeves and it is the colour of her eyes.

'Malcom, I don't understand what is happening?' She looks around her and they are no longer in the Underneath, but in the Canopy. 'Is this it? Is this where we will stay from now on?' She asks and rubs her hands over her arms. She is cold and she isn't sure why. 'Where are the twins?'

He takes off his suit jacket and helps her put it on. He is standing behind her, wraps his arms around her again and gently kisses the side of her neck.

'Look down Bonnie,' he says and her eyes follow his. She can't see them, but she can hear them. They are breathing heavily and they are absolutely terrified. She pulls away from him suddenly and faces him. 'We need to do something Malcom!

They are in trouble!' She shouts and starts looking for a way to get down to them.

'No Bonnie, there is nothing we can do for them. We can only watch.' He replies and this angers her.

'What do you mean we can only watch?' She snaps. 'Those are our children and it is our duty to protect them!' Her face turns red with anger and her eyes are glowing.

'Yes darling. But we are dead. There is nothing we can do for them now,' he replies calmly and gives her a soft and apologetic smile.

'No!' She starts to cry, but she sheds no tears. She puts her hand up to her face. 'Malcom no. I am sorry, but I change my mind. I choose them, they are my children and I need to go back to help them,' she says and gently touches his face.

'I know Bonnie.' He takes her face into his hands and gives her a big kiss. 'Perhaps we should go for a little walk?'

She frowns at his suggestion and grabs his shirt and makes a fist. 'No! I don't want to walk. What is the matter with you? I want my life back! She had no right to do this, she owes us. She needs to make things right! He is going to kill them all!' Her voice starts to deepen and she is angry.

She closes her eyes and looks for mother nature. She finds her at the far end of the Canopy. She is grey and sad and she is watching in horror as Azrael wreaks havoc upon the Earth.

'You can still stop him you know? You can make this right. Send us down to the ground and help us stop him?'

The grey changes to a soft orange and then to a warm yellow. 'Dear girl, I have already helped you, why do you think you are here?'

'I don't understand? What are you saying?' She asks confused. She looks at Malcom, but he is staring down at the ground with a concerned expression on his face.

'Bonnie!' He calls for her. 'It is time darling!' He stretches out his hand. 'Come, let us go now.' He is suddenly in a hurry and she places her hand in his, as quickly as she can.

'Go where Malcom, I am confused, where are we going?'

She asks.

'We are going to finish this fight!' He says and jumps out of the Canopy, holding onto her protectively.

They land on the ground and can see Cassiel lying face down on the ground. He isn't moving and has burn marks all over his body.

'It can't be!' Azrael screams and the look on his face is priceless. 'You are dead, I saw you die!' He screams in horror. But *that* arrogant smile is still on his face.

Malcom lets go of Bonnies hand and takes a big step forward and is suddenly at the same height as Azrael, even though Malcom is actually much smaller in reality.

'The art of deception father.' He shakes the smile off of Azrael face with that simple sentence. 'Eventually your luck will run out and today, right here and right now, you have run out of luck.'

'Careful boy!' He attempts to reprimand him and uses his arrogance to try and intimidate Malcom. 'You forget who your talking to!'

'No Azrael, I have not.' He looks over at Bonnie and she is just as confused as he is. 'Bonnie darling, come here and join me please.'

She walks forward and takes the hand that he is holding stretched out towards her. It all hits her at once, the moment that their fingers touch, and she now understands what is happening. Malcom did die, Azrael was correct when he claimed to have killed him. However, what he failed to realise is that mother nature had a sudden change of heart and she no longer wants to help him. She wants to help them now. She created a monster and he will destroy her if she doesn't stop him.

CHAPTER TWENTY-TWO

Azrael doesn't believe a word that they say, he is too arrogant to think that they could beat him at his own game.

'Mother nature is ignorant, just like the rest of you. You are bluffing!' He scoffs back at Malcom. 'Even if she has changed her mind, it wouldn't matter. I have conquered this place and it belongs to me now!' He replies and his eyes analyse his surroundings. He is feeling unsure of himself and both Bonnie and Malcom can sense it.

It starts to snow harder and Azrael wants to fight. He isn't ready to give up what he has accomplished. He turns on his heels and charges at Malcom and knocks him out of the way, with one big thump. His eyes are wild and it is clear that if he is going down, he will take as many of them with him as he can.

Malcom gets up and brushes the dirt from his clothes. His shoulder is dislocated and he struggles to click it back into place.

Bonnie stands motionless and watches them both, she doesn't fight him. Something is wrong, there is something unfamiliar in the air and she has no idea what is it, but the whole situation feels very wrong.

Malcom pounces onto Azrael and starts punching him with all of his might. The two of them carry on fighting, neither is stronger than other suddenly and they keep going back and forth. They grunt, they bleed and they posture, but nothing really happens.

'What is the point to this?' She asks mother nature or the Tree of Life, she isn't sure who she is actually talking to or who can hear her. She doesn't get an answer, so she turns around and walks away, slowly towards the big hole she created in the ground.

'Where are Samira and Kismet, Tree of Life?' There is silence for a couple of seconds and then she suddenly hears a voice.

'They are tucked away in the holding area of the Tree, down at the roots, exactly where they belong. There is no way for them to escape dear girl.' Her reply is warm and comforting.

'Good.' She replies and glances down into the hole. She can't believe just how big it is and what she did, how she fought and more importantly that she died. The sequence of events bothers her, she doesn't like the fact that she was brought back to life, without her permission.

'I never wanted to come back, why did mother nature bring me back?' She asks whoever is willing to answer her.

'She didn't Bonnie. You never died, you only thought you did. It takes a lot more to kill you than what you experienced dear child.' The voice startles her and she looks around to spot where it came from. It was loud and from a man. She knows the voice, but she has also never met this man, this she knows for sure.

She scans all around her and sees no one at all. She looks up into the clouds and sees the silhouette of a man, he is in his forties and has a kind and gentle face. She squints her eyes while she stares at him.

'Father? Is that you?' She asks and already knows it is him, before he even gets the chance to answer her. 'Where are you?

Please come here, so we can talk. Her hearts begins to race at the thought of him and she is very excited that he is reaching out to her.

'No Bonnie, I can't do that, but you must know something. Something has happened that changes things, it has never happened before. A betrayal so treacherous, you would never expect it.'

'A betrayal?' Who would betray me? Mother nature has come to her senses, we have stopped the Heaven Bearers and their plans, except for Azrael.' She pauses and glances over towards Malcom. They are still fighting each other and she rolls her eyes like a child.

'Who is it father? Is it someone I know? Perhaps I can put a stop to it before he or she even gets the chance to betray me?' She asks and looks back up at the sky, but he is gone. 'Father? Please come back and finish what you were trying to tell me.' She asks calmly, but the sky is clear and the clouds reveal nothing anymore.

She traces her eyes along the firmament and looks for him, but he is no longer there. Her mind starts to race with confusion and she wants to know who is going to betray her. More importantly she wonders if she can stop him or her in time? *What if I can't?*

The sky starts to rumble and her heart stops. 'What is coming for me now?' She mutters and the wind starts to howl. She watches heavy-looking clouds roll in, but they are calm and still white coloured. She looks all around her and the dust in the air blows past her patiently, it is in no hurry to disappear.

'Bonnie!' Malcom shouts and she returns to her senses and runs over to him. 'Look up.'

She turns her eyes up towards the sky and there is a terrifying crack and they watch as the firmament opens up slowly. The colour drains from her face and she holds onto his hand tightly.

'What is coming for us Malcom?' There is fear in her eyes and she can sense Malcom is worried too.

Azrael backs away from them slowly and smiles. He is completely arrogant and they know he had something to do with this. But how, she wonders?

She realises what is about to happen, that he wants to escape and she knows she needs to stop him.

He lifts off from the ground and stretches up his arms. It looks like someone has tied a rope around his shoulders and is pulling him up and away.

'No!' She shouts and takes a big leap towards him. She manages to grab hold of his legs and with all of her might, she tries to hold onto him and pull him back down to the ground. He kicks her hard, in the face and she loses her, already loose grip, and falls back down to the ground. She is all of a sudden weak! She has no strength; her powers are dwindling and she doesn't understand why or what is happening.

'Bonnie, are you okay?' Malcom cries out and immediately runs towards her. He scans her over and notices she has a cut on her nose, her palms and knees are grazed and they are bleeding.

'I'm weak Malcom, I couldn't stop him! What is happening to me?' She asks and they watch him escape form the Earth through the firmament and is closes up again with a loud bang. She wipes over her nose and she notices the blood all over her. She starts to screams hysterically and as loud as she can, but she barely makes a sound and her voice doesn't travel far at all. Her eyes don't light up, nothing happens.

'She betrayed us again, mother nature! She said she was going to help us, but all she did was lie and let Azrael escape!' She shouts at Malcom and she is angry, but she doesn't scare him.

Malcom doesn't know what to say, he is just as angry and he wanted Azrael dead, more than anyone. He knows he must respond to her somehow, but before he even gets the chance, the entire Earth starts to shake. It is nothing like they have felt before, it feels more like the Earth is shifting on its axis. Leaves starts to fall down from the Canopy and surround them. As they land next to them, they quickly turn a light brown, then grey and eventually black and shrivel away. They disintegrate and turn to dust that mixes in with the dirt.

'What is going on?' She asks and watches as large pieces of branches come crashing down and create dents into the ground all around them. A branch narrowly misses her and she freezes in fear and she doesn't know what to do.

'Malcom!' She cries out.

'We need to get up and find cover Bonnie!' He takes her by the hand and they start to run, but she can't keep up with him, she is too slow.

She is a mere Tartarian girl and possess no powers or abilities. He has no other choice, but to pick her up and carry her to safety. They reach the edge of the mountain and hide under a small rock ledge and watch how more branches crash down, split the ground and create clouds of dust all around them.

She sees *that* bright, blue butterfly again. It flies up to her face and gently flaps its wings and hovers, while it makes eye contact with her. She wonders if it is trying to talk to her, because she can't hear anything or understand it?

'I can't hear you. My powers are gone.' She says and frowns. 'I don't know what to do, what is happening?'

Dead birds start to thump down and one lands at her feet. It is white and black and its neck is broken. The butterfly flies away and she watches it head upwards towards the Canopy and she knows she must follow it.

'The Tree of Life! She is dying.' Her words echo all around her and she understands what her father was trying to tell her. Someone is trying to kill the Tree of Life. 'Malcom, we need to find her and save her. If we don't Earth will implode and we will all die.' Her eyes don't flash *that* colour like they used to, but there is sparkle in them and its her fighting spirit shining through.

He takes Bonnie up into the Canopy and she looks around for her, among all the dead leaves and broken branches. The Tree of Life is lying on the floor, in the form of the old lady that she remembers talking to, and she is clutching onto her stomach. She is bleeding and Bonnie runs up to help her.

'We need to stop the bleeding.' She says, as she takes her hand and presses down hard, but the blood starts to flow more.

'What happened? Where is mother nature? Where is she?' She asks her with a clam voice, but her eyes are a dead giveaway as to how frantic she really is inside. Her adrenalin is pumping hard and her hands are trembling.

The Tree of Life tries to talk, but nothing leaves her mouth. She struggles to lift up her hand, but manages just enough to point it towards the dark end of the Canopy.

Bonnie follows her movements and is terrified at the sight of the darkness, but she knows she has to act quickly and save her people. *This is her chance for redemption.*

'The staff! Malcom, I need the staff. Where is it?' Her eyes muster up a faded, gold flash and she can feel it is near. She stands up and walks down towards the darkness and Malcom grabs her by the arm suddenly.

'Bonnie no! You have no powers anymore. You need to stay here and take care of the Tree of Life. Let me handle this!' He pleads, but he knows she has already made up her mind and won't listen to him. Not this time, too much is at stake.

She shakes her head slowly and her eyes are cold. 'We don't have time, she is dying and mother nature doesn't have much time either.'

'Follow me,' he says and takes the lead. His luminous green eyes light up the darkness that lies in front of them, just barely. She follows him slowly and carefully, concentrating hard on sensing the staff. She sees the blue stones slight up, one by one and her heart begins to beat with relief. She approaches the staff, bends down and picks it up gently. There is a bright, blue flash the moment she touches it with her finger tips and it causes the Canopy to vibrate hard. The Vibrations cause all the remaining leaves fall off, until there are none left. For the first time in history, since the time of creation, the Canopy is bare and naked. She feels a soft hand touch her back and she turns around to see the Tree of Life smiling at her and she is no longer bleeding.

'Tree of Life, you are okay?' She looks over at Malcom and then back at her. 'What is happening?'

'Everything is okay now dear. Look –' She waves her hand around in front of Bonnie. 'The darkness is gone and the leaves are budding again.' Bonnie reluctantly looks around her and notices the darkness has completely dissipated, there are green buds on all the branches and they are growing into fresh, new and healthy leaves.

The Tree is healing itself and Bonnie knows it will all be okay.

Malcom sighs out in relief and rubs his hands over his face. The blue stones on the staff stop glowing and they both stand there and watch in awe as the Canopy heals itself, completely, within fifteen minutes.

'I still don't understand what is happening?' This time Malcom is asking the Tree of Life and her eyes turn sad and dreary.

'The war is not over I am afraid. It has only just begun.' She replies and disappears.

HEAVEN BEARERS :THE AGE OF DECEPTION

BOOK 2

TEASER

The town square is packed with people of all ages and races. The Tartarians have accepted the Phoenicians and Humans as their equal, after all their beloved new Queen is married to one.

It is mid-summer. The sun is shining brightly, the air is fresh and the wind is completely still. There is happiness, awe and excitement in the air, everywhere, and even the clouds have formed neatly in the sky for this important day.

She takes her position next to her husband and they each hold one of the twins, firmly in their arms. Amelia and Amile are only three months old and Bonnie is about to be sworn in as Queen of the great, new *Empire of Tartaria* and protector of the Earth.

She is wearing a simple, yet elegant champagne coloured gown, with long sleeves and a low cut neck line. She is wearing a shiny, cushion cut purple stone around her neck and her hair is neatly styled up, so that only a few strands shape her pretty face. The top of her head glistens bright, as the light touches the diamond tiara, that she is wearing. It is the exact same one she wore on her Union Day to Malcom and belonged to his mother.

She is beaming with excitement and purpose. She waves to her people and they cheer with joy and hope and it echoes all across the city.

'Queen Bonnie!' The crowd cheers gracefully and her eyes scan over them as they wave and gesture for her attention. She can see so many happy faces that she doesn't recognise at all, shouting out to her, wanting her attention and she feels completely overwhelmed.

Malcom gives her a gentle and reassuring smile and takes Amile from her arms so that the proceedings can begin.

Cassiel stands up, walks to face the crowd and holds up his hands to calm and quieten them down. It takes a few minutes until there is complete silence and he waits patiently for them to settle down. He proceeds to take the Staff of the Elders from the mahogany table, covered with a silver linen cloth and he holds it up with pride. The crowd starts to cheer uncontrollably at the mere sight of it and he hands it to his *new Queen*.

'My Queen, Bonnie, wife of Malcom Harrington and ruler of the great Tartarian Empire.' He places it gently into her hands and gives her a respectful grin and slightly bows his head in complete submission to her.

Bonnie gracefully accepts the staff from him and it lights up slowly. Each stone shines a bright blue and the illumination causes the crowd to keep dead quiet as they stare in awe and relish in all its glory.

She takes a deep breath and can feel Malcom in her mind. 'You look absolutely stunning in that dress Bonnie, I can't wait to take it off of you later.' She gives him a reprimanding look and he winks back at her. Her smile is stretching from ear to ear, she has everything she could have ever wanted and much more. 'I do love this man,' she mutters just loud enough for him to hear and she takes three steps forward to address the crowd.

'Thank you Tartaria!' She waits a moment for the crowd to settle down a little bit more and feels their infectious smiles penetrate her soul. 'Thank you all for coming today and accepting me as your new Queen.' She looks over at Cassiel and he takes a step forward with a big smile and stops in position, slightly behind her. The crowd starts to cheer again and he relishes every moment.

Cassiel has always wanted to rule, he dreamt of this day since he was a little boy and deep down inside it saddens him that he isn't standing next to her as her husband, but merely her advisor.

He places his hand on her lower back and with the other, he waves to the crowd. He can feel Malcom's eyes bore into him, but he ignores him completely. He can't have her, but this doesn't mean he won't try bis luck from time to time.

Cassiel suddenly drops his hand from her back and flexes his fingers and his smile softens slightly. Malcom chuckles to himself softly and can't help but grin. He knows Bonnie wasn't having any of it and must have given him a slight electric shock.

'I stand before each one of you today, whether you are Tartarian, Phoenician or Human, and I declare that we are all equal citizens of the great Empire of Tartaria. We shall all share in her good fortune and her riches. I declare peace and harmony, which will be achieved as a matter of the will of our hearts.' She swallows hard suddenly and gazes in silence for a moment. 'We have achieved a new covenant with mother nature and I look forward to a healthy and trusting relationship with her.' Her eyes flash gold and the memories of that dreadful day replay in her mind.

'To the covenant!' The crowd cheers in unison and the strength of their cheer gives her goose bumps. They run all the way down her spine and she has never felt so much purpose in all her life. She is proud and amazed at the love and trust that is radiating from the people that stand before her.

'We must, however, not forget how we reached this point. We lost many good and innocent souls. Fathers, mother, siblings, children and loved ones.' Her voice breaks with emotion and she needs to clear her throat. 'I implore each of you to bow your heads now, as we remember them and together share a minute of silence.' She bows her head and the crowd follows her lead and bow their heads without hesitation.

She is thinking about her father in this very moment and she can't help but wish he was here today. She can feel Malcom comfort her thoughts and she raises her head again.

'Citizens of Tartaria, the war is not over! I wish I had better news, but I do not. I cannot claim to know the day or the hour, nor can I tell you whether it will be soon or in many years to come. But the Angel of Death has escaped through the Firmament and I know he will return one day and try to lay siege to our new Empire, *our home.*' She takes a deep breath and scans all the faces in the front row. 'He will not succeed again, not this time. So, let him come!'

The crowd cheers hysterically and the sound echoes back and forth like ocean waves crashing up against a rock wall, at the edge of the shoreline.

'Bonnie, it is time.' Cassiel gestures for her to get down onto one knee, so she can take her oath. He takes the staff from her and holds it out in front of her.

'Please place your hand here my Queen and repeat after me.'

She places her right hand gently onto the Staff of the Elders and makes full eye contact with him. His eyes draw her in completely and time stands still. Images flash before her eyes and she knows that destiny was real, she was meant to be his and she doesn't understand why destiny didn't succeed. What stopped it, she wonders? And quickly shakes the thought away.

'I, Queen Bonnie Harrington, the duly elected ruler, do hereby swear my allegiance to the Empire of Tartaria. I promise to never lie, cheat or deceive in any way or form and await a slow and painful death, if I break my oath.'

She suddenly pulls her eyes away from Cassiel, she feels nauseous and wants to puke. There is a presence among them, she can't see or feel who it is, but she can feel him or her and she knows that this presence is *pure evil.* She tries to regain her composure and musters up a smile, but it feels fake.

"Someone will betray you." This is what her father told

her and she now knows that he is right. There is someone here that will betray her and her body tenses up, because she knows it will be someone who she will trust and not suspect.

She can feel Malcom focus his gaze at her, he is trying to read her thoughts, but she blocks him out completely and pretends her mind isn't wandering.

They finish the proceedings and she stands up, proudly next to Cassiel. They wave one more time and, in that moment, she is very glad to have him share the responsibilities with her, although not officially. He loves his people; he would die for them and this is what is needed to rule the Empire well and most importantly, fairly.

Malcom and Bonnie leave New York and go back home to their mansion in Montreal. They have spent two weeks there and she looks forward to the change of scenery. Bonnie doesn't want to live anywhere else; Montreal is *home* and it always will be. She kicks off her shoes and Jane suddenly appears from nowhere and helps her with Amelia.

'Thank you, Jane. It has been a long day.' She says as she hands Amelia to her. She is fast asleep and she can't help but smile at her angelic, little face.

Malcom follows Jane upstairs with Amile and they put them both to bed. Bonnie walks over to the kitchen and makes a pot of mint tea and takes it with her upstairs. She runs a hot bath, while she sips the tea and climbs in. The warm water feels good, it relaxes her body and she stairs at the light bulb up on the ceiling and grins. She closes her eyes and relishes the moment, the fact that they won, at least the first round.

Over the past few months, they changed many of the repurposed buildings back to what they were originally built for. Unfortunately, much of the knowledge has been lost. But they are working hard to learn all that they can, from all the different books in the libraries, that managed to survive all of these years. The library in the mansion proved to be very helpful. The big book, the one that was stored in the glass case, is full of knowledge about the harnessing of free energy. They have translated some of it, but not all. Yet.

They have figured out how to produce a basic form of free energy, enough to light up the houses and automate some things. They plan on harnessing all forms of energy in the future and she allows her mind to imagine what Tartaria will be like then. Excitement runs thought her body and she can feel it radiate and dissipate into the water.

Malcom walks into the bathroom and interrupts her thoughts. He walks straight to the bathroom sink and washes his face, but he doesn't join her in the bath. He changes his clothes and goes straight to bed. She takes her time and eventually joins him in bed as well. His back is turned towards her, the exact same way he used when he wanted to avoid her and she knows something is bothering him.

She strokes his back with her finger tips, but he pretends to be asleep and she decides to leave him be. He will talk to her about what is on his mind, when he is ready. She lies on her back and closes her eyes, thinking about all the things she wants to achieve as Queen.

She wakes up in the middle of the night and she is soaking wet. She is as pale as her white bed sheets and she can't breathe. She isn't crying, but she is terrified. She tries to call out, but she can't make a single sound and she tries to reach out to Malcom with her hand. She flops her hand on his back and her clumsiness wakes him. He ignores her for a moment, but can sense something is wrong. He turns around and sees the look on her face.

'Bonnie, what is wrong?' He sits up and looks down at her, while she gasps for air. She still can't breathe and Malcom realises she is turning blue from the lack of oxygen. He Pulls her up and over him and starts to rub her back. This isn't helping, so he applies more pressure and gently thumps her with a flat hand.

'Breath Bonnie! Calm down and take a deep breath.' He presumes she had a nightmare or a possible panic attack and keeps rubbing her back.

Her gasps are getting more desperate and painful, as she tries to grab onto the air around her and she clutches his arm, digging her nails into it. He remembers the day she choked on the piece of chicken at dinner and takes her into his arms, just like he did then. He holds her tight, with her in an upright position and uses his full might to try dislodge whatever is stuck in her throat. She completely stops breathing and goes limp in his arms. He drops her to the floor and gives her mouth to mouth, but nothing is helping. His eyes turn luminous green and he pounds down hard onto her chest.

'Bonnie, you need to breathe!' He nervously calls out to her, while he gives her chest compressions and watches her body move mechanically as he pushes down onto her. Her eyes turn gold and it illuminates her face. She has black marks all over on her neck and there is a white foam at the edge of her mouth. He looks at her emotionless face and doesn't know what to do. He stops giving her chest compressions and puts his hand on her cheek, she is still warm. He pulls his hand away suddenly and realises she is burning up. She feels as hot as coals from a fresh fire.

He remembers what she told him, that is isn't so easy for her to die. She explained what happened the day she thought she died, how the soil completely filled her throat and lungs, but she didn't choke.

He picks her up and puts her into the bath and lets cold water run over pale and lifeless body. He pushes her head under and doesn't know why he is doing it. He watches her face and the black marks on her neck start to turn blue and he realises the marks are actually words. He doesn't recognise the language, it is not Tartarian.

The gold colour in her eyes fades and her eyes become dull and blank and the look of them makes him throw himself back against the wall in horror.

'Bonnie!' He sits on the floor and can't move or think. He stays there until the morning and doesn't move a single muscle. He is in shock and is utterly devastated. This time she is dead and *he couldn't save her.*

Jane knocks on the door. 'Mr and Mrs Harrington, is everything okay in there?' She asks politely, not wanting to disturb them. They didn't come down for breakfast or check on the twins and she thought their behaviour was odd. She knocks again and listens carefully for any sound. She gets no response and decides to walk inside.

'No!' She cries out and sees Malcom seated on the floor and Bonnie lying dead in the bathtub, she is lying flat on the bottom of it and her eyes are still wide open. Jane rushes over to her and pulls her out of the bathtub, lays her on the floor and tries to get her to breathe.

Malcom sits there and rubs his hands over his eyes and face and feels completely dead inside.

'There is absolutely nothing you can do Jane. She is dead, I have tried already.' His voice is empty, yet raw with anger, frustration and hate.

'How did this happen?' She asks him while still staring at her lifeless face. Her expression is blank, but her lips are a blue-purple colour and she knows she choked to death.

'Look at her neck,' he replies and points with his right hand at it.

Jane turns her head slightly to the side and notices a weird inscription on the side of her neck. 'What does this mean?' She asks surprised by what she is seeing.

'I was hoping you could tell me?' He replies, his voice is a mere whisper.

Jane sits down next to her and tilts her head even more to the side, so she can have a good look at what is all over her neck. 'No, I have never seen something like this before. It isn't Tartarian!' She rubs her finger over the marks, but they don't smudge. She shakes her head in confusion, the reality is starting to sick in and she starts to cry at the sight of her dead Queen. She instinctively wraps her arms around, like a mother would a child and cries out in sadness.

'Oh Bonnie, dear Bonnie!' She holds her for a couple of moments and says nothing else.

'What do I do now Jane? How do I explain this?'

She lays Bonnie back down on the floor and looks over at him, with a completely blank expression.

The wind starts blowing hard and the curtains are swaying in the wind. She gets up to close the window, when an owl lands on the window sill and shrieks. She jumps with fright and tries to shoo it away, but it doesn't move. It shrieks again, this time much louder and it is so loud Jane blocks her ears.

'Shoo, you stupid thing.' She shouts at it. She takes a hand towel from the rack and tries to smack it away, but the owl digs its claws into the window sill, as hard as it can, and refuses to move.

'Owls are a bad omen. Did you know that Jane?' He asks and gets up from where he is sitting. He grabs the owl and a single, white feather falls off from its body and floats down towards the ground. His eyes watch it carefully and it lands on Bonnie. He remembers the very first night he spent with her and wonders if this is the same owl that frightened her then?

'Did you see that?' He mutters and takes a step closer towards Bonnie.

Jane looks over at Bonnie and frowns in confusion. 'Mr Harrington?'

'Shh. Just look.' He says and bends down watching her hand carefully. 'Her fingers, look at her fingers,' he tells her.

Jane focus her full attention on her fingers, but she doesn't see anything.

'Mr Harrington, I think you want her fingers to move and so they are. But it is not real.'

'No!' He snaps at her. 'Just watch Jane.' She swallows hard and does what he asks her, albeit very reluctantly. There is a slight twitch in her hand and this time Jane sees it too. Her frown suddenly disappears from her face and her cheeks fill with colour.

'I think, I...she moved, I saw it!' She replies suddenly.

'Bonnie, wake up! Listen to my voice and come back to me.' Malcom leans down beside her and gives her a gentle shake. 'Bonnie, please wake up, let me see those beautiful blue eyes.' He stares at her, rubs her cheek and gives her another small shake, but nothing happens.

Her eyes suddenly flash bright gold and it is so intense Malcom lets go of her at once and turns his head away from the blinding light. Her head drops down onto the floor with a bang and she doesn't make a single sound. She lies there staring up at the ceiling and it looks like she is smiling at someone. Malcom traces her eyes with his, but sees nothing there on the ceiling. He remembers the story she told him about when she was a baby, the night her parents were fighting about who or what she is.

"There is something wrong with her. She is pure evil." That is what her mother said at the time. He looks at her carefully and realises she was party right, there *is something wrong with her.*

ABOUT THE AUTHOR

Janine Helene

Janine Helene is a qualified lawyer and writer. She grew up in the city, but currently lives on a farm in South Africa and is part city girl and part cowgirl. She has a passion for agriculture, history and romance.
Her writing is based on some of her own life experiences and she enjoys sharing her life lessons with her readers

BOOKS IN THIS SERIES

HEAVEN BEARERS

It is 1834, the sky suddenly turns dark and snow starts to fall down. The Tartarians are scared, they have never experienced snow before and wonder what is happening. The sand begins to lift up from the ground and rain falls down, like a flood and mixes with the sand. A wave of mud covers the entire earth, leaving more than half of all life forms dead. In the meantime, a race of beings have taken over what is left of the great Empire of Tartaria and murder all who oppose them.

The Great Reset Of 1834 And The Mud Flood

Bonnie is a shy girl living in an orphanage. She just turned 18 years old and must marry a man and produce children. This is her duty. Malcom, her husband is a mean man, he wants to get her pregnant as soon as possible, so that she can produce a Human, that is the goal. Humans need to mine the resources of the Earth for the Heaven Bearers and make them rich.
Bonnie, however soon realises that she is no ordinary Tartarian girl and she is not prepared to further this sick goal of creating a race of slaves.
She decides to fight back and take back what his rightly hers, only to learn about who she really is and what she has done.

The Age Of Deception

The war is not over, but the Empire of Tartaria still stands, for now. Bonnie is not herself; she is acting strange and it scares her, what is she? War is looming, she can feel it in the air and she knows that she needs to do something and stop him before he enters the Firmament, but she isn't sure how.

Azrael is waiting for his day of revenge and someone close to her is helping him. Will he succeed in destroying the Empire for good?

The Prophesy said so, but she has since learns that reality is stronger than destiny

BOOKS BY THIS AUTHOR

The Kate Hayleigh Trilogy

30 Three and Me (Book 1)
Third Time Lucky (Book 2)
Three Things (Book 3)

Kate is a city girl from South Africa looking for something, a purpose in life and the right man. Like most of us, she knows there is more to life and the prospects excite her. She meets the man of her dreams and moves to Montana, where they plan there lives together.
Something, rather someone, is lurking in the shadows and wants to to destroy everything she has worked so hard to achieve. What will happen to Kate and will she be able to hold onto the things she wants most.

Romance - Adventure - Family - Love